The
Murder
of
Kaelin

Steve Dreben

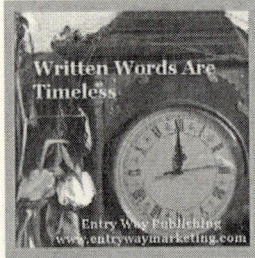

Written Words Are Timeless

Entry Way Publishing
www.entrywaymarketing.com

Publisher: VicToria Freudiger
Entry Way Marketing and Publishing
www.entrywaymarketing.com
entrywaypublish@aol.com
Editor: R. D. Foster, Editor-in-Chief
Assistant Editor: Kristi Bishop
Cover Illustration: Juan Rodriguez
Cover Design: Delaney-Designs
Printer: Apex Book Manufacturing, Inc.

ISBN: 978-0-9793944-9-2
ISBN: 0-97939-449-X

Biography of the Author

Author, Steve Dreben, graduated from the University of Illinois, as well as The London International Television and Film School where he received honors and various awards during his Master's Program.

Steve majored in Logic/Philosophy/Science at the University of Illinois, and directing, editing and writing while in London, England. He has written twelve original screenplays, two teleplays, one play, two children's books and a recently published novel, "Compromised Positions." The author has won the International Cine Golden Eagle Award as well as the American Documentary Film New York Festival Award for "Huichol: People of the Peyote."

Aside from being a writer, Steve is an independent businessman and a Horticulturist. He works substantially in the financial industry and in mortgage banking.

Steve's a family man with three children, two of whom are college graduates and one is in the twelfth grade.

This author has won both of his prestigious awards through practical experiences and his eyes see deeply into character shattering most of the usual screens. His personal philosophy supports a populist view and he's proud of being a progressive environmentalist who balances ideas before he votes them. Steve works each day in a practical world while interacting with many people and making his voice heard. In a society of many 'blind faiths,' he tries to open the box, or separate the 'iron vice' of conformity in order to let truth enter when and wherever possible.

Prologue
February 6, 2001

The "Murder of Kaelin" is a true story mixing place and characters. Part of the chronicle that follows is a tall tale, while some is real, with much of the storyline caught in between. Some of Kaelin's characters and places are fictional, though they do represent certain people and the way they truly exist, both then and now. Many of the names have been changed or have been altered for obvious reasons.

This story exhibits some hard clues or various pieces of substantial evidence outlining a gruesome murder, which took place in a rural Oregon county in the late fall of 1996. From best guess, it can be surmised that the murder of a young girl, itself took place somewhere in the mountain ranges, and the body was pillaged and dumped. Over time, the effects of decay and animals gnawed away at the evidence.

One of the real issues portrayed in "Kaelin" is that people in the county where she was raised knew the girl and loved her. Some of the locals were quite close to her. Many of them continue to miss her young womanly charms.

At fifteen, Kaelin had quite a reputation with both the adult population and her many peers. Her mother, Peggy T. Bradley, married twice and gave birth to three more children after Kaelin's father disappeared some time during the mid-1980s. Peggy was a chiseled-face, classically built countrywoman from German stock, with long auburn hair. Somewhere in her middle-forties, Peggy loved and was extremely devoted to all her children. Although she usually kept to herself and her own family, Peggy's entire family's history went back one hundred and fifty years in the river valley where she and all her children were raised. They were pioneers, native Easterner/Westerner all mixed into one strong family alliance, the Bork family.

In many ways, Peggy and Kaelin Bork (her oldest daughter), were outcasts in the valley, mainly due to the fact that most of the Bork's had otherwise achieved wealth or social status. Although Peggy was an educated woman, she was nonetheless poor. She was the type of woman whom the rest of the family would avoid in a small town the size of Pullman, Washington.

Peggy's first cousin, Lucinda Bork kept her name for nearly twenty years after she was married to Sheriff Miles T. Carson's brother, Will. Lucinda and Will were greatly in love when they first met. Their happy relationship continued for a good ten years of marriage. After that period of time, both partners in the marriage started to discover who they actually were and their marriage became radically independent.

Lucinda and Peggy Bradley were nieces of Nathan Bork, the most famous and powerful man in the county. Nathan was a rancher, hunter, businessman, and fisherman. He served as county commissioner for five terms before settling down as a rancher at the ripe old age of seventy.

It could be said that the valley was a mix of some odd and some old homestead families. Still, there were the new families coming in from Washington. A few of them were small-business type people; however, there was a dash of other sorts, ranging from general laborers to skilled carpenters.

Miles T. Carson was the dominant law force in Wallowa County, a county that was very rural and somewhat poor. He had strong personal connections in Pullman, Pendleton, Portland, and Spokane. Miles was a rural sheriff with a flair for the modern. As sheriff, he used his powers both internally and externally to get what he wanted. Sheriff Carson's goal was to get what he knew could be done within the community politics. All municipal employees had to watch themselves in regard to the county 'powers' that literally controlled the valley. Miles was a perfect servant of those powers, and that went for most of his staff, with the exception of Buck Parrish, who thwarted a 'cut' of independence above all local citizens.

Buck Parrish was an ex-rodeo bronc rider who became a deputy sheriff in 1985 after a wild Appaloosa crushed his ear and part of his skull in the "Pendleton Roundup" of 1983. People said Buck had a small metal plate buried in the side of his head. The plate caused him to be stubborn as a mule and he was plagued with severe headaches. It's said that when old Buck got onto something, he was like a small tick on a big dog, one would have to pull him off with large tweezers.

In 1996, Kaelin Jones disappeared from the valley. Her body was never recovered. During the years in between Kaelin's disappearance and her recovery, clues began appearing. The clues suggested a possible murder, in the same way as something quite strange emerging from the deep bat caverns and old mining shafts that were dug during the turn of the century.

Some of the information regarding Kaelin's murder was hearsay, while other data was hard forensic fact. Yet other 'stuff' came from a local psychic's haunting dream image, vivid details of the child's raw murder.

No one knew exactly how the investigation started or who tipped it off, but by the time it ended; solid proof that a murder had been committed was now without question. Kaelin Jones had been brutally and crudely slaughtered in our valley during the late weeks of October 1996. The community chronicle depicts actual events, with names and places changed to protect people who did their public duty without concern for their own well-being.

Introduction

    "The Murder of Kaelin" is a fictionalized account of a scenario that is repeated far too often in America; the disappearances and/or deaths of our runaway teens.

    The story line represented in "The Murder of Kaelin" is about the disappearance of one of rural Oregon's special young women. Kaelin, a fifteen-year-old adolescent left home one evening, never to return or be heard from again. In the fall of 1996, this young lady disappeared and in time, human remains were found in the nearby mountains that could have been the scattered, skeletal remains of the missing girl, or that of so many other missing girls her age.

    Kaelin Jones' disappearance wasn't given the national attention that some missing children's cases are given, but her disappearance was noted nonetheless by those who loved and cared for her. This precious teen's absence from the lives of the people in the St. Joseph, Oregon area is still felt today, as each runaway occurrence has a ripple effect in the lives of those involved.

    In telling Kaelin's story, the author, Steve Dreben, has created a fictional cast of characters, places, and events that represent what might have happened in this one case, in order to facilitate understanding and compassion for the tragedy that is the runaway dilemma in America today.

Brief Report

...by Arthur M. Bell, journalist
and community radio news host

Fiction and non-fiction, truth and non-truth yet the subject and the content of all truth may indeed be fiction or in fact, this work of fiction may be quite close to the truth. All characters in this novel are as true as characters can be, but the names aren't the same as the people they represent. Names have been changed to protect all innocents. Contents of the story are both real and present. The actual murder(s) in question has never been solved; therefore, all places, names, and references remain fiction.

Wallowa County is a magical place in Northeastern Oregon where the fictional story takes place. It is a majestic region of untapped contours still as remote from urban civilization as any forested place within the developed world. Much of the story did happen and details of the events are as 'real' as any mediated present-day news report. Most of the fiction in the documentation of the story will fill gaps where the mind demands knowledge within fiction.

Outside of the novel, truth still wonders in the same darkness as ghost vapor in Mountain Meadows. It is dedicated to Kaelin and her kindred sisters, who brought her back to life, and to my loving wife and to Peter Matthiessen for the charm and style of 'Mister Watson'.

"The Murder of Kaelin" is particularly dedicated to the tens of thousands of lost young *runaways* whose fates are usually never known. My dedication goes out to a multitude of young ones who disappear into the dark of our cities and to those who crawl into the black places in our rural forests whose destinies are as acrid as tortured victims 'round the world.

~~~

Prelude 1996
"Deputy Buck Parrish"

It all started one day while I was investigating a robbery that had taken place at McHenry's Last Store. There was evidence that some kids had jimmied the backside of an old cedar door. They had eventually worked their way into the old metal safe. From what I could immediately see, they stole a few hundred dollars, some canned goods, a few pieces of jerky, and two full boxes of twenty gauge shotgun shells. Old Bob McHenry was beside himself. Never before in the history of Inmaha had such an awful crime taken place.

"Buck, now, this is straight talk, 'cause I want you to hear me. Them kids robbed me and you'd better track down and find these son's-a-bitches, or I'll do what I can to have you and Sheriff Miles T. Carson removed from office. Get my meaning?"

"Bob, I'll just have to be real quick about finding all them clues I need for this here massive investigation. Then we'll dig into it a bit more. We'll just see what comes up-"

McHenry interrupted. "You'd better have all my stuff back in this store in ten days, Deputy, or we'll see who pays for it. Buck, we'll see!"

Well, no doubt McHenry was a pretty tough old hoot and he usually did exactly what he claimed he'd do. He was not the first, nor will he be the last man in Wallowa County who lived by the old western plain's principles; and for sure not many of those fella's remain.

After several calls to local lawmen in towns within the county looking for possible descriptions, I worked up my brief report while sitting in the patrol car with the map light on and a small flashlight on my report book. As I started the motor, a young woman in her early teens knocked on the window of my car as a few massive raindrops began crashing on the windshield. I'll never forget the look in the girl's eyes and the expression on her face. Her mouth was cut back in a fearful way and the girl's brown eyes looked sad and her wavy black hair was messed from the downpour. The fear, the look of deep fear 'popped outta her pupils'.

I'd known Tammy Bork since she was a babe. She was fifteen at this time and was from one of the best and oldest prominent church-going families in these parts. In fact, the Bork family had been in this area since Nathan Bork settled in 1848. He was one of the first 'croppers' in this part of the state, and was from one of the first families in the Whisky Valley.

I remembered asking Tammy to sit in the seat next to me to see if I could help her and to simply get the hell out of the rain. She slowly went around the car like something had recently shocked her badly. Afterwards, she sat down at the end of the seat crouching close to the door. The child kept her hand on the metal door handle looking as if she was ready to jump out of the vehicle at a moment's notice.

Even after I asked her to tell me what was bothering her; she said nothing. Tammy stared out the dark window, occasionally looking down at the lights on the dashboard. Several requests later it was easy to see she was in a state of shock.

Everything I said was of no avail. I asked Tammy if she wanted to go home and offered to drive her anyplace she needed to go. Again, the teen remained silent. With my engine revved up, I put the safety belt on Tammy, switched into gear and headed down Little Sheep Creek Road, or Highway 350.

From the time we passed the old Gray place, on the way to Tammy's home, ten miles away, the girl said nothing. My passenger simply stared out of the windshield and watched the rain. Soon, she began to shed tears, which slowly rolled down her cheeks, smaller droplets becoming larger ones. She was in obvious emotional pain and sobbed like a young woman who'd just lost a loved-one. No matter what I said, no matter what I did, I couldn't help her and was unable to contain her weeping. For me, it was clear that old Buck Parrish was one of those old-thinking men who couldn't handle a woman's tears. It was like a piece of me fell away with every breath of Tammy's emotions.

By the time we finally arrived at the Bork place, her eyes were as red as a just-butchered, hung hog. Slowly, I took her down the sidewalk to the door of the house and rang the bell.

Tammy's mother, Lucinda Bork, came to the door and peered out at her daughter. She opened the door quickly and took and comforted her child within her arms. Lucinda called old Jeffery to the door to deal with me.

"Hi, Buck. Do you know what this is about?" he asked.

"No. Jeff, I haven't got the slightest clue. She was just sobbing and said nothing at all, all the way here. Still, I knew for sure that you'd want me to take her home."

"You did exactly what I'd expect you to do, Buck. I appreciate your help. I'll call you on this tomorrow," he said.

Jeff Bork closed the door real hard and I remember turning away scratching my head, because I had no idea what had happened out there. I didn't understand the crime site or the incident with Tammy. Neither made any real sense at that point.

Driving back home, I kept thinking about Tammy's tear shedding. I had no idea what had caused this young woman to be so upset. My own daughter was just a year shy of Tammy Bork's age. She had known her well at school and always had fine things to say about her. I'd known the Bork girl all her life. She was someone in the community that we all knew from a family we all grasped and respected. Her family was a peg in the community structure, an old family with solid public connections.

That night as I lay in bed with my wife, Martha, I found myself speaking to her about the incident, which was something I normally kept to myself. She listened as I told her I was anxious about Tammy. Martha told me about seeing Tammy and Kaelin Jones walking down Hemmings Road towards Reverend Chrisp's New Church.

"The two of them," she said, "were talking intently to one another as if something had just happened." Martha also noticed how the girls were holding each other's arms as they walked.

Neither she, nor I, could really make heads or tails out of the whole thing at that point. She grabbed my shoulder and pulled me towards her as I turned to switch the lights out and received the comforts of a fine woman.

one

Arthur M. Bell
Summary of the Disappearance

The facts surrounding Kaelin's disappearance, from a journalist's point of view, are a mix of fiction, fantasy, psychic revelation, religious insights, gossip, and small-town journalism. The only thing that remains an absolute fact is the disappearance of the girl, and the various accounts surrounding her 'murder.'

Perhaps the most accurate description on the murder came from one of our local psychics, Millie Roberts. Her specific account and details, along with the other super-varied data, had the FBI on a massive, non-stop evidence hunt. Local authorities had been working on the case in secret for two years since her Christmas eclipse. Very few pieces of evidence had ever appeared within the seven hundred and some days from Kaelin's sudden exodus.

At first, the local police had conveniently looked at her case as just another common teen-runaway problem. Yet during those two-plus years that were spent grinding stuff out, tiny fragments of lucid evidence and other details began to emerge like pus from an infected wound. It seemed as if the scabs were covered, yet the dermis was still infecting the whole case with puzzlement.

Of all the people in the county, it was Millie Roberts who seemed to keep the case alive. She said she was always dreaming about Kaelin and was able to hear things coming from somewhere. Maybe the dead do speak to some of us? It's strange regarding the amount of detail Millie was capable of uncovering. Her description was colored in a way it felt as if she was there and it somehow made a believer out of many of us who didn't believe in those tales at the time. Millie sure had a way of expressing herself. She was a woman as solid as a rock 'til those dreams about Kaelin started seeping through her head some three months after the disappearance.

I remember the night she came into my newspaper office, the infamous *Republic Enterprise*. The lights were on in my office and I was working hard on a new piece about falling barley and alfalfa prices when Millie walked in the room. She was definitely in another state of mind, a cloud-like euphoria.

What portion of the story was true or false I'll never know, but Millie certainly was sincere. I never met a woman surer of an account on any subject other than Millie Roberts.

That might have been my first major experience with the murder of Kaelin: a gruesome tale of hatred and loathing coupled with a twisted sense of self-righteousness conveyed through the angled mindset of each killer.

"Kaelin was picked up by a man whom she knew well. She was drugged by this man using the precise amount of drugs to keep her mind conscious and her body sleeping." Millie had described in great detail for almost one hour, the precise nature of the killing courtship prior to the eventual slaying. All her words and gestures seemed 'too real' to me, or at least it did during that unforeseen night.

two

Sheriff Miles T. Carson

Three years ago, I first met Kaelin. She was a very shy young one who usually wallowed ten-to-twelve steps behind her mother while sucking the end of a small blanket.

Lucinda Bork asked me to come out to the house and talk to Tammy and Kaelin about drinking and whatever. She wanted me to discuss some of the runaway girls that the old church had helped take care of up in Inmaha. I parked in front of the Bork home and slid quickly out of the patrol car leaving my black metal flashlight on the seat. I asked the Bork family if I could talk to the girls 'kind of privately' somewhere out on the screened-in back porch, to which they said 'yes', and that's how our first, little private conversation began.

"What makes you girls want to go to that house up in Inmaha, especially during the night to cuss and drink?"

I'd think drink and maybe smoke with those runaways, eh?

"Don't your parents provide enough for you all to do around here?" Or, I'd say, "You think you need to go up there do you? You know I can't prosecute you now because of your ages, but you'll see, in a few years there could be some real trouble."

Tammy Bork was a feisty outgoing mule-headed girl with one hell of a fire in her spirited belly. At twelve years old, she said pretty much what her dark brown eyes and red hair prompted her to say. The girl was one brawling little critter even at that age.

"Sheriff Carson, do you want me to make something up or do you want some real stuff?"

"I'd like some real stuff, thank you. It's a lot easier facing that than the usually country cock-and-bull stories."

Kaelin just sat back in the girl's chair. I remember her chiseled nose twitching, her hazel eyes and auburn hair poking upward and her staring at my face. She was a beautiful little thing even then. There was something about her eyes and dark eyebrows. The child had the ability to draw a man into her when she looked straight at him. I'd spent a lot of time during my twenty-four years as a lawman by investigating things and I had a keen sense of people. This young woman had something real attracting going on for her. Yes, something surely attracting. This attraction could easily get her in trouble with the wrong kind of man, a man who was strictly drawn to the sex of a woman, not the whole composition. This type of man would be particularly scary for a young woman such as Kaelin. I've seen the nature of pull she had many

8

times, and I've confronted it investigating a lot of cases, including murder. After many years in the field, I'd come to know exactly what I was saying.

Another thing that I remember about that night, as I talked to Tammy and Kaelin, was their power; they weren't even a touch afraid of my big Carson body, or even me in fact. We sat there for a half-hour talking about many things and skirting many issues until Kaelin turned to me and said, "Sheriff Carson, we just plain like getting high and laughing with those girls. It hurts nobody and it only helps us."

"I see, but let me say this much, girls. If we catch 'ya coming from Inmaha drunk or high in any way, we're 'gonna stop you just plain sure as the sun's rising tomorrow. Plus, I think I'll have a talk with Sister Mary about your little trips and the fact that you're getting high. Knowing Sister Mary like I do, and I do know her, she'll want to do something about halting your little adventures. You might not know this, but it's damned dangerous for you girls to be out on the highway in the dark hours, especially if you're hitching on some of our back roads. None of those places up there are safe like most of the county was twenty years ago. There's a lot of madmen roaming the highways and backwoods today."

"We can take care of ourselves, Sheriff. We don't need any big men coming along to protect us," said Tammy.

"When you're eighteen, not many of us will be able to do much about your running around, but 'til that time, the two of you are grounded! I'll be visiting Sister Mary Espanola real soon to make sure both she and you understand what I'm saying. Do you understand my words?" Sheriff Carson asked.

Well, the two of them moved around both sides of me and headed into Tammy's dark bedroom. The Borks came out of another room carrying a tray of crackers and iced tea. I sat down with them for a while and told them about the 'police grounding' and then explained what I'd be planning to do next with Sister Mary. As with a lot of good people in the valley, they thanked me for stopping in and 'taking the bull by the horns' and making solid points with the girls.

I remembered those candy-sweet faces on both girls that night. Tammy and Kaelin were sweet people beyond their own nature. Both girls were smarter than their years could bear, usually a sign of trouble to come.

My instincts told me at that point that some kind of bind was brewing in the future for all of us sitting on the porch that night. I knew it deep within me. I knew it like my Great Uncle Kit knew it prior to an Indian attack. A man had to move by his guts on the frontier in the same way as he had to move today. Those frigid mountains were there on the horizon a hundred and fifty years ago like they are today; time becomes nothing to an easy-blowing frozen-topped mountain range.

Yes, I remember driving home thinking about Tammy and Kaelin the whole time. I also thought about the way the girls looked and remembered their smiles. The girls had a youthful coyness. My wife, Jenna, and I discussed those girls. I explained to her how I was bothered about their generation being seemingly more lost than the last one was. My wife listened as I explained how their plight got to my guts. I shared with her how people their age shouldn't have to be afraid in a small place. It was now a period of time when they should get as much pleasure out 'a life and play as much as humanly possible. For the first time in many years, Jenna seemed to side with my sentiments, which was totally unusual for her. Most of the time, I was the bad 'badge' who knew little about people, especially women.

We continued talking about young people in the county 'til deep in the night. My wife became weary.

She grabbed me and we rolled over just far enough to snuggle as close as a man and woman could get.

three

Buck Parrish

I remember taking the back road to Inmaha that day; yeah, I swung around the road north of Enterprise toward Findley Buttes. Usually it was a hard hour's drive, maybe even an hour and half's drive through a lot of wind and rain. Can't say I remember a time going to Inmaha during the summer or winter when it didn't rain for a short time at least. For a part of the road, maybe ten or so miles from Sister Mary's, the road turned to dirt. Pavement ran out and the dirt and rocks appeared like something pushed up from the earth. Under the tires, it was hard lava rock and broken granite mixed with dirt. The shelter for runaways was hard to get to in the deep winter unless one was using a snowmobile or dog sled if you could still find one.

As I neared the girls' shelter, five miles away, I spotted a large elk eating some fall berries near a recently downed tree. I pulled off the road and sat there for a while just looking at that big 'fella munching away like he didn't have a care in the world. This particular section of the woods was not too far from Hell's Canyon Park. There were a few Elk, Goats, Bighorn Sheep, Black Bear, Cougar, and Lynx, roaming mostly unmolested even after the hoards of hunters in the woods during various seasons. The Federal Government hadn't let anyone shoot the animals since the late seventies. It surely was a good thing, a real good thing; otherwise, there'd be none to see anywhere. Once I hunted like most people in these parts. I mounted my trophies, but all of a sudden, something in my head said killing these magnificent animals didn't make any sense, so I stopped mounting trophies. Maybe I stopped killing creatures after I talked to Sister Mary. Yes, maybe it was after my chat with her; I just don't remember the date, except that it was nearly twenty years ago.

Sister Mary Espanola was half Nez Perce and the other half was a mix of Spanish and Scottish. Her father was married to the baby sister's daughter of Old Chief Joseph of the Nez

Perce. Her father was Edward Aneroid, the son of one of the great trackers in these hereabouts, a man known as Kyle M. Aneroid. Sister Mary was a strong-hearted daughter of one of our finest lines of folks and was the spitting image of her father and grandfather. She had all of the gumption of both.

In this part of the world, family was real; it meant something. In Wallowa County there was still an interconnection of people, people and their past. We still had timely connections of both dark and light. It was a powerful human linkage. Fact was, I could still think of that time in the late fifties when I was just a kid and I remember old Kyle Aneroid coming out in town on certain tartan holidays blowing his bagpipes. He marched down the street one day just after the Korean War had ended. Kyle marched down First Street Enterprise right close to his son who'd just returned from the war with half of his left arm blown off.

To this very day, I can remember that old man blowing his bagpipes as if he were warning us about a kind of mountain storm coming down from the Wallowa's. I watched him as he hit one note after another with the force of a hurricane. Each note became clearer and more beautiful than any music I'd heard before or since that time.

I'd seen the storm clouds brewing in the northeast and watched them blow over Summit Ridge. Well, that giant Elk slipped quietly out of the meandering forest shrub as the rain began to set in; half-awake, I turned my head away. The beast was gone. He had gorged enough on wild blueberries and I hadn't been able to stop thinking about it.

The runaway thing had begun to get to me; so many young kids running away, leaving their homes and going to other places, anywhere away from where they'd been. These days it seemed like nobody knew where he or she was any longer, or who they were, or where they came from; not at all like in my younger days. Nothing was the same; nothing was the same as the way it had been even in Wallowa County.

During my youth, while growing up in Joseph, we had been pretty poor but the family was linked. The community was solid. All of us knew who we all were; somebody was always there looking out for one another. There were always neighbors caring about neighbors, which meant there was something somewhat binding about our community during those days. We were raised with something that tied us all together as a place and as a people. Seems as if a great deal of that is lost now even within the county. In fact, even the local Indian had a hold on life. We all lived more or less like an Indian in those days. Most of the hatred of the past wars had healed by the late forties or the early fifties. Most of it had been forgotten with few scabs left showing.

Anyway, as I neared the settlement where Sister Mary lived with the runaways, I couldn't help thinking about sweet Kaelin. She had been a person to reckon with, even at fifteen. What an individual spirit she had. The child had stunning green eyes to go along with her long, shaggy, auburn hair. Often, she even appeared to be a striking young woman. I heard she had been smoking pot and drinking pretty heavy before she disappeared, but that was what most of the kids got into in these parts. As law officers, we sort of let 'em get through it before we even started to get serious about punishment. The law out here still wasn't similar to that in the big cities where the Fed's force their way on the youth, cracking down on everybody in draconian ways. In these parts, we still had a strong sense of common good along with a sense of law. We had laws that were made to serve people not for people to serve the law.

Sister Mary had taken her mother's name after the older woman's death many years ago. The two of them were about as close as any mother and daughter I'd ever known. She was like the squaw princess one sees in early Remington paintings and the drawings of many plains artists. Until the day she died, Mary's mother had a full bonnet of beautiful black hair. Maria Espanola's face was chiseled in time like the cliffs of Old Wallowa's Matterhorn. That mountain stood tall like that old woman; it was ten-thousand-four feet in height, and with her being six-feet tall, I often felt the same sort of majesty. They say that she was from full-blooded stock of the Nez Perce and the Blackfoot. The rising sun and old dog soldiers mixed on dark nights and there was Maria. I felt warm inside thinking about her.

All of my family, as well as most of the town and county, attended her funeral at the aged Catholic Church in Joseph.

Hers was a service to remember. It was a mass of local, and not so local, people that she knew. A lot of people loved and respected that old woman. She always had something concrete to say, not that she said very much, but when Maria spoke, she said exactly what she meant to say.

As a young man in high school, I was about as nuts over Maria as any man could be. I was completely taken by her. Yep, I was a real goner. She and I played as kids in those mountains. While the two of us swam naked in the streams, we never thought of sex, or never let it get in our way, at least that's the way I thought then.

Sister Mary was still a most striking woman. She reminded me of the fifty-some-year-old actress, Barbara Hershey, but her mouth was not quite as large. Her hips; those hips of hers were far fuller. They were more like a woman from these parts closer to the earth. Mary had a figure when she was younger that caught most men dumb. She'd looked at us with those brown eyes and they'd overpower any one of us like good homemade fudge syrup over ice cream.

As I drove up to the door of the runaway house, I noticed two of the girls were sitting to Mary's left in a wicker couch on the screened-in porch. After I opened my car door, I waved at Mary. She smiled real deep as she always did when we hadn't seen each other for a period of time. No doubt she and I had a lot of past together, might have been some love still holding between us, but those kinds of things could never be spoken of, especially to a Sister of a Jesuit Order.

"Hello Sister, what ya been doing since I saw you last?" I remember nodding ever so gentle towards the young girls.

"Oh, just doing the usual things. I'm taking care of the young people's needs and the homestead. What else is a woman like me going to do 'round here, Buck?"

On her left was Terrie Conson, one of Kaelin's best friends and runaway buddies. She looked somewhat scared. I could see it in her bright-blue eyes. "How you doing, Terrie? And Tilly, is that right? Is that your name? Tilly?"

"Yes, that's my name, Mr. Parrish, and how come you know it?" she asked.

14

"Well, it's my job to know all the girls who stay here; I believe the Sister's got about twenty-five of you girls here now, right?"

"Actually, Buck, there's twenty-eight of us. We had three new arrivals last week. I'll have to introduce 'em to you later," Sister Mary informed me.

"I've actually come up here to talk to you and Terrie 'bout Kaelin Jones. She's been missing for several days now, as you may already know."

Tilly replied, "Yes, we know; probably know too much 'bout Kaelin, Buck. Maybe we know too damned much."

"Sister, what is it that you know? Do you or the girls know where she is, when she'll be back, or where it was exactly Kaelin ran off to? Do you know much about that?"

I watched Mary's eyes. She was always easy about speaking to others close to her with her piercing dark-brown eyes. "Come inside, Buck. Let's chat a little prior to any conversation that you may have with the girls."

We both got up and walked to the back of the old house, which was actually a big lodge. In fact, it was built with human working hands 'bout one hundred years ago by her grandfather who used the largest Ponderosa logs ever used for construction in these parts. At this point in time it would take a volcano set off right under the damned structure to shake it in any direction. The house was still as solid as the Wallowa's and was solidly built by a real craftsman who knew his craft and his tools. It was one wonder of a lodge.

The two of us, Sister Mary and I, sat down in her office at the back end of the lodge and simply stared at each other's faces. My hat was off and I could easily remember how I kept twisting my fingers. "Miles and I have a strong suspicion that Kaelin's gone for a long time, probably never to return. Do you have the same concern?"

Mary got up and went to her desk and pulled a letter out of a small locked drawer and handed it to me. "Buck, take the unopened letter to Sheriff Carson. As he reads it, listen to the contents, but make sure he's the one who opens it first."

The Murder of Kaelin

"Mary, I'll do exactly that. Do you know anything further, or do you have any other information about Kaelin? Is there anything else you can tell me?"

"Yes, we'll talk further after you and Miles T read the letter. It may help," she offered.

"Well, it's always good to see you, Mary. Everything else going pretty well out here?"

"Yes, as well as ever. In fact, maybe better than it's ever gone before now. However, right now, a bunch of the kids are scared 'cause of Kaelin.'"

"Scared of what? Scared of who? Me? That's what you're talking about isn't it, Mary?" I inquired.

"No, not you in particular; anyone in authority in the county. They're scared of anyone who is part of, or close to, influential people hereabouts; so I guess that includes you. Either you're one of them or you work for them in some capacity, or you work against 'em and that may be another kind of problem," she warned.

For the first time I'd ever noticed, Mary looked self-conscious, almost self-inflicted with something she seemed to be hiding from the outside, which did seem to include me. I said nothing more to her at that point. Instead, I just got up and asked her if I could have a private conversation with Terrie. She gave me her permission and I tipped my hat to her. Within a few minutes, I headed out to talk to Terrie who was now sitting alone. I eased down on the wicker couch to her left side.

"Terrie, when's the last time you saw Kaelin and just as important, where'd you last see her?" I took out my police-issue memo pad and began taking accurate and copious notes describing anything she said, and depicting any obvious expressions she exhibited. These notes were a real help to me. I'd used them before in many investigations and they were extremely useful.

The girl sat up and looked forward for a few seconds. Terrie began speaking straight at me with no hesitation. "Mr. Parrish, last time I saw Kaelin, we was just strolling down about three hundred feet from Pastor Chrisp's New Church."

"Did you see anything unusual around you, maybe some foreigner? Did you see any cars parked nearby with the sort of person who might be interested in pretty young girls, like the two of you?"

"No, I didn't see any other cars 'cept the usual ones driving in and out of New Church," Terrie answered.

"How'd the two of you get from here to the church that day?"

"Miss Cruthers brought us down from just in front of her mailbox. She drove us all the way to the north end of town. We walked hand-in-hand to the front of the church."

"I ask again; did you or Kaelin see anything different? Notice anyone unusual parked in the area around the church? Was anyone staring at you from somewhere? Did you feel anyone?"

"No sir, Mr. Parrish; can't say I saw anyone or anything out of the ordinary prior to leaving Kaelin and running down to the children's center just below the church's center building."

"When exactly was that, Terrie?"

"It was right about a week ago today, Mr. Parrish," she answered.

I stared at her for several seconds and noted her blinking more times than usual during our discussion. Also her hands seemed wet and she kept rubbing them together as if she was keeping something inside. "Okay, Terrie, then I'm off to talk to Miss Cruthers as long as I'm up here. But you do understand you and I'll be talking about this again real soon?"

"Sure, Mr. Parrish, I understand and I'll be expecting to see you another time. It was good to talk then." Terrie nodded to me while drifting slowly down the side of the porch. She headed towards the small lake at the far end of the property.

There was a big water swing there; I sure remember it well. I called down the hall to Mary. She came out of her office and stood there in the semi-dark shadows staring at me. "Bye, bye, Buck Parrish. Sure, I'll be seeing you soon, won't I?"

"Yes, you will; no doubt. In fact, I'll be up here next week. Got to do a little work in between."

17

Sister Mary smiled at me in her friendly manner as I stepped down the old porch stairs and trotted toward the patrol car. From the corner of my eye I could feel young Tilly Wallis staring at the nape of my neck. I got in the car and drove away. From the side mirror, I watched Tilly emerge from behind a middle-sized sugar pine. She gazed at the dust kicking up behind me.

four

<u>Willa Shannon</u>

I recollect the night Terrie and Kaelin wandered into my store. As I calculate, it was the precise night Kaelin disappeared. From what I recall, all three of us were talking about some local herb. Yes, I believe it was a unique high-desert sage, which just grows at the foot of these Wallowa's. I remember talking to the girls about the mental alertness one gets while using the herb with a salad or another food. In fact, one can get the same reaction from a tiny spoonful of the extract. It's funny how we got into that subject. Not a whole lot of people were interested in my oils or extracts but those young teens sure were that night.

You know there was something about that night which was quite strange. I recall seeing an old '57 Chevy parked just outside the store. The car was parked in the far corner of the parking lot with its dim lights on, but I wasn't able to see anybody on the inside. Normally, I wouldn't have thought anything about it 'cause lots of people have old classic cars around here. Yet there was something about this car that was quite different, something quite unusual about it. I did finally get a glimpse of the driver but it wasn't a very clear view, and at first, I didn't think I knew him. Still, his hat, as I flashed on it, well, I somehow connected it to someone familiar. It was a hat, which had a shape to the head I'd seen before. Yes, I was sure I'd seen the hat before.

At the next moment, the two girls redirected my attention to some fine Dutch chocolate, which had just arrived from Europe. This was a chocolate I'd gotten from some locals who ordered a bunch of it for Christmas presents. There were a few who could easily afford this stuff, but only a few. Most of the people in these mountains would buy the cheaper brands; some would even prefer Nestles or Hershey's to the good stuff. My business was always good around Christmas. All of the people wanted some different type of gift for someone, but I'd always get more orders for chocolate.

The two girls that night just kept looking at that chocolate like they'd never seen anything like it. They looked like their mouths were just watering for a bite. Guess I got a soft spot on my old heart for these young girls; life grows up fast on all of 'em, especially now.

They asked me, "How much is a piece of that chocolate, an ounce of that chocolate, Willa?"

"Well, my dear," I said to Terrie Conson. "I sell that Dutch stuff for about two bucks an ounce. How many ounces of it do you want?"

I think back at the two of those girls snickering and digging through their tight blue jeans as they kept staring and digging for enough money to buy a piece of that chocolate. I moved my hand at that point to a broken piece of chocolate at the corner of the candy display. "You girls see that broken piece there? Well, I'll make you a deal on that piece, 'cause it's broken. I can sell it to you for a buck. You two got a buck between you?" I asked Terrie.

The two pretty girls dug even deeper into their jeans. In fact, they kept poking around through everything they owned 'til they finally came up with one dollar between 'em.

"Is this what you said you'd take for that broken-up piece of chocolate over there, Willa?" asked Kaelin.

"Yes, you two give me a dollar and both you and Terrie can enjoy that fine piece of Dutch chocolate."

The joy in those two girl's faces as they walked out the door headed west towards Pastor Chrisp's church was a delight. Funny thing is I still remember the fine chrome on that Chevy, as it turned and headed down the same way as those two young ones, I especially recall those back tail lights; they were real dark red and fin-shaped.

Kaelin was such a lovely girl. She was pretty in a deep sort of way like a natural mountain kind of beauty, with deep, dark-green staring eyes in a fully formed face with fine features like Old Ella, the grandmother of Tom Onaban- that old woman was pure Creek, diamond-pure Creek. Old Ella had a face like nothing else I'd ever seen around here. That young Kaelin reminded me of her.

I knew Old Ella well before she died; she and I spent a lot of time talking in those days. I recall how we talked about the settlers 'round here, white, native, and black. We spent good times talking about all the people in eastern Washington and northeast Oregon, sure did. She was a knowledgeable old woman, Ella was. The woman had her faculties 'til she died. Nobody knew how old she really was, but the best guess was about middle nineties. She was one of those fine 'real' human beings who one has got to learn how not to forget nowadays. It seems like everyone is not anywhere too long, and then they leave, off to Portland or Seattle or another big city. Guess I'll remain here with the store and my memories, good and bad, 'til they bury me somewhere near these mountains.

five

Shawna Thore, FBI

The first time I met Jillian Douds and Millie Roberts, I'd just finished a run up to the upper end of Main Street, and I'd come back around the backside of the town for a second time. I'd known ever since running track in school that a brief run or workout prior to a meeting would help keep me far more alert and on my toes.

For the meeting, Deputy Parrish sat on my left side, just to the north side in front of a framed window. I'd used this conference room for adjunct meetings when I was first stationed in Wallowa County. We chatted for a while about all the new crime in the valley and the odd kind of druggies that seemed to find a home in the rural areas. Parrish was the type of authentic man I could still talk to; he was hard looking. He had deep chiseled grooves in his cheek flesh. It was easy to see his nose had been broken in his early days of semi-professional boxing. The deputy had gone two years to junior college where he majored in Criminology. Having been in his trade for twenty hard years, he was experienced and skilled. Parrish was six-feet tall with a solid sturdy physique for a man in his early fifties who had done little formal exercise in his recent past.

Deputy Parrish confronted me with some questions and idle chitchat about a few illegal aliens from Mexico who continually crossed the borders between rural Oregon and Washington. "Lot of 'em worked in the fields around Kennewick," he said. "Some of the smarter ones drop a little dope on a few of them who need to make some extra money distributing the stuff."

"Found a man named Alfredo F. Gonzalez, chopped and hacked in half. We found him up by the old Joseph graveyard. We thought he was buried to his waist, but when we pulled him out, he had no legs. His trunk and half of his body just sat there propped up rigid by a stake, which went through the lower section of his body to his heart. The other half was parked about twenty feet from his other parts. Legs up, balls out and spiked again with a stake up through the spine holding the lower half of his body up; never seen anything like it," he claimed.

"Did they do a full post-forensic on the body parts?" I asked.

"Yes, we shipped it all to Pendleton where they have facilities for full postmortem forensics. We came up with a lot of solid information from the examination," Deputy Parrish said.

"Like what, other than the usual who, what, when, where, and how?"

"Actually we were able to detect the blood types and the records of the men, or at least one of the men who killed Gonzalez, through DNA tests that we ran and re-ran. And as I said, through these tests, we were able to track three men to a gigantic farm in eastern Washington, about a hundred miles south of Spokane. Seemed like these men, or the killers, were part of a much wider operation, one that was based in Vera Cruz, Mexico. By gathering different evidence, the authorities found matching hair samples and blood at more than one scene. The police in Vera Cruz were most helpful in identifying them for prosecution and deportation," he said.

"Surprised the police down there were clean. Usually, they're as tied in as the cocaine overseers who manage the huge cartels," I said.

"Didn't matter anyway; 'cause we caught 'em in Kennewick, Washington. We were transporting them to a stock county compound when we got a report that the bus exploded and all the prisoners and two guards were killed. They were blown up like so much raw meat," Deputy Parrish said.

"Any evidence left linking the explosives or the device, or the bus parts to anyone?"

"No local money to continue the investigation, no motivation, and you guys asked all the local cops in the area to "cease all criminal pursuit," Parrish said.

"Did you stop?"

"Yes, wasn't any money or time to investigate nothing; the state boys would pick up on the guards but that was a joke. Nobody pursued anything 'cause we all had easier collars. You understand what I'm saying?" the deputy insisted.

I looked up at the door as the clerk announced the arrival of my other witnesses, Jillian Douds and Millie Roberts. I asked both women to sit down next to me at the south side of the small coffee table. Millie was dressed in a purple top and wore small lavender earrings. Her hair was frizzy and wild and her eyes were very red but not the redness caused by 'coke' or any other drug concoction.

Jillian was like most medical people, set and professional, ready to balance her emotions, energy, and skill. She wore a fine antique-style dress, which was dark brown and long. It looked nice with her earrings that were draping and shaped in a three quarter moon design.

The girls greeted each other cheerfully and sat down quickly across from one another for a few seconds of usual silence. I brought out my recorder and note pad and asked the two women if they minded the recording. Neither said 'no' to anything, so, I turned it on.

Deputy Parrish twisted a pencil in his hands. He kept looking down at those large man's hands folded partially against his knees. "Good to see both of you ladies. I hope you don't mind my being here," he said.

"Don't mind you, Buck, but we sure don't want to explain anything in front of Deputy Byron Frank," explained Jillian.

Parrish asked, "Don't like Deputy Frank? Why is that? What'd that old Byron boy do to you?"

"Just don't plain trust the man, Buck; never trusted him. As far as I'm concerned, he could be deeply involved in some of the local activities," she said.

"What sort of activities? What are you talking about? In fact, why have I been invited to this meeting in the first place?" Deputy Parrish asked.

Cops always protect other cops, especially when they lack respect for the subject officer. This certainly was the case for Buck Parrish regarding Byron Frank. Frank was a sloppy, overweight former security guard who ended up working in the state prison system as a corrections officer. He was let go after six months under clouded circumstances. That's when Miles T. Carson picked him up as a deputy, which was just after he won

24

the last election. Old Mr. Frank, and Miles' father, knew each other quite well. They served side-by-side in the trenches during the Korean War. Something sure binds people close together during times of war more than any other time in a person's life.

"Never mind any thoughts about Deputy Frank; 'cause if he were here, neither Millie nor I would be sitting at this table, period," Jillian insisted.

"Let's get on with the meeting; we all know what we're here for, don't we?" I interjected.

"Jillian and I went trekking into the upper back country of Hell's Canyon, up there near Hat Point, one of those side roads west and down a ways on towards old Horse Creek. We took an old logging road off Horse Creek and traveled about a mile and a half into the woods. As usual, the wind never stopped blowing," said Millie.

Buck Parrish sat for what seemed like forever staring at Millie as she recounted the story of their trip up into Hat Point. He knew the area as well as anybody in Wallowa County and listened as though he was mapping their journey in his mind. Buck was still one of the best trial lawmen in what was left of the rugged West and his reputation could only be matched by two Indian half-brothers, the Onaben boys. Frank Onaben was half-Nez Perce and half-negro. His half-brother, Billy was a full-blooded Nez Perce with a family history tracing back several hundred years. These two brothers shared the same father.

Now that was a pair of brothers one could never forget meeting, thought Shawna.

"We made a camping site not far from the old logging path," Jillian explained. "The road had become more a path than a road at that point. It looked as though the weather and time had gotten to it. Millie and I pulled a couple of sandwiches from one of the packs. She and I started discussing where exactly we were while trying to read one of the old Pittman mine maps, which were never that accurate anyways."

"What'd you talk about other than an occasional Elk and a few jumping Bighorn Sheep? If you're lucky enough to even see one," inquired Buck with his shy humor.

"As you know, Buck, the summers are fairly cool up there at Hat Point. The trees are so big you hardly see the sun. The wind never stops, the mist always follows, and then the cold rain; the same sequence, different day," Jillian commented.

"Know the weather real well up there. That's where old Nathan Bork and I used to hunt and play, as kids; know it well. So what's the purpose for the two of you being there?" he asked.

Jillian simply looked across the table at Millie, seeming to wait for a gaggle of words to flow out of her mouth. Nonetheless, nothing came out; not a sound was made. Millie sat still and stared off in space. No one in that room could know where she was, much less penetrate that silence.

Her explanation continued; "Listen and listen well. Millie and I searched the area hard for several hours, several hours indeed. I searched the higher areas and she took the lower ground. We made a pact to meet at the campsite at two thirty."

"What were the two of you searching for? And by the way, Shawna, I still don't understand why you invited me to this meeting; or to any other meeting unless there was something important to reveal." It was obvious Buck was a little perturbed. "Okay, let's get to the point here, ladies. What did you find up there?"

"I climbed to the top of an eastern ridge just above Horse Creek. In fact, I was about two miles up from base camp. After reaching the upper ridge, I was totally exhausted. Still, I thought I noticed something cream-colored lying between two rocks in an offshoot gulch feeding Horse Creek," Jillian explained.

"Tell him what you picked up from the dirt, Jillian. Tell 'em straight and voice it now," said Millie, somewhat elusively, but poignantly.

After a few seconds, Jillian began again, "Just adjacent to a rock cranny, cut into a little pool area was what was left of a human foot; four metatarsals and the phalanges of the right foot," she confessed.

"Did you find any other body parts? Did you look further for more?" asked Buck, now very interested.

"Yes, another twenty feet down the feeder gorge, I found a talus bone and one cuneiform bone, which comes from the toe bone, I believe," admitted Jillian.

Knowing she probably had more information, Buck drilled her more. "What did you do with the bones, and what drove you out there in the first place? Why'd you two head out there looking for bones?"

"I pulled a plastic bag from my desk and placed it gently on the table. The women had given it to me right before Buck arrived for the meeting. It was pretty obvious to me that these were weathered bones from a teenage adult's foot. It was a metatarsal, best guess from my anatomy course, and the next questions required forensics and forensic pathologists." She was tiring of the conversation and her leg began shaking some.

"Had you seen the bones before, or is this actually the first time?" Buck asked Shawna.

"No, Buck, I've never seen them before and they were brought in just prior to your arrival; maybe ten minutes before," the FBI agent replied.

Buck Parrish was obviously angry. He hated being placed in second position, especially in his home territory and especially by the FBI. If I had it to do over again, I might have presented it to him in a different way, but for that moment in time, I had to live with its reality. He was one of the few local law officers that I had any respect for, and my methods at that meeting did leave something to be desired.

"Jillian, tell me something. How and why did you and Millie decide to head out toward Hat Creek in search of Kaelin's body?" asked Buck.

Jillian gazed at her friend for several seconds before replying. It was as if she looked to Millie to re-express something lost in the conversation. "Millie had a dream. No, maybe a revelation would be better regarding Kaelin's disappearance. And in the revelation, we were led to the bones stuck in the pool by Kaelin herself."

"You say that you found those bones up on east Horse Creek through a dream, or maybe I should say a revelation? Is that right?" Buck asked in disbelief.

27

"Yes, it was through the revelations that Millie had that led us up to the bones, to the discovery of poor Kaelin's lost bones, of finding her foot and the child's *image revelation*. Yes, that's how we got there," Jillian said.

"Image revelation? Now what in God's sweet world is that? Are you talking about some kind of ghosts being here?" Buck asked.

"Listen, Deputy Parrish, you can call it what you will. The young girl talked to me. She talked to me direct and in front of me. I saw her, spoke to her, could have touched her," Millie claimed.

"Did you talk to Kaelin? Do you have any proof that a physical being was there other than what you seemed to talk to? Do you have any evidence of any of this?" Buck inquired.

I sat back in my chair not quite positive of what to do regarding any of the conversation to that point, so I intervened. "Buck, I called you here to listen, to take what you can from the meeting, then make a decision. Nothing more."

He stared at me the way men sometimes look when they feel belittled by a woman. I had always tried to handle these types of situations gingerly, but every time I got into one, I ended up with myself tangled in a seamen's knot.

"Might be I can help a little here, Deputy Parrish. You and I have known each other for a good many years now, haven't we?" Buck nodded to Jillian as he sat back in his chair, pulled out a pouch of tobacco and paper, and began to roll one.

"Jillian, we can just finish what we've come here to say, make our little statement and get the hell out," insisted Millie.

Buck and Millie were two people at that point in the meeting who one could say they had reached 'the ultimate head bump.' I did all I could just to keep them sitting together at the same table during that meeting.

"We'll leave some of the bones we have so you can run tests to see if they are Kaelin's. If there are any further questions on the experiences Millie or I had, you can call me or leave a message," Jillian declared and stood to leave.

Deputy Parrish wasn't finished, though. "We have several other questions to ask you. This interview is not over."

28

Jillian answered. "Yes it is. We volunteered to help catch the murderers. In fact, we came down here to detail our findings to both of you and as usual with the law, you're giving us a hard time."

The room was silent as Buck Parrish diligently and with great precision finished rolling his cigarette. He lit it, and took in a deep, long drag.

I was almost ready to end the meeting, but it was a courtesy to the local law forces for us to continue. Part of my job as a representative of the FBI was to remain objective and make the local law part of operations. The girls' disappearance did take place on county turf, and in law enforcement, a common courtesy prevails.

"Could we continue the conversation with Agent Thore, and she'll tell you all about it later?" inquired Millie.

"No, my dear, I'll be part of any conversation about any disappearance in this county, even if what disappeared is only a stinky skunk! The law here is the sheriff's department, which I represent. We are the number-one group to consult within this county and that's the way it is!"

"Listen Buck, if you have a problem with our story, let us complete it with Agent Thore. Afterward, she'll inform you of the outcome," Jillian sternly suggested.

"Go on with your story, Jillian. I'll sit back and take notes, but I want that damned bag'a bones when all's finished with these conversations, okay?" Buck demanded.

"Alright, as long as you listen fairly and let us complete our story," Jillian shot back.

Again, a time of gentle silence passed between the women and Deputy Parrish. It was as though they had reached a covert agreement between themselves.

"Alright then; what led you to the location, Horse Creek Canyon that is?" Buck asked.

"We were told exactly where to go, Millie had every detail of the location mapped out for her by Kaelin, or her image, let's say," said Jillian.

"Did you find any other items? You know, articles of clothing, jewelry, or anything else of a personal nature in the surrounding area?"

"Not much. The only thing we found was a shirt that she had sometimes worn. Actually the shirt was turned over to Deputy Byron Frank about a year ago," Jillian further informed.

"Byron Frank got a shirt from you that you say was Kaelin's and he received it about a year ago? And where did you discover that shirt?"

"My daughter, and her friend Daniel, found it up the northwest section of Heaven's Road, just two miles out of town," Millie replied.

"Was that before or after your dream revelations?" Buck questioned.

"Before – actually the kids found Kaelin's shirt about thirteen months ago while playing some games up the upper section of Heaven's Road."

Buck Parrish took a slow drag from his cigarette and wrote everything down on his pad, detail-for-detail, and kept asking questions. "Yes, well tell me a few more details about Deputy Frank and his supposed possession of the missing girl's shirt?"

"You see, the children brought it right up to the Sheriff's half-way station where Byron usually visits for a couple hours each day. That station is within walking distance of my house," Millie explained.

"Did you see the shirt? Did anybody other than the kids see the shirt?"

"No, to my knowledge nobody but the kids saw the shirt, 'cepting of course Byron Frank."

"Did the children mention any stains or anything unusual about the shirt? For example, was it torn?"

"No, don't think there were any stains on the shirt according to Daniel. Nothing was torn about it. But, I'm positive it was Kaelin's shirt all right; she wore it a lot. It was her favorite," the girl said, her eyes becoming moist.

30

"Jillian, did you see the shirt? Did you see or handle anything belonging to the girls other than the bones in question?" the deputy asked.

"No. Nothing. The only thing I ever handled which belonged to Kaelin were the foot bones in question here."

"You're sure and you're certain that these are Kaelin's foot bones? Even before forensics has a chance to examine them?" Buck asked the woman.

"Buck, I'm as sure of the validity of these bones as anything in my life." Jillian didn't like the tone the deputy was taking. "I feel these are her bones sure as a witch wand finds sunken streams. That's how certain I am. And, Buck, there's no real proof, just my deep gut feelings."

"Shawna, can you sign for the evidence in question here under the FBI's control, and if you're unable to accommodate, please let me sign under county jurisdiction?"

"I can, Buck, but I'd prefer, in fact, that Millie and Jillian officially hand the bones over to you under county control, which would be officially acceptable."

Buck pulled the bag full of foot bone evidence over to him right next to his note pad, and then prepared a formal evidence receipt and handed the stamped yellow copy to Millie. "This is written proof that all pieces of material evidence are in our possession for now until all formal examination is complete. Understand?"

Millie nodded, as did Jillian. At that point, it seemed that each woman had a solemn way about her. "Can we leave now? Millie and I've got other things to do? Do you have anything else to ask, Shawna;" or Buck?" Jillian asked of them.

"No, if there's anything else, I know where to find you," Buck replied and stood, signifying the meeting was over. "Oh, just one more question. Do you have any other pieces of evidence in your possession?"

"Yes, I have two other bones which may add to the case," admitted Jillian.

"Okay, why not hand them over now if you still have them?"

"No sir. We'll not hand them over until you prove the first two are human, and preferably of course, that the human being was Kaelin Jones," said Jillian.

Buck Parrish clinched his teeth on the stub of his cigarette. He did all he could to contain his anger.

"Illegal possession of evidence is a crime. Are you aware of this, Millie?"

"No, Buck, I didn't know. But I do know that when you acknowledge what we've told you, we'll withhold the other bones no matter what you invent."

"Invent? We'll see what you ladies withhold, but in the meantime, I'll take what you ladies have presented here today and see what the lab has to report." Buck held the bones up in Millie's face, trying to make a strategic point, but the gesture was lost and there was no humor left in the room.

Buck Parrish had done a good job keeping a lid on his great temper, as good as any man I'd ever witnessed. At that point in the discussion, we told the two women to leave. As soon as they went through the door, Buck and I planned our next course of action regarding the disappearance of Kaelin.

"I'll take the evidence to Pendleton for one test," Buck explained. "No need to go to Portland. Pendleton has most of the lab equipment now, so I don't see an immediate need for your people, at least not yet."

"Alright, Buck, we'll do it your way, but if you need our lab, it's open to you. In the mean time, we'll continue our investigation of Pastor Chrisp and his congregation. There are a few on the mighty board that we'd surely like to know more about."

At that point in the discussion, I was able to envision Buck's complete anger and frustration as he grabbed the plastic bag of evidence. I watched as he shoved them into the pocket of his jacket, while removing the cigarette from his mouth. He then pressed what was left of it into the glass ashtray and flipped me a signaled 'goodbye' using two fingers, similar to the Army salute.

For several hours after the meeting, I was unable to get the 'revelation story' of Millie's out of my mind. It was as if someone had set me atop a wooden merry-go-round horse and slapped it so hard that it seemed to be in perpetual motion. For me that meeting with Buck Parrish and the two women was one of the strangest witness-encounters of my life. Nothing we had gone over made any real sense, and as it was at that point, I was never truly able to see how it would.

six

Jillian Douds

I guess the time had finally come. We had been playing tag, Millie and I with Kaelin's murder for over a year- ever since Millie's first dream or whatever one might call it. I often recollect those trance-like dreams such as that first night she called me over to her house; the first exposure I had to that solid magenta-colored rock crystal. I was sitting with my husband at ten that night watching a video-film about some new horror flick in Bosnia, a film called 'Pretty Village, Pretty Flame'. The telephone rang. My husband stopped the tape and passed the phone to me.

"Millie was on the line and she sounded farther out there than usual," he said.

There were several times I resented Jason's comments about Millie but I knew he was a slightly jealous man. Usually, he got jealous about anyone with whom I had close relations. My caring about other people and having friends seemed to be a problem for him. I always thought it was quite a normal reaction for men to feel that way when they perceived someone's getting between the two of you. Women could relate well to special people in one's life. We had that type of intimate ongoing friendship, nothing kinky you know, just a real distinctive thing.

When we got together that night, I found Millie lying on her California King bed. She was grasping a large crystal against her stomach using both hands; her face was reddened as if she'd been crying for quite awhile. Her eyes looked as if she 'piped it' more than usual for a night, meaning she'd felt she needed a little pot to clear her mind. Millie was extremely distraught. The teen had been moved by something strange, something that had really gotten to her and she was quite agonized by it. I approached her very gently and at the same time, took her quickly into my arms and kissed her lightly on the forehead. After my genuine kiss, after all we were just close friends, she hugged me quite hard. Obviously she was pleased that I was there in that room that night for her!

"I love you for being here, Jillian. I've talked to her. I've talked to Kaelin; she came to talk to me. We spoke of many things and we talked about the disappearance and the time period she'd been away from the Wallowa Valley."

"Kaelin spoke to you in the same way that I'm speaking to you now; is that what you're trying to say?" I asked Millie.

"She spoke to me just as we are speaking now. However, it started first up the road on one of my walks, up Heaven's Creek Road," she informed me.

I looked at her somber, bloodshot eyes as she looked right up at me. For a few seconds, I thought before speaking, "Well, tell me what'd Kaelin say when you first met her? What'd she look like?"

Millie stared off into space for several brief seconds while focusing hard on the center of my face. However, she didn't see me. In fact, her eyes seemed to get redder and redder. It was if she was getting deeper into a self-propelled trance. "Kaelin walked up to me. There was some sort of color spinning around her. She wasn't a 'real person' like you or me. At this time, she was a spirit image; that's the best I can describe it for you Jillian," she explained.

"Let me ask you again, Millie, what did you and Kaelin talk about that day?"

The girl sought something deep inside me. I could just feel it in her eyes. Next, she grabbed my hand and placed it on the crystal. "Feel yourself in the stone; feel it warm you. You will see and hear with me as I try to bring you there with me; yes, I'll bring you there."

I laid one hand, then the other one on each side of the large crystal rock; it did have a certain bizarre feel about it. Something, let's call it a warmth, rushed through my fingers and up my arms- it was like a strong static electric shock. I waited for Millie to say something or come forward with additional words describing her meeting on that deserted creek road, up on that road with Kaelin. Naturally, at that point, I was very skeptical yet the crystal rock did pulsate. Funny how super warm that rock was that night, though it could have been the excited body sweat coming off Millie. I asked her what I was to do next. Again, there was a period of dead silence.

"Just keep your hands close to mine and wait for fluid images. Close your eyes. I know it'll all come to you," she promised.

I waited for anything, just anything to happen. My excitement caused me to feel as if I'd just received my first Christmas morning doll. "We're out there, standing out there together in the cold frosty night drizzle. We're eye-to-eye with Kaelin now."

Images started flashing in my head. I was conscious, yet in a dream-like condition. It felt as if I was standing in between awake and asleep. A series of stark images rattled through my head. Suddenly, I found myself standing alongside Millie and Kaelin. At first, I tried to wake myself but was unable. I was standing on the dirt road, old Heaven's Creek Road with Millie and Kaelin. It was extremely dark that evening.

"Tell me what happened to my sweater. Please tell me how I got so soaked; my body is totally soaked and my clothes are all torn up," Kaelin begged.

"Honey, we know nothing about your sweater and even less about your dampness," said Millie. "You look so lost, Kaelin, do you have any idea of what happened to you?"

Kaelin only stared at me for several seconds. It looked as though she gazed right through me. She then began to cry as though she had no idea of what had happened to her; more than that she had no idea of what she really was. The image was glaring at me and the spirit of the girl was extremely strong. The spirit of her ghost was right in front of me; there was no doubt about that. Truly, the more I peered at her, the more convinced I became that the vision was indeed right there in front of me.

"I want to be with Tommy and Brandy, two of my closest friends, and there's another girl I was like a sister with- Terrie Conson--where are they?" Kaelin had asked us.

"I imagine that Brandy and Tommy are at their homes. However, no one has seen Terrie for several days. Sister Mary believes that she too may have run away. They may be out searching for her right now."

Kaelin began laughing and screaming all at once. Her head bounced back and forth while uttering something about wanting to party with her friends. The spirit of the missing girl told us how much she missed her friends. Kaelin even said that Terrie was staying protected with the old tribal people by Medical Springs. No one could find her there so few could ever get through and Medical Springs was a very sacred place to the Umatilla and the Nez Perce peoples. They buried many of their dead in that place and had prayed near there for many centuries.

"I have to find my friends. It's cold out here and the forest is very lonely," she said.

"What forest?" I asked. "What forest are you coming from?"

"They threw me down a cliff somewhere about seven miles south of Hat Point."

"Tell us exactly where to look. We want to find you. Maybe if you tell us, we can find something of you?"

Kaelin danced away. All of a sudden, I seemed to be looking at Millie. She was lying near me and was snoring while holding tight on that crystal rock. For me, that may have been the most unusual night of my life. However, as I was to later discover, it was only the beginning!

seven

Shawna Thore, FBI

Some time in late May, Jeb Hirsch, a longtime agent and friend in the northwest called me one afternoon while I was in Seattle, Washington. He asked me to come to Pendleton, Oregon to discuss an important call he'd recently received on a disappearance/possible kidnapping. I drove down immediately to his office where we discussed the case he had in mind.

Jeb had been with the agency for at least twenty-five years. He was in his early fifties and had jet black-gray hair. His bony nose supported a set of pigeon eyes. He wasn't an easy man to stare at; few people did. We talked about a strange call, which came from Millie Roberts and her friend, Jillian Douds.

"Shawna, I want you to meet with two local women and somehow out of this critical conversation, we might be able to get a clue or two about the New Church of Wallowa and one or two of the 'blessed deacons'. Do you get my drift, my dear? Also, I want you to have Deputy Sheriff Parrish at the meeting."

"Sir, I don't understand. Why don't you let me use our standard interview tactics undisturbed?"

"I believe we could learn to achieve much more by having Mr. Parrish at the meeting, better than having some loose-tongued legal cowboy sidestep our purpose. Better that we stop him from finding some blind steer to wrestle than letting him waste more of our valuable agency time."

"Let's not be unkind to our local law enforcement brothers, sir. Mr. Parrish certainly has his jurisdictional place at any meeting in this county."

"Yes, and you will have him there but do brief him prior to any meeting," suggested Jeb Hirsh.

When Hirsh made himself clear on all points, all who listened surely understood exactly what he was saying. He was a powerful speaker, especially for an FBI man. "As you know, at this point in the investigation there are activities beyond our first glimpse. There are things going on at that glorious bastion of biblical hypocrisy. Now, it's time to get to a little substance."

"Yes, sir, but wouldn't it be better to have Deputy Byron Frank? He seems to have the capacity to alienate everyone, so he's just a tobacco chewing stained shirt charmer."

Hirsch stopped at the door for a moment and then he peeked back inside the room. "I suggest you keep those tiger-jawed teeth of yours for a boyfriend; maybe a sharp tongue will do; just get Parrish on the phone and get him and Millie to the meeting--now!"

I watched him step through the door. Jeb never joked about his position on a case. He was the regional station chief and I knew exactly what he wanted. We both knew the best person to get something on the table quickly was your's truly.

Buck Parrish was an easy man to take. The fact was I even had an attraction towards him. If he wasn't tied up, I sure would be the 'front-line woman' to play with his zipper, sure would. It took me a couple of hours to call Millie Roberts and Jillian Douds. First, I had to formulate a written plan prior to getting everyone together.

I called my old friend Marty MacArthur, a top agent in D.C. who worked with 'sane' known psychics. He had developed a priority list and Marty was as sharp an investigator as I'd ever met in the service. He and I had our 'bedding time' together but that little affair had ended or 'rock-ended' some ten years earlier. Unlike many affairs in the agency, he and I had kept irregular contact. After a long conversation with him, I was able to glean an affective approach to our oncoming meeting interrogation with the two local women, Millie Roberts and Jillian Douds. According to Marty, the best approach would be to push them gently towards their real concerns and then delicately nudge information out of them regarding Reverend Chrisp and New Church of Wallowa.

Marty gave me some recent detailed information about a new line of investigative science called 'psychic mental space'. He taught me the best way to recognize a true psychic personality and her story. The bureau had used these types of methods with people they'd investigated five years earlier, so why not apply the best of this data to the situation at hand? Even Marty was interested in the New Church and Reverend Chrisp. Marty offered to help me anytime I needed him. The commitment was an unusual indulgence for him. For the immediate moment, I brushed all outside interference aside.

The next day, I called Parrish and the two women and made arrangements for Millie and Jillian to come down on Wednesday the twenty-seventh of November. I mentioned to all that I'd like them to bring every bit of the evidence, insignificant or not, and anything they had written or taped on the subject of Kaelin's disappearance. Both women agreed to the meeting as did Parrish and that gave me two additional days of research time to prepare myself.

Marty had always said in or out of bed. "A good agent always prepares oneself," prior to any interview. I never quite forgot that statement because it always helped me reach new career goals within the bureau. The interview would 'turn the case around' for me as well as for most of the inside and outside agents assigned to the case details, or who were just working in areas uncovered. Millie, Jillian and Parrish would never completely understand the tactics employed by our interrogation techniques. They were subtle but they worked on both the unconscious and the conscious sides of the brain.

My training in the bureau would help me uncover many items a 'normal' police investigator would miss, and the technical follow-up we had achieved in the FBI was quite powerful…nothing in the world matched it.

eight

<u>Judge Hamus A. Buchanan</u>

I knew Peggy MacCloud as a child. Perhaps she was the brightest young person I'd ever known. Her father, Peter, was my oldest friend and the last living man in the MacCloud line. Peter and I fished every river 'round here from the Snake to the Walla Walla and everything in between. Old Peter MacCloud died as a man, died as a scout in Italy in World War II while serving his country in Patton's 2nd Infantry. Peter could use a rip-sharp knife and a rifle as well as any full-blooded Indian in these parts. Peter was able to run as fast as any man he knew and he was able to fight better than most. There had never been a student like Peter at Brown Cougar High; probably never will be again.

We were told that Peter was killed by Germans using a land mine planted in some bushes. He never knew what hit him. The news came from Joseph 'bout Peter in February 1944, as I remember; and many a man in northeastern Oregon and western Idaho cried openly about Peter. Mr. MacCloud was a lifelong friend and when he died, it left a permanent hole in me, which I shall probably never fill. That son-of-a-bitch, man, I loved him with my whole heart as many did. I would've done anything for him or his kin as he would have done for me and mine. So it goes on with Peggy and Kaelin.

Sixteen months ago, as I recall, it was November 1997, and old Sheriff Miles T. Carson outlined the case for me right in the judge's chambers. I sat there for an hour listening to dead ends, follow-ups, and non-evidence. At that time, I asked Miles T. to put Buck Parrish on the case kind of on a permanent, or at least a regular, basis regarding as much time as we could allow him to be spared on any case. Of course, Miles T. agreed with me that we had little to go on, and I told him that warrants were open to him as he needed them to be regarding any legitimate matter within the ongoing investigation. Naturally, Sheriff Carson got my full meaning in this matter and this was the last of any discussion on it, within or outside my chambers.

After several nowhere reports from Buck Parrish directly, I asked him to use his spare time only when a real clue appeared that he could follow up on favorably. Sometime after the brief meeting with Miles T. Carson, I personally met with Peggy MacCloud Jones Bradley. The two of us had quite an eye-opening discussion.

Peggy walked into my courtroom chambers, which was situated next to the big county courthouse. I had been in that particular set of offices for nearly twenty-five years and it always felt like a home away from home. A lot of business was done there during those years. All sorts of people and all types of cases were tried and many men and women were sentenced there. Yes, there sure was. A lot of years rolled by, and I was feeling reflective.

My good wife, Sarah, was deceased at that time. She had died of stomach cancer in 1993. My son, Charles, had been killed in 1968 by a bamboo knife trap in some remote South Vietnam jungle area near Khe Sanh. Karen, my youngest daughter, a personal friend of Peggy MacCloud, had moved to Europe in the mid 70s. She lived in the southern part of Norway near Bergen. In the last nine years, I've visited her there twice. I have two grandchildren from her: Becky and Nels, lovely young children, lovely Norwegian Americans.

The Norwegians are naturally cold people…you know native cold folks just like my grandchildren. My daughter, Karen refused to ever return to the United States. She felt that the U.S. Government was rotten and some real ugly people had taken over just after Mr. Reagan was elected. At the time, I felt she was somewhat 'crazed' but at my age, I'm now beginning to have some of the same thoughts, and I'm a judge? Rural people seem to get an open and stark view of things up in these parts. We're isolated. Even with the Internet, we still have a life outdoors. We smell life, we live life. We still refuse to buckle to blind consumerism, yet it creeps at us anyway.

Peggy and I sat across from one another and talked of old times. We chattered especially about Karen, Charles, and Old Peter, her father. I couldn't help but to express how Old Peter and Karen both occupied a vacant spot in my chest; three damned holes next to each other right around my heart. So

Peggy and I talked of a common past and we babbled of the present. We even broached the future.

"I spoke to Buck Parrish about Kaelin the last time we met thirty days earlier. He's followed up on every piece of evidence, which he or his support has unearthed. Most of the so-called leads seem to head nowhere, I'm sorry to report."

Peggy stared at me for several seconds trying to hold her tears back. She tried to pry enough voice power from her clogged throat to speak openly and clearly. "Judge, you've known me most of my life. You knew my father and my family beyond that. I need your support here, some solace. I've got to know what happened to Kaelin. The girl didn't just disappear or runaway like they say; not Kaelin. You know her; she's not a runaway. Is she, Hamus?"

Abruptly, Ms. MacCloud grabbed hold of me and began sobbing against my shoulder. I held her in silence for several minutes before we resumed our discourse. "No, I can't say that I've ever seen that girl as a runaway, and I've counseled a few in this court, that's for sure. Seems like there's a definite breed that continually shifts towards being a runaway or not. It's just not the normal kids with normal-family lives; that's for certain. Not solid American family children; they rarely runaway!"

About the time that Peggy looked up at me again, it was if I was some sort of newly unearthed Kennewick man. The girl looked at me in a way that made me feel as if I'd just been exhumed from nine thousand years in a rocky grave. My ideas and my mind do get closed sometimes dealing with some of the rabble of the planet that come into the court; yes, sir, sure do see the dregs sometimes!"

"Judge, I need your help. You should know me by now and you know that I'd never ask for anything. However, I've got to find the body. We need some kind of proof that's Kaelin's gone. I've got to find the people who did this. I must have something!" Peggy cried.

The pain I saw within her as a mother, as a person, and as a human shook me. Her emotional state was even grievous for me to view. I had seen this woman grow up and at times had her on my knees like one of my own. Damned war! War strips a great deal from people; all wars! Well the country did need to protect itself from some of the foreign slant-eyed animals. Though I guess wars are a necessary part of life. Aren't they?

"Well, my dear, I've personally instructed Sheriff Miles T. Carson to keep up the search as long as necessary. He'll keep searching as long as I'm the residing judge within these county lines."

Peggy continued. "I've been told there's some new evidence that was handed over to the FBI by a couple of our local women?"

"Yes, that's true. Two women, one kind of a wacky thing did happen over two odd animal-looking bones that were sent for analysis a couple of weeks ago. We're still waiting for the confirmed forensic lab reports."

"Judge, I've waited without word and without much for just over two years now."

I didn't want to excite Peggy in any way; nor stir her hopes on false evidence, so I was demure with my answers. "We're really hoping the evidence found isn't some old animal bones. I told Miles and Buck to get immediate word to me when they discover. Of course, you know my opinion, my dear, but kidnapping is a major crime and if we had evidence, strong evidence, we could bring in the federal folks in force."

Peggy's blue eyes began to cloud over like mist over azure pines while she stared at the old wooden courtroom floors. "It's been said that Kaelin might have crossed over the Washington border line up by Anatone, just off Highway 129."

"Where'd you come up with that tale? There's no evidence that points towards all of them or anyone related to her being up that far north."

"There's some real wild and sparse country up there between Anatone and Paradise," Peggy explained.

"My dear, you know how your father and I used to fly fish up there. We packed it in many a summer and fall. Often, we were so cold up in those creeks, it felt as if it were July." I remember how I started to laugh 'cause those were fine times old Peter and I had fishing in those roaring gorges. That old boy, Tom Onaben used to come up there guiding and fishing with us sometimes. What a guide that old Indian son-of-a-bitch was. He knew that area all the way from berry bush to mesquite shrub."

"Judge," Peggy asked, "can you order those two Indian guide boys, Billy and Frankie Onaben up there 'round Horse Creek to search around themselves if the bones prove real? Promise me you will; okay?"

After thinking about it for a while, I looked out of the chamber windows at the distant mountains. Never before now had Peggy ever asked me to promise anything. Actually, my position was never to promise, but looking at that young woman with those mother's eyes, how could I say no?"

"I can personally swear this, if the evidence turns out to be real or is confirmed by tests, I will have the Onaben boys hired to track the whole bloody county, if necessary. I'll make sure the full resources of both the county and federal folks are opened to support us as soon as we have some substantiation."

At that point, Peggy stood up and walked behind my desk and hugged me hard just like she did when she was a youngster. I felt more from that hugging at that moment than I'd felt in years. Words had no place in that special crystalline gasp of time.

nine

<u>Tommy-Boy Wenaha</u>
[to Buck Parrish]

I got a call first from my Uncle Teddy Cochran. He asked me to go with the Onaben family on the track for Kaelin. He said something about Horse Creek and that cut-up old northeast logging road that beat up ancient switching road that winds down into Hell's Canyon.

Billy and Frankie Onaben moved quickly in their Jeep Cherokee. They passed by, going toward the Little Sheep Creek River coming down from what's left of Witman Cut Road. Ma and old 'Poky' my half-Lab, half-Bloodhound mix followed in an old pickup truck as close as we could. A pebble or a flying rock flew against the window; we just kept 'a moving.

Brady Thompson was sitting in the seat next to me about as strapped into his seat belt as a teenager could get. "That's real rugged terrain back there. I remember it well. We did some shooting up there with my dad; a couple of years ago. I recall going up there with dad, just him and me. I was real small then but I have it all etched in my memory banks, 'cause we saw the first real cougar I'd ever seen."

I've been up there myself a couple of times. One time, we tracked a cattle-killing cat up Cow Creek. That damned cat was a tricky one. My uncle and I took three days to finally corner him in one of those small box canyons up there; it was quite a trap for him, that's for sure. That was when old Uncle Teddy was able to target any animal; he wasn't a politician yet; I guess you lose your aim when you go into state politics. Anyway, old Teddy M. shot that cat right between the eyes as it leaped towards the two of us. Son-of-a-bitch cat dropped dead in the air before hitting a rock with his head; real solid shot, real dead cat. Those cats when boxed in with no escape will attack to get free even when there were no odds for 'em. What a fine shot Teddy M. made, I'll never forget that one. May have been the last time old Teddy M. killed anything 'cepting his own gut.

"He's still drinking a lot, is he?" Buck interrupted.

"I heard he stopped for a while during his time in Salem," Brady commented.

I told Brady that was only a rumor; never met a true blood of any sort that ever stopped drinking. Booze is a blood thing for most of us. Anyway, as we headed up toward the canyon roads, which were still filled with heavy fir and lone pine, I couldn't stop my mind from dreaming about those times Kaelin and I spent together in those woods. We walked hand-in-hand and shared a joint or two next to those running creeks and waterfalls. She loved the smell of those high pines. The girl enjoyed the winter snows and the game birds that came out during those months. Kaelin and I spent a lot of time back in those canyons about a year before she disappeared.

"You don't have to talk about Kaelin, Tommy. Why don't you just tell us about the track. Don't crush your heart if you can help it," suggested Brady.

Now, as it was, Brady and I could have possibly been the best friends Kaelin had. The three of us had been close buddies since the early days of grade school. I remember the three of us playing in the schoolyard. We were all about seven. I don't think I remember any other kids as close together as we were.

"Well, I was only two years older than the two of you and I remember her having a thing for me," Brady bragged.

"Is that so? Well, that girl loved from the heart. There was never any pretense about her. Kaelin knew who she was and where she was going every step of the way. The only time she ever got messed up was on that mescaline I gave her two years ago. I'd gotten it from some half-breed Hopi trader that had passed through here, so I gave it to her. I thought Kaelin would like it, and she did. She and Terrie Conson went up somewhere back of East Creek Summit. Terrie told me that the two of 'em almost died that day on that high. They were naked and danced like bears in the cold summer ponds of the creek. I should have been with them. Maybe none of this stuff would have happened if I had been with 'em then."

"Go on with the story, Tommy Boy. Don't get sentimental on us now. You'll be grabbing a bottle, and then it's all lost," warned Brady.

At that moment, I looked at Brady. I knew he had some difficulty getting those words out but they came; yes, they surely came. So at that exact spot, me and Brady stopped racing those four-by-four Indians at the northeast edge of Sheep Creek 'bout right near the fork where it meets the southern edge of the Little Sheep Creek River. There was a plan figured out by Billy Onaben and to some degree, brother Frankie. We all knew Billy was the brains in the family, but Frankie always had some words.

"Have you ever been with the Onaben brothers when Billy had an idea that Frankie didn't agree with or ever said no to?"

"No, can't say that I have, Tommy. At least I can never remember him saying no," admitted Brady.

"Well, we all split up to meet at the lower part of Horse Creek. Oh, about three hours, we'd split in all, 'bout three hours." Tommy replied.

I took my Husky/Aussie mixed breed on the ride and the Onaben brothers took their specially trained hound dogs that always ran ahead of them by about two miles. One could hear those damned hounds crying and yelping through those rocky creeks and gorges for miles. Of course, next to me, Billy was considered the best native tracker anywhere in our three local counties and Southern Washington State. I'd take my Old Poky as he was against the best dogs the Onaben's had!"

"When you were working with the Onaben brothers, getting back to the tracking story, did you find anything of Kaelin's?" asked Buck.

"It took about two and a half hours of hard moving 'til we got to the spot they said to search thoroughly which was 'bout four and a half miles from Hat Point. It got real cold out there. You know how fierce the weather is, how it changes in seconds up there. I searched through those rocks, up those jagged ravines and gaps, in dry riverbeds and inside gorges. Neither Poky nor I came up with anything. I climbed up one dry water fall leading up maybe several hundred feet, maybe even a thousand feet up from the creek's edge. I did find some newly chewed on Elk, which could have been something else," Tommy replied.

"Nothing else, my friend, 'course this was only the first major search up in that area we were going to be involved in, but there were to be at least three more," said Buck.

Brady looked around us for awhile as though he was somewhere in deep thought, but I knew better. He was simply staring at space trying to make sense of whatever he'd say next.

"Did the Onaben boys find anything substantial other than the old elk bones and unnamed rocks?" Buck asked.

Tommy agreed, "The surprising thing is, yes; they did find a small shirt collar. It seemed as though it had been ripped off someone's Oxford shirt. It was all discolored and had been in the weather. Sometimes, things like clothes get weathered. They lose all their dyes but it had some scent left."

Buck asked, "Do you think the Oxford was Kaelin's?"

"Didn't know for sure; but all of Billy's hounds did find the scent familiar and those are real solid bloodhounds, well-trained and line-bred," Tommy replied.

"Did Billy or Frankie say anything to you about where they found the collar?"

"Yea, they said they found it next to a dry rock bed about a hundred and fifty foot just above Horse Creek," said Tommy Boy.

"So, it was some kind of dried-up rock ravine 'bout fifty meters above that spot along Horse Creek?" Buck inquired.

"Yea, that's where they said they found it or the hound dogs found it."

"Did they find anything else or did the dogs pick up anything else around there?"

Tommy Boy answered, "Nothing; nothing at all!"

"Billy or Frankie Onaben say anything else to you about that piece of cloth, anything at all?" Buck continued his questions.

"No, nothing really but Frankie did make one odd statement. There was a part of a broken heel print against a gray rock, not exactly a normal stone. It was more like dry-hard potter's clay. Those Onaben boys never said much. But, when they did, it usually meant a whole hell of a lot," Tommy Boy answered.

"Did they cut it out and take it with them?" asked Buck.

"Yes, they did, but I haven't thought about that cut-out section of clay heel print until now, and who knows what they did with it," said Tommy-Boy.

We drove back real slow through creek beds and all the way back; the dogs were strangely silent. When we returned, I was told Billy had Frankie took the collar and most probably the clay-print over to Deputy Parrish. At least the collar evidence was packed in a plastic zip lock bag. I don't know about the clay-print.

No one actually said much for thirty minutes prior to our arrival in town. They dropped me and the dog off, and Billy shot north over the ridge. Old Frankie rolled his cycle out from behind the Sheriff's building and slammed off in the opposite direction. I recall the cloud of fine dust that 650-Honda made as old Frankie pushed off towards that shadowed ridge. Guess there was some actual truth to the story Millie and Jillian told 'bout Kaelin to those Feds. Turns out those dreams aren't just so much bullshit. Naturally the Indians been talking 'bout their dreams for years, saying the same kind of thing about visions. Of course, no one hears them either.

ten

Jeb A. Hirsch, FBI
June 1997

I can recall standing there on the old Wallowa County Courthouse steps reporting various updates on the disappearance of Kaelin. Art F. Bell, the local news celeb and radio talk show host, was standing directly in front of me with his recorder rolling. At the end of the day, clouds had gathered in the eastern vistas and even in the summer months, it looked like snowstorms. For a few seconds, I felt as if I was flying up there in the thunderheads, like some kind of Harrier Hawk gliding down from cumulous heads.

Before becoming the lead FBI man in the region, I'd fly a glider up there once a week or maybe twice a week. I learned pretty easily how to fly gliders and learned to love 'em. In fact, flying to those places was the most meditative time of my life; probably the most relaxed I'd ever been. The silence seeping through those thunderheads between the rocky outcrops of the Wallowa Alps, that's what they called them, now that was a time remembered.

The state's evidence brought in by Tommy Wenaha and the Onaben family proved to be the foot bones of a girl about the same age as Kaelin.

Art F. Bell asked, "Have you people run all the DNA tests required to define the white cells and blood type?"

"The full compliment of tests has not been run, but I can assure all of you, as spokesmen for the Bureau, we will run all the necessary tests to develop a complete profile."

"What exactly do you mean by a complete profile, Agent Hirsch?" Twila Grey inquired. She was a local television news cute-face. The girl was someone I felt attracted to, but I had always remained objective regarding the citizens within my posts. What we're talking about here is this; the Bureau will do everything in its power to apprehend the culprits in the alleged kidnapping of Kaelin Jones."

"Will the FBI spend Washington resources on a case this small that involves a nobody fifteen-year-old from Wallowa County Oregon?" Art asked.

"Yes, to all of that stuff, Mr. Bell. We have already identified the bones found as being those of a human female between the age of fourteen and sixteen years old. We'll make a positive statement regarding all confirmed evidence within the next five days."

"Will you conduct another press conference when your evidence is proven proof positive?" Brad Williams, a Portland reporter inquired.

"Yes, we will call another press conference as soon as we have confirmed scientific data regarding our current hard evidence."

At that point, most of the press people were finished. They began drifting down the courthouse stairs heading in all directions before the rain began falling. It reminded me of a group of scattering young hens flying into their shelter during a semi-frozen downpour. Chickens, for that matter, most birds, avoid that kind of cold, except certain species of Northern Territory animals who become quite accustomed to it.

"Hey, Jeb, are you going to make a statement regarding some of the other disappearances at the New Wallowa Church of Christ?" asked Mr. Bell.

For several seconds, he simply stood directly in front of me. Twila was to the right of him. A marked silence fell between all of us.

"We've been following various telephone calls and stories regarding the New Wallowa Church of Christ and Pastor Chrisp. For four years, we've been gathering data ever since the church began to grow larger."

Mr. Bell snapped off the switch on his tape recorder before he spoke next. "Off the record, Agent Hirsch, are you actually investigating the New Church?"

"On the side and very off the record, Mr. Bell and Ms. Grey, we are not openly investigating the New Wallawa Church. However, if evidence is uncovered that implicates the church in any way, we'll be right there, I can assure you."

"You scared of deacons, Mr. Hirsch? They got you all freaked out politically. Too much influence?" Art Bell inquired.

"No, Mr. Bell, that's not the case at all. We have not been investigating because we have no evidence and consequently, we have no reason to investigate."

"I've heard differently, Agent Hirsch, but then again, my information just comes from small-town gossip."

Carefully I watched Bell's face twitch and his mouth twist as he shoved a note pad in his jacket pocket. He shot two victory fingers in my face as he always did after a no-nothing dry media interview. While he walked away, I studied Bell's odd gate. It was a walk he had acquired due to grenade shrapnel in his left leg that happened somewhere in South Vietnam in 1968.

Twila asked me to have lunch with her at Olsen's Café. I accepted the invitation, which was another chance to be alone with her. Still, I realized she was probably trying to pull more out of me regarding the New Wallawa Church and its known cadre of special deacons. We strolled across the street as small raindrops began to pepper the asphalt. I threw my rugged squall poncho over Twila's head, no more than twenty-five feet from the café's front door.

eleven

<u>Annabelle MacCruthers</u>

Occasionally, some of the girls, friends of Kaelin, would come up here to the pure-air country, and would help me tend the animals. Kaelin was particularly fond of the horses, especially Esconshia, which was by far her favorite animal.

Terrie Conson and Tilly Wallis would usually run over to the goats. There was something about those Arabians' they loved to watch. Since the air up here is so good, it draws people. When people can breathe better without artificial means; or Yoga, for that matter, they feel better. Purer oxygen helps them to naturally feel better. Then again, maybe it's the air at 5,200 feet that does it. To me, it's the perfect level, the absolutely perfect elevation.

It wasn't long from the time the girls arrived, maybe two or three hours passed when a small blue Ford pickup pulled up next to the inner gate of the ranch.

Whenever I'd see Kaelin, maybe two, maybe three hours, after that, Tammy would arrive and not long after that, I'd get a visit from Terrie Conson. Now, on that lovely fall day, in early September, the sun peaked large over Mt. Howard. The sun pushed glorious orange-red streaks down its many crevasses. It sure was unusual the way the sun darted through the Lone Pines and the few Ponderosas still left standing. Maybe because they were some kind of seed trees; that's why they let 'em stand. Who really knows? As the sun passed behind the western section of Mt. Howard, the air began to fill with its customary chill. I knew the girls at that time were ready for some hot chocolate, a little yap, and some homemade cinnamon buns. Dora Moss, my old cook baked those old buns the Oregon way. They were big buns. She made them excellently and they were always solid eating, not too sweet. The buns were perfectly moist in the mouth and went down easy. After she died last year, we tried to duplicate her recipe for those buns, but we didn't get too far. Her buns were the very best ever!

As soon as we had entered the old log house, Terrie seemed unusually nervous. I can't say that I'd ever seen that girl shy about anything, but that day there was something sure 'a bothering her. Tilly and Kaelin went at those big buns, two or three apiece.

The darkness of the fall sky was almost on us as the last rays of the sun kept popping through the windows. The rays against the walls of the room created mini-prisms everywhere. Terrie sat back in her chair right next to me and stared at the prism colors breaking at the apex of my high ceiling. "Annabelle, I'm sixteen now. Do you think it'll be all right for me to have a bit of that wine you're drinking?"

I didn't think about what Terrie asked very long. Dutifully, I got up and went to my cupboard and took a glass out and poured it for her. Both Kaelin and Tammy Bork asked for some of the red wine. So, without much hesitation, I brought out three more wine glasses. When placed in front of the girls, Tilly was the only one to place her hand over her mouth. Soon, I poured the wine for the other girls. She was the only one to refuse to drink that night.

There was a silence between the girls that I hadn't observed before; a kind of quiet came over our little group that night. The girls thought of me as a friend and older woman who loved animals and children. They expressed a comfort with me that they seldom felt with other adults, especially men. Kaelin knew Buck Parrish pretty well, and she knew him to be a kind man. She also knew him because for years, her mother and Buck 'saw' each other, and as adults, they had remained good friends.

Kaelin said she felt good about Buck every time she ran into him. Usually, he watched out for her because of her mother, maybe *too much*; or so she had said. Kaelin sure enjoyed that house of mine. She loved her mother real deeply and she also felt close to me. Except for her intimate friends, the girl was a real loner.

Terrie stayed quiet for several minutes during our girl-talk when she abruptly blurted out a surprising question. "How would you take a Deacon of the church making strong advances towards you?"

"Wouldn't think all that much of it, dear; but tell me what you're really saying?"

"Come on, Terrie, tell all of us what you're really saying," demanded Kaelin.

Tilly and Tammy glared at Terrie sitting back in a relaxed state while she sipped her glass of red wine. "One of the Deacon's drove me back from Sister Espanola's. He drove me directly to The New Wallowa Church. The same deacon put his hand on my shoulder. Afterwards, he brushed past my breast and laid that same hand on my left thigh. We talked about my experiences at the church and he told me how all the deacons loved me. I was told that they loved the kind of girl I was and they thought a lot about me."

"Was there any more to it than that? A little feel?"

"Maybe, but no feel, really?" Kaelin replied.

"So, you were, or he was getting a little sexy with you. Is that what you're saying?" Tilly questioned.

"I can't say who it was. I'm sworn to say nothing about the incident, especially who it was with me on that day. I'm afraid to say anything specific."

Quickly, I could see a deep sense of fear come over that young girl's eyes. She needed a little more wine to loosen up the story even more. We joked around with her for a few minutes before she blurted out some pretty strong words. Kaelin looked at me and then she glanced back and forth from me to her friend. Her bright green eyes kept moving. It was almost as if she didn't want Terrie to speak further. I watched 'fear,' a kind of dread crept into her face. Watching animals all my life made it easy to see a face, which had 'a cup a fear' blooming within it.

"That old deacon grabbed my knee next and told me how excited I made him feel. I said nothing, just kept staring at the lights and the trees passing through the windshield in a constant glare and blurred image."

"What'da old Deacon do next? Did he slide his fingers past your thighs into your open skirt?" asked Tammy.

At this point, I was able to see how interested the other girls were and how excited Tammy was in particular. "Yes, Deacon slipped his fingers under my skirt and into my underwear. The man started telling me how much Jesus loved me and he told me that we would have to pray together to show our mutual love for Jesus; and we had to give our love to Jesus

57

and at the same time each other. His face was very red and over-joyous as he pulled his vehicle off the highway and shot down an old unused logging road just off Highway 82," said Terrie.

"So what in the hell happened next?" her friend Tilly asked. All the girls were completely enmeshed in the story. Everyone waited nervously for her next words.

I remember how Kaelin's lips quivered; I could see her heart move directly to her lips. She tried to do anything in her power to stop Terrie from continuing the story. I just caught Kaelin signaling her friend to stop talking. It was quick but I caught the signal from the corner of my eye. Terrie slouched back in her chair as if she were really feeling the wine, maybe she was a little high, but the conversation immediately changed to chit-chat and horseback riding after that gesture from Kaelin. What really concerned me in the conversation was Terrie's sense of angst. The God-given fear in both of those other young girls eyes, Tilly and Kaelin's.

No one's heard much of Tilly Wallis since Kaelin disappeared. Some said she ran off because she was afraid of being next. And after that night together, on the ranch, I could understand it. Might even be some real truth in that 'pack a fright' those girls sensed that evening. There might just be some actual reason for jitters, I'd say.

twelve

Pastor Parham A. Chrisp

We started on the side of the Grand Ronde River, near Wildcat, in a small cedar church building, which was a shack really. That old place we worshipped in was a special place for all of us, and at that time. we referred to it as The First Church of Christ in the Woods. That little church was originally built by the people of Wallawa County 'bout the turn of the century. Even then there wasn't too much Christianity around these parts 'cept a couple of settlements to the east and northwest of Wallawa. Most of the people who lived in these parts even in those days were bare-assed-near-naked heathens. They were from the Nez Perce and some of those other kinds 'a tribes.

My father was a self-taught preacher; come from the 'tent and court circuit.' There was a time the preachers would preach on the porches of the courthouses in the small towns of the nation. Others, including my father, would use tents. My father Rev. Charles B. Chrisp was a man greatly inspired by 'the word'; all the magic religious prophecy comes from 'the word'. But talk of my father, that's not the purpose here now, is it? You know I asked Agent Thore if she was interested in the church's history; that is The New Wallawa Church of Christ. As I remember, she was quite interested. She was almost as interested in the church and its activities as she was in the questions regarding the disappearance of Kaelin Jones.

"Tell me, Pastor Chrisp, you're saying that you and some others, current members of the new church actually started the original church from scratch?" asked Special Agent Thore of the FBI.

"Yes, Ms. Thore, there was a group of us who built the church out a nothing; some old wood borrowed from members. And as we built her, we held sermons in tents that were put up near the fields and streams around here. Of course, we put up on the adjoining two acres of property, which was gifted to us, and was then doubled by old widow Bork, Lucinda's grandmother. Our members are generous and give all they can in property and valuables. There's nothing cheap about the people of Wallowa."

I watched Agent Thore take copious notes while we spoke. She additionally asked for the meeting to be taped and I openly granted her that wish.

"So, in fact, was it Olivia Bork, one of the town's founders from our records, who deeded the land and the remainder of her property up there to the New Church trust?" the FBI agent inquired.

"She did; actually Olivia first deeded it straight to me and I deeded it directly to the New Church trust."

"What trust are we talking about here, Pastor? According to the county records, you are the total owner of that property."

"No, Ms. Thore, the land and now an adjoining one-hundred and sixty acres are actually owned by a combined trust called The First Deacon's Associated Trust."

"All right then, the deacons of the church or the FDAT, as it's called, actually owns all the property and controls all the church's business?"

"Yes, that's true, Ms. Thore. I can see that you've been doing a little research. I think you might have hit on something."

I remember how surprised Agent Thore looked as I opened our conversation on the subject of research. It was then she stopped her recorder and asked me an off-the-record question.

"Pastor Chrisp, if you object to anything here regarding any element of what we're investigating, please alert me immediately."

At first, I said nothing; I just lifted my hands and raised two fingers in a V-shape and gave her that old salute, the old V salute. After that, Ms. Thore snapped on the recorder and continued, "Is Dr. James Oliveson the current president of FDAT?"

"Yes, he is," I answered, "and Judge Buchanan sits as the co-president when Dr. Oliveson is unavailable. Yet, my dear; let me assure you that it takes two signatures to purchase anything sizable or to release large amounts of money."

"Can you supply me with a full and up-to-date list of all current members of the Deacon Association and members of the FDAT?"

"No," I replied, "unfortunately, not until I inform all the deacons of your request, and then I have to have a unanimous vote on the matter."

"So, Pastor, let me see if I've got this right; you're refusing to give the FBI a current list of all the deacons?" Agent Thore asked.

"That's right. I can't give you anything on the Deacon's Association without their prior knowledge and permission; that is part of their rules and the by-laws of their church contract."

Agent Thore was frustrated and perturbed. I could see it in her face. Something about what I said to her really bothered her; yet, we continued with the interview.

"Tell me something, Pastor, did you see Dr. Oliveson on the night of November 14, 1997?" Thore asked.

"My dear, regardless of what television movies say one can do, it's quite impossible for me to remember a specific night. Why that night anyway?"

"That was the night Kaelin disappeared. It was the exact night when she vanished from the face of the earth."

"Well," I said to Olivia, "I can't really remember exact dates. Why don't you let me do a little research on the subject?"

"Sure, you do that, Pastor, and while you're digging through your notes, let me know if Amos T. Blackburn was in attendance the night of the seventeenth of November."

I was quite hesitant at that moment to comply with Agent Thore's wishes, especially related to any direct deacon activities, but I told her I'd look into it.

"Can I ask you three more explicit questions, Pastor Chrisp?"

"Yes, but if the questions are similar to the last one, I may not be able to openly comply."

"Do the deacons, or have the deacons, ever worked closely with the lost teenagers of Sister Espanola's Inmaha Mission?"

"As a matter of fact, they do. They have worked supportively with the children. In fact, they have given charitably to the Mission; that is the FDAT. I can tell you that much. Additionally, the Sister's mission works with many 'wayward' girls and many 'a young woman was 'saved' as a result of the deacons' efforts. It is their giving, my dear, that is the true work of Jesus Christ!"

"I'm sure of that, Pastor, but can you give me a list of the young women the deacons have helped during the last three years?"

"Maybe. I'll do my best to obtain the information for you. Now, do you have another question?"

"Tell me precisely, Pastor. Will you identify the names of all the girl exchanges between the church's halfway house and Sister Espanola's Mission?"

"That is difficult data to gather my dear." I replied, being as direct as I thought possible. "I'll see what I can do. Third question?"

During that part of the conversation all I could think of doing was getting out of the discussion. Getting back to my work was a great idea.

"Pastor Chrisp, can you tell me the name of the deacon in charge of transportation for the teenage girls? Was he the only person involved? Was there a backup deacon?"

"Nathan Bork was the deacon in charge of transportation and all that. The backup deacon was always A. T. Blackburn because of his religious convictions and his civic status as Volunteer Civilian Chief Deputy Sheriff. That position was one of the highpoints of A.T.'s life. He was really proud as a man could get over that honor."

"Pastor Chrisp that will be all the questions for the moment. Please call me when you have the answers to the first two questions and anything else you might want to bring to mind."

I recollect how, Ms. Thore, or Agent Thore, I should say, started gathering up her interview instruments. I watched her as she slowly headed for the church office door and stopped to comment. "Pastor, we'll be talking to each other in person or by telephone in the next ten days. I want to thank you for your time."

Funny how the agent said that; I wasn't really sure of her sincerity but it was a fine way to end a grueling conversation. As she left the church building, I slipped into the rectory and immediately began praying. For me, many times in my life, a good solid prayer has given me solace. It has always been one of the best ways to ease personal tensions. As I started getting into serious prayer, Dr. Oliveson walked into the rectory. As he crossed my path, our eyes exchanged a certain brotherly warmth, which can only be understood by intimate church members. It was the end of a hard day and Dr. Oliveson was the right man to empathize ways. He and I prayed together. The two of us prayed for the lost girl. We stayed in the rectory communing for another two hours.

thirteen

<u>Sister Mary Espanola</u>

The day was cold and clear, one of the rare days for Wallowa County, totally free of clouds. I stood at the side of the corral looking at the skies when Agent Hirsch and Buck Parrish started walking the rim of the corral towards me. Deputy Sheriff Buck Parrish and I had known each other extremely well as children. We had even shared beds together for the first time, as first-need young lovers. Yes, Buck was my first and only lover prior to becoming a nun. As a matter of fact, in many ways, I can still say honestly that we're still in love. That love now is a kindred type of love, shared between great friends, great comrades who follow feelings and solid human instincts together, who share a common will.

Occasionally, Buck would traipse up to Inmaha late at night and visit me. He always came when the need for companionship arrived for either of us. Funny how he always knew when to come. We'd usually share old times and a glass of wine. Our favorites were Washington Cabernet or Merlot. He and I would discuss anything and everything of interest in the world. From time to time, I'd play some Gilbert and Sullivan opera, as they were the one group of opera composers Buck did appreciate. The rest of them, he'd tolerate for me usually as background music. Yes, we enjoyed many lovely conversations. Some would be serious and others not so serious, some joyful and others painful. Still, the two of us were always able to share our feelings with each other. We never spoke of our relationship twenty years prior. There were times I wished we had just cleansed the air of any 'old stuff' that might be still webbing its way between us.

After some quick internal thinking, I walked up to the two men that were approaching me from the north side of the corral, which was next to the main dormitory building. It actually was a large converted home where the majority of the girls lived.

"Why don't the two of you come up to the 'big room' where we can talk private? It's probably the most secluded place in the compound."

"Not a bad idea," agreed Agent Hirsch.

Buck nodded to me but said nothing. However, he did tip the rim of his worn old black Stetson. With a wide smile, he followed Agent Hirsch and me into the house.

It took a while for us to get to any meaningful conversation. We simply sat there chit-chatting about the school, the weather, or some other general kinds of discussion. Finally, Agent Hirsch asked me if it'd be okay to record the conversation between the three of us. He said the tape might be used for back-up evidence. It was at this point that the interview got down to what I call the urgent level. I didn't really know a great deal about recordings. Also, I wasn't sure about the process in general. Still, I trusted and loved Buck. If he thought it was acceptable, then I'd go along with it.

"Think I should allow Mr. Hirsch here to record me?" I asked him.

"Yes, I think you should do the recording. It's justified at this point in the investigation of Kaelin's disappearance. We're now compiling a history of related and specific events, Sister Mary," Buck encouraged.

"Sister Mary, can you tell me something about the date of Terrie Conson's disappearance from the compound?"

I looked over at Buck, took a sip of good red wine, cleared my throat, and formed some solid thoughts. "We were having our first snow, which fell sometime in early November 1997. I don't remember the exact date of our conversation, but it was quite early in the month. I believe it was two or three days after Kaelin's reported disappearance."

"How did you notice the first signs of her departure or disappearance?" the agent inquired.

"Sister Mac McCormick informed me of the situation two days after the girl vanished."

"Are there any employees here, other than Sister Mac McCormick and Injun Tom that is, any other people who live and work here?"

"They're the only two people who work and live here fulltime, but we do have steady volunteers who come up here four-to-five times a month each. Those volunteers are men and women who support the girls and me with their time and money; usually, it's two regular women and three men."

"I see. During the month that we're discussing, how many of the volunteers are now a part of Pastor Chrisp's' church?"

I looked over at Buck Parrish who'd just started chewing on one of our fresh jellyrolls; I guess I was silently asking him for some kind of support. Buck looked down for a moment and then stared directly into my eyes with those smiling 'blue soul's' of his. At that point, I felt perfectly comfortable going right into my story.

"We'd had several additional New Church volunteers that month, some of them I hadn't seen at the compound for several weeks," I told them.

"Like who, and can you give us the names of each person specifically?" Buck inquired.

"Actually, it's never been necessary for me to remember that information. Sister Mac McCormick keeps a complete journal of all visitors and volunteers. Each person must sign in if they're active with our mission boarders."

The moment I finished my last sentence, Agent Hirsch turned off the recorder and looked over at Buck.

"Can we borrow or copy the journal, Sister?" Buck asked.

"You are welcome to copy it, but it isn't supposed to leave the mission. Nevertheless, we do have an old Xerox copier, which was donated to us. It's in the office. However, I'd have to charge you fifteen cents a page."

"Sure, Sister Mary. Here's five dollars, Sister. Let me know if that doesn't cover the costs," Agent Hirsch generously offered.

We made several copies of the timeframe that was two weeks prior to Kaelin's disappearance, some copies of the exodus week and then a set of the week following that one. Buck and I entered the big room again and sat down to continue the interview.

Passing the list to Agent Hirsch, the FBI agent, Buck said, "According to this list and these signatures, Mr. A.T. Blackburn, Pastor Chrisp, Lucinda Bork, and Dr. Oliveson (all from New Church) were official volunteers or had been guests the week of Kaelin's disappearance."

"Whatever's in there, Agent Hirsch, is in there. Nothing has been changed or altered; and that book is kept under strict lock and key at all times."

"Who has a key other than you, Sister," Buck asked of the nun who was beginning to tire of the investigation.

"Only Sister Mac McCormick. She's the only other person allowed to open the locked drawer." Sister Mary stated.

The conversation continued until Agent Hirsch brought up a specific date or the most likely conceived night of Kaelin's eclipse.

"I was here that particular night, but busy; so, Sister Mac McCormick was solely the one who saw A.T. Blackburn pick up Terrie Conson and Tilly Wallis. Is that what you want to know?"

"Yes, and I'd also like to know if Dr. Oliveson or anyone else was here that night or during the day prior to the seventeenth," said Agent Hirsch.

"Well, two I remember were: Dr. Oliveson, bless his generous soul, and Pastor Chrisp, the day before. Also, Lucinda Bork dropped by as we recorded in the journal. All the girls were, and are, extremely fond of Lucinda; she's a real leader to them. Lucinda is equivalent to a big sister. She and Nathan have always helped the mission, plus they give generously both in their time and they donate several thousand dollars a year."

"You say that only Mr. A.T. Blackburn was here the night of the 'departure'?"

"Yes, he picked up the two girls and took them down to the church where they were to meet with Pastor Chrisp and Chief Deacon, Dr. Oliveson."

"Dr. Oliveson wasn't around at all that day or night, was he? The day of the seventeenth?" asked Buck.

Sister Mary answered, "No, as I said before, the journal is as accurate as we can get it. There's so much work around here; that's the best we can do."

"I understand your mission here is to receive wayward girls from New Church's sanctuary in Promise?"

"Yes, that is correct. We do take in wayward teenaged females from their halfway house located in Promise. In fact, Terrie Conson and Tilly Wallis came from that exact sanctuary, nearly a year ago."

"Sister, thank you for all the open and straightforward information you have given me. You have been very helpful. May we call again if we have additional questions?"

"Please do. Of course, Mr. Hirsch, I'm open to whatever is necessary to assist you in finding these girls, both of them, or all of them; if there's more!"

I recall Buck turning and winking at me as he and Mr. Hirsch began walking towards the front door. Suddenly, he stopped in his tracks, came up to me and kissed me on the forehead. "Thank you for your help, Sister, we do appreciate everything you're doing."

For one brief moment, I was taken back by Buck's sudden affection, while at the same time, I tried to figure precisely what he really was trying to say to me.

fourteen

Annabelle MacCruthers

It was so clear that day. I drove fifty-one sheep across the ridge arriving just north of Maxville. My ride was Zena, a fifteen-hand fine Appaloosa/Arabian mare. She herded those sheep well, followed the lines of the ridges, and just kept pushing. 'Course, young Tanya, my sheep dog, a young Great Pyrenees, was my pride, for guarding and following mountain sheep and goats. She was a perfect breed. The other dog, Manya, was a half-Collie, half-Australian Sheep dog. That dog was fast and smart and worked as hard as any man I'd ever hired. Both dogs worked as a well-coordinated team. At the end of the day, whether out in the mountains or at home, those dogs deserved their vittles.

"Never heard the word 'vittles', did you, Ms. Thore? Now there's a bunch of words disappearing from the English language these days, that's for sure. Also, there are some good humans disappearing. That's also for sure, Ms. Thore. That girl Kaelin, now she was sure a soft heart. She was right down to the spirit core that she was. It is a damn shame the girl vanished. It was almost as if some circus magician dropped in from Boston or New York and just zapped her out of the "big tent" in front of us?"

"Why were you moving your sheep across the ridge that day, Ms. Mac Cruthers? Was there a special reason for that?" asked Agent Thore.

For several seconds, I looked over at Ms. Thore and tried to make some sense out of what she was asking. My problem was only that God's truth would come out of my mouth 'cause that's all I knew.

"As I was riding, I remember getting bit by some grass wasp that day. Half the left side of my cheek was still swollen from it. 'Ya see, I was just trying to settle a trade that I made with Billy Onaben. It was for seven well-fed good solid quarter horses for fifty well raised sheep fully woolen," I explained.

"Sounded like a good deal for you and not so good for Billy Onaben," she stated.

"It does depend on how you look at it, my dear. Also it depends on what your needs are. The deal was a fair part of that I can assure you."

"How'd you get so many sheep in your truck? Or did you just keep hauling ten at a time back and forth?" Agent Thore inquired.

"Nathan Bork loaned me his semi-rig, which carried all fifty-one sheep with some room to spare. That's how I did it."

I watched Agent Thore write every word down as though I was saying something important like talking to some local judge.

Almost without pausing, Thore continued the questioning. "I understand that area north of Maxville up to Promise is some fairly rough country for traveling."

"Not that rough. Sure, it does have its snakes and holes and the other usual obstacles common in these parts; but nothing really unusual 'ceptin the panthers and an occasional Timber Wolf."

"Didn't all the Wolves get driven out of this area or out of these mountains long ago?" the ever persistent agent asked.

"Not totally true; some actually floated in from Canada and Northern Idaho, but wolves are some smart animals. They kept hiding them from man and dogs, like the panthers do."

"Why do you call the cougars, panthers?"

Proudly, I answered. "Because that's what they are and that's what they descended from. Those cougars, or mountain lions, are just old panthers. That's all they are, nothing more or less. Now there's an animal that just loves sheep next to a doe. Those panthers just love my sheep. They're its favorite prey. So one's got to keep constant vigil and sleep near 'em, even if you have a dog like my Tanya."

"I see, but I hear those panthers rarely surface for a good shot," said the agent.

"Only when they're really hungry; then you occasionally see them. Usually the animals prefer to stay real high; at least the ones that live up here. Aside from that, Ms. Thore, you really don't want to see 'em. That day, up in those ridges above

Promise, there was a big one, about a two-hundred-pound male. I saw him jumping across the boulders. Next, I saw him climb a large dead Oak. That Oak was a fat one and he could easily get lost behind it. They kind'a blended together. Those cats have a natural mesh color to 'em, and they move silent like a soft breeze. They can nearly completely camouflage themselves in the mountain shadows."

"On another subject; yet the same, can you tell me what else you saw on the way to Promise that day which was unusual?" Agent Thore kept up the questioning.

"The New Church you know, keeps a young girl's retreat up there around Promise. There's always someone driving up there. Plus, there's always somebody driving back. But, seldom do you see someone moving far away from the road. Nowhere to go up there really unless you have a destination," I told her.

"How well do you yourself know the country up there? By this time, you must have seen a bunch of it?" the agent asked.

"Well, Agent Thore, I can say that I've been there all my life. The ground I know, and I know the mammals and the reptiles, most of the birds. The road is something I know like part of my left hand. Only Billy Onaben or maybe his half-brother, Frankie, knows the road better. Those two guys are about the only two I can think of right now that might know it better."

"I see. Can you tell me what you saw on the seventeenth and about what time you saw it?" Thore prodded.

Nervously, I answered Shawna Thore. "One of my sheep ran astray and Tanya took off after it. She took off like any really good sheep dog should have. The horse and I kept moving the other sheep up towards Peter's Glenn. About two miles northeast of Maxwell, just west of Mud Creek, I saw Amos T. Blackburn was tracking down some logging road adjacent to the creek."

"Was there anyone in the truck with him?" Agent Thore asked.

"Yes there was. Looked like a young girl 'bout the same size and had facial features similar to that of Kaelin. The girl, whoever she was, was just staring out the windshield into space sitting right across from Amos. It did at the time seem strange to me that Amos T. was heading down or across one of the logging roads that cuts through to Mud Creek, 'cause there's nothing there!"

Agent Thore continued jotting down her notes in that book of hers just as fast as possible. I offered her a drink of cold nectar but she didn't even hear a word I was saying."

"Tell me, Ms. MacCruthers, could you clearly identify Kaelin in that truck? Would you act as a witness if I asked you to?"

I answered, "I'd say to you or anyone else that I'm eighty percent certain it was Kaelin 'a sitting next to old Amos T. Blackburn."

Agent Thore continued the interrogation. "About what time was this? Tell me as close as you can and try to be precise, Ms. MacCruthers."

Annabelle hesitated, but soon began again, "Oh, it was about four in the afternoon. I remember from where the shadows fell that day. In fact, from where the sun cast its long arm against some of those rugged cliffs."

"So let me repeat what I think you're saying. You believe you saw Amos T. Blackburn and Kaelin Jones riding together in a truck heading towards Mud Creek about four o'clock in the afternoon of the seventh day of November?"

"As I said before, I'm almost positive it was Kaelin and I'm absolutely convinced it was Amos," she answered. "You see, Ms. Thore, picking up the girls from Sister Espanola's place and transporting them back to Promise was a common thing you'd see up there."

"Yes, I'm beginning to see that. Now was there a great deal of this kind of transportation going on up there, this transporting back and forth?" the agent inquired.

I looked up at Agent Thore not sure of what she was asking me 'cause I wasn't real positive she was really listening anyway. Almost every other day, Amos T. himself or Pastor Chrisp or even Dr. Oliveson could be seen driving those girls from one runaway house to another.

Agent Thore asked, "Anyone else from The New Church or any other place involved in driving these girls back and forth between the shelters?"

"As a matter of fact, sometimes I'd see old Sheriff Will Carson drive one of the girls up there or maybe two of 'em. One time, in fact, I recall even seeing Judge Buchanan drive two of those kind a girls up there to Promise."

"What was the purpose of all the transporting between these places?"

"I believe it was some kind of church and mission exchange program set up by Pastor Chrisp, his deacons and Sister Espanola. That's 'bout all I know," Annabelle explained.

"Does The New Church, as you call it, maintain a special resort up there near Promise for young runaway girls?"

Annabelle spoke slowly, "Yes, they've had a facility to help runaways from all over the country. I believe it's been going on up there for about four or so years now."

"What do you think Kaelin was doing up there?" the female agent asked the woman who seemed to be tiring.

"I imagine Kaelin was probably visiting her friend Terrie Conson, that other disappeared young'un." Annabelle's comeback seemed short and to the point.

"Right, and does Mr. Billy Onaben or his half-brother have much to do with The New Church's place up there near Promise?"

"Correct. Occasionally, he and Frankie work the ranches around the shelter," she exclaimed.

"Shelter? It's a shelter you say? Why is it called a shelter?"

"'Because they help comfort and strictly maintain the place for troubled and lost-runaway girls.'"

Agent Thore simply smiled at me while closing her notebook and turned off her recorder. Shawna said that she'd talk to me again soon. It was one of those real friendly meetings, better than most one has with the law, but I can't help feeling as if I didn't help her much. She did say something direct about

73

talking to those Indian brothers Billy and Frankie Onaben; that I do recall her mentioning to me.

fifteen

Billy Onaben
Notes: A.M. Bell

Billy Onaben and his half-brother, Frank, lived just above the northwest section of the Grande Ronde River seven miles from Promise. Most folks in the county considered Billy the finest tracker, bar none. Well-known, and the not so well-known hunters hired him at various times for some pretty fancy prices.

He's slightly pocked face and his eyes, which were like a Falcon's when he looked at you, penetrated deep. Frankie, the quiet one, was a head taller than Billy. He was quiet and was trained for fighting and survival in the old Nez Perce traditions. The two men were direct descendents of Chief Joseph's younger brother, Dark Horse, who was one of the great Nez Perce soldiers. Dark Horse had survived the battles with the U.S. Army.

This particular part of Wallowa County was extremely populated with large numbers of roaming puma, noted for occasional attacks on man if one was startled with prey. Puma or cougar attacks are rare in the United States. There has been only one attack for every ten years of history in all of the lower forty-eight states. The big cats are far more afraid of man than man is of the large cats. When the cougar was last seen, or at least its tracks were seen, especially in the old days, the cats were tracked by the Nez Perce. They used a dead animal's carcass from the paws to the skull and teeth. The Nez Perce wasted nothing. They used all they could forage from the forest and never took too much. Today, they would be near perfect environmentalists.

The puma's role was as a hunter to keep the deer in check. Of course man was to keep the old puma in balance. Except for the poisons, and man, the big cats had no natural enemies. Still, I suppose humans and toxins are about enough for any animal.

The Onaben brothers lived together; however, only the two of them remained since Frankie's divorce in the mid-

75

nineties. Nobody knew much about his wife other than she was full-blood Indian and part of the new breed of woman. Life out there was too much for her; at least that was Frank's story.

Their ranch occupied one hundred and sixty acres on the 'upper cold' country of the Grande Ronde River. That was the part of the river that cut north to the edges of the Wenaha Tucannon Wilderness where wolf sightings were common even before any government introduction. Folks up there in the upper river valley areas had a great deal of respect for the Onaben family. Some of the neighbors were real warm towards 'em. In fact, they were as fond of those boys as any family who braved those woods.

Billy and Frankie were part of one of the most honored Indian families in the northwest. Whenever visitors came to the pine-log-ranch house they'd usually be greeted by some kind of stretched skin sitting on the front porch. They might even be set off by the smell of Indian fish smoking away in their ancient knife-carved cedar smokehouse.

On the day that Deputy Parrish, as well as Special Agents Shawna Thore and Jeb Hirsch, arrived at the Onaben's place, a Puma skin dazzled them. It was stretched across the side of the round porch, cranked tight on long poles for maximum drying.

sixteen

Sheriff Miles T. Carson

The ranch that my brother and I share, which was passed down from my grandfather, is considered one of the largest and best cattle ranches in northeast Wallowa County. In total, it occupies nearly two sections of rolling, and sometimes flat, but fine, grazing land. The ranch is almost ten miles southeast of Joseph and runs along both sides of the Little Sheep Creek. Initially, the land owned by the Carson family had been quite a bit larger, but pieces and parcels had been sold over decades, leaving what amounted to the ranch as we see it today. My people have lived here a long time, and even with selling off of parts, we've managed to leave prime parcels to our grandchildren.

After my father died, I became head of the whole clan, and both the Frank and the Carson families generally listened to what I had to say and followed it to the letter. My popularity grew both within my own family and also with the county-folk after I ran for sheriff and was elected to that post. Getting the post wasn't easy. It was necessary for me to socialize more than I wanted to with the right kind of people in the county; if you understand what I mean?

*Note: (Miles Carson had a great deal of money behind him both from his own bank and the various contributions of the landed gentry and the business owners of the county. He was everybody's sheriff except the Indians who knew him and his family for what they really were, 'haters'. The only natives Miles ever got close to were the Onaben's who he always hired as hunters, guides, and trackers for any occasion he needed them.)

People have always asked me what I was most proud of regarding my family heritage, and each time, I tell 'em, in descending order, my ranch, my heritage, my gun collection, my trophy room, and my daughter, Sherill Lee. Right now, she's away studying Agriculture and Ranching at the University of Idaho.

*Note: (Sheriff Carson's wife, Donna was killed in a car crash in the middle eighties and Miles never re-married. His brother, Will Carson, a deputy sheriff, was married to Lucinda

Bork. Tammy Carson Bork was their child from their first marriage. Will and Tammy didn't get along very well and she preferred her mother and her step-uncle, Nathan Bork. Titus Bork, Lucinda's second husband, was run over and killed by an eighteen-wheeler truck in the early nineties over on Highway 82. He had stopped to fix a tire. According to articles on the subject, it was a rainy night and the driver never even saw Mr. Bork, nor the parked car in front of him. The death and where it took place was something out of the Kirk Douglas movie, "Lonely Are the Brave." Titus, a fine finishing carpenter, was killed instantly and thrown one hundred feet into a grove of log pine. During the years of marriage, and following Titus' death, his brother, Nathan, got real close to Lucinda and Tammy. He almost took his brother's role, it could be said, but Nathan and Lucinda preferred to remain single; they both believed marriage was bad luck.

My niece, Tammy, usually stays with my brother, Will, at the ranch during the summer. She and my daughter share experiences. Those two girls have been close from birth although Tammy is a lot younger than Sherill.

*Note: (The summer, or yearly, stay by Tammy was on her father's and blood uncle's ranch called the Big Horn, which was named for the sheep that still roam wild in the area. The sheep roam mostly in the Hells Canyon National Recreation acres where they're safe from human predators; at least most of them. When Will made out his will, he left everything to Tammy. 'Someday', it has been said, she would inherit his 200-acre ranch, plus all the buildings and half of her dad's section of the Big Horn Ranch. The ranch was a 360-acre parcel just east of the main ranch. The Carson's also had other ranches they owned in Washington, Idaho, Montana, and central Oregon, but their real pride was always the Big Horn. This was the original family homestead, which was first settled by Kit Carson and his brother, William.)

I clearly remember the day when Will and I were out on the far eastern side of the ranch shooting some assault-type weapons. In the fancy shooting range, Will had me design and build for him at the far-eastern corner of the Big Horn, he used that range a good deal of the time; it was like a place for him to relax his nerves. In the process, he became quite proficient at using assault weapons.

"Was Will ever in any war or was this assault thing just a hobby for him?" Arthur asked.

"No, he never served like I did 'cause of an accident he had when he was a kid. In the accident, Will damaged his knee, real bad. He was thrown from a huge bronc against a hitching post, broke the post and his knee pretty bad."

"Did he do anything to the horse that had thrown him?"

"No, sir, Will's a real horseman, and a good ranchman."

Old Buck Parrish was driving in a dust cloud up toward the sound of all that shooting. It looked like his truck was out to see where all that noise was coming from; or it sure did look that way. Buck was one of those guys who just didn't take kindly to the assault weapons. He was aware that both Will and I enjoyed firing those things; still, I think Will actually loved those guns. A man over time can fall in love with his guns; funny how that works sometimes.

"Never knew men fell in love with hard steel, something non-flesh-like; seems kind of odd to me."

"You mean you never fell in love with a hobby? You were always a reporter and that's all you've ever known?"

"No, I did have my hobbies like plastic model planes. I used to love to put 'em together piece-by-piece, but I was a kid then!"

"Doesn't matter whether you were a kid or not, if you love something non-flesh like, then you love it. Leave it at that, Arthur, and I don't want this subject printed if you get my meaning?"

"Yes I do. No, this subject is for me, and for you, and your brother if he ever wants to discuss it further."

"My brother won't talk about it with you or no one else; it's something interior in him. That's the end of it, and no further discussion on this subject will be tolerated today or tomorrow," said Miles.

"Now, it is true that Old Buck did know that Will would, on occasion, hunt puma and sometimes bear with those weapons, which is a legal practice in Oregon at least, as long as one doesn't use dogs. But you know the law, Arthur, don't you?"

*Note: (One thing was true, thought Arthur. Will and Miles always used the Onaben boys when they felt the need to hunt. They'd use those trackers about every three months that's how often they had the need to hunt I guess. Buck Parrish was usually, and maybe always, invited but never accepted. Nor did he ever arrive just for the fun of it.)

I continued watching Old Buck drive his jeep up the road. Some dust clouds came up from the surface although it had rained some thirty-six hours earlier. Buck was one hell of a steady driver; he never faltered at the wheel and would be able to take almost any road and hold his own in a chase. My brother Will was getting real good with his AK-47. For me, the rifle was next to impossible to use, I never really found the damned target. I invited Old Buck up that day to give me a complete report, short and specific on the Kaelin Jones matter. More than that, I wanted to hear about the FBI's work regarding The New Church. I had a few friends who attended and loved that church, and I was especially fond of Pastor Chrisp. He and I would have a great time on occasion. We'd have dinner, maybe play poker at Catty Brugel's Dining Place just south of Lostine. To both the pastor and me, that woman served the best Porterhouse in the whole three-state area. Nothing palates better than a good solid piece of meat. Her steaks actually tasted so good you'd want to pick it up and eat it by snapping at the bone like' ya love a good woman. There's nothing like a steak cut right, fresh, and fed proper; besides, the fact is that the portions were manly. Think I'll talk my brother into going down to Catty's and grab us some of that fine meat she serves. Yep, right after we finish here.

I'd been following Buck's reports on the Jones case for two months. He and I would often meet for lunch or I'd see him in my office or privately, like in the back part of the county jail. All of us in the county were real concerned with Kaelin's case. I had personally known her mother since she was a teenager, maybe even before that. She was a solid part of the community so Kaelin's disappearance had additional input. I recall sitting at the round house, next to Buck, watching. Will blasted at those targets with those bloody assault weapons. Have to say this, I had a special respect for Buck Parrish. He was perhaps the best "country cop" I'd ever known. I was gladly paying him a grand more a year, to come up here from Baker County. As far as I was concerned, Old Buck was a fine investment. I've known many men and how they worked. I learned to smell out a good one; the fact was Old Buck was even a better cop than my brother, which was saying a lot. Yet, I'd never say something like that in front of my brother that would hurt him. That bastard brother of mine could be hurt too easy by me that was for sure.

"So what do you have to report, Buck? Do we have the damned thing solved yet, or are we any closer?"

"I'd say we're a little closer. But the darned truth is, Miles, I just can't get my hands around anything concrete."

"What about the church thing? That agent, what's her name? Thore? Is she any closer to the meat? By the way, I hear she's a pretty fine looking filly. You haven't had a chance to enter the contest have ya, Buck?"

"No, Miles, you know me better than that. No matter how I'm viewing things when I'm on an investigation, a woman agent still looks like a cop to me, and that's not a turn on, especially on a case such as this one."

"Sure, Buck. A man's got to look after the business of the case first; he surely does. There shouldn't be no funny business when it comes to tracking, right, Buck?"

Old Buck just rubbed his fingers across his knuckles. He wasn't interested at all in neither my joking nor my direction down that little road.

"Shawna Thore is pretty good at groping, Miles, but she hasn't quite gotten to the 'quick' yet."

As we talked, we both watched Will load and re-load three more weapons for testing. One of them, of course, was that Israeli machine pistol. I can't remember what they called the damned thing, but it was sure both quiet and deadly. Nothing like actual testing grounds to really work a weapon and that part of the Middle East is just such a place. And those Jews know exactly how to create silent weapons; they must have thought of the Nazis every time the workers in the foundry poured the melting steel.

"So, Buck, at this juncture, do you see any key points here I should know about? Don't want to get into a real embarrassing situation do ya, Buck, 'cause that's where we're going here?"

"Yes, Miles, I understand perfectly well about your situation, but first, let me give you a few minor facts plus a couple of personal insights."

Again, Buck Parrish was a great cop and always honest to the core. Still, he had no idea of what kind of political pressure I was confronting regarding this damned disappearance.

"As you already know, Miles, we've been looking up Mr. Blackburn's rectum like good little proctologists. We've been searching all the cavities for quite some time. The problem is we've found very little."

As Buck talked, I kept peering out the window at brother Will blasting away with his weapons. I was impressed with his deadly accuracy, especially while watching him use the Russian machine pistols.

"Let me tell you this, Buck, I need something here and now. The damned pressure needs to be relieved. They're all coming at me now, particularly the Buchanan's and Bork's, never mind all the people they know. Judge Buchanan even called me yesterday on it; I was in the goddamned bath and I still had to take the call."

"Did he ask you anything specific? Or was he talking about progress in general, and maybe your rubber ducks?"

I always liked the way Buck threw in a bit of humor in almost every situation, but at that point, I could have used a lot less of it. "I want you to know, Buck, that old Buchanan's down my backside with a corkscrew. We've been following the exploits of Blackburn for two years now and the Judge demands a little progress. He wants answers."

"Yeah, Miles, he wants answers; he should. But at this point, nothing we've delved into has created any sort of light, not even a faint glimmer of anything solid."

"Nothing solid you say, well what about the deacon, what's his name, Dr. Oliveson? Do we have anything reasonable on his whereabouts that night?"

82

"Yes, we do have a witness who spotted Amos Blackburn and the good doctor in a jeep 4x4 up near Onaben's ranch 'round Promise."

Will kept shooting his two Russian-made weapons from the center of the target range. I yelled out to him, "A couple more volley's like that and they'll recruit you for the Israeli Commandos."

I watched my brother laugh, which caused me to laugh. Buck only smiled. At that point, I picked up a good deal of tension from old Buck, unusual tautness for that lawman.

"Buck Parrish, you find a woman yet to crawl in with? I must say it would make you feel a lot better, less stressed."

"Not yet, Miles. I've been somewhat too busy now to spend any real time with a woman and I guess I'm far too particular after Julie. Don't think I'll ever find another Julie."

"No, but if you'd get your butt out there then you just might meet another rock-solid woman like Julie. You just got to get out there. Listen, Buck, I'm putting on big bar-b-que on the twenty-first. We'd sure like to see you there, okay?"

"Sure Miles, why not? Guess I got a few moments free in between cases. I'll be there, Miles."

"Hey, Buck, I want you to give me all the stuff you've unearthed up to this point. Whether it's real or potential, no matter, just raise that lid up for me a little."

"By the way, Miles, I've had Billy Onaben checking into the interior workings of the deacon's group at the New Church."

"Onaben? Now you tell me. How do you expect that hateful group of boy scout deacons to let an Indian, any Indian, get anything out of them intimate like?"

"Funny thing about that, Miles, and I thought the same way you do about the whole thing, but those deacon's were convinced that Billy could bring something unique into the Deacon's Association."

"This whole damned story gets harder and harder to believe, Buck. Still, for the moment, I got nothing better than going along with you on it. So what's Billy uncovered? Give me anything substantial; I'm getting tired of all the bullshit!"

I watched Buck's face, his eyes backed off on me the way he always did when I pressed him on something.

"Betty says all those deacons are involved in something pretty ugly related to those teenaged girls up there at their retreat. It might just be exactly what you suspected, Miles. Sex ring, a frickin' teenaged sex ring."

"Yeah, Buck, and with all the publicity and raw shit that goes with the exposure."

"I'd say we're real close to opening it all up, Miles, and from the situation within that church, we believe there's a link to Kaelin's disappearance."

"So the girl exposed something beside herself. Ha! She knew too much about too many people and so the story goes that they disappeared. Kaelin went missing just like those generals did in Argentina. It was Argentina wasn't it? No matter, Buck. Difference is, she's one of ours and that's simply not forgivable. Do you understand precisely what I'm saying here, Buck?

"Yes, Miles, I understand completely. Besides, whatever happens, it all better fall within the words and codes of county and state law."

I smiled at Buck, while I shook his hand. My instructions were for him to report back to me privately in one week. He nodded, walked out and then jumped straight into his jeep. Buck moved down our dirt road pretty fast.

After several minutes, my brother walked up to me and asked why old Buck didn't stick around for a little fun blast or two as a little shooting always calms the nerves. I told Will that Buck had very little time to do his job at this juncture and that time was even getting tighter and tighter.

Will smiled and snapped another clip into his AK-47; no doubt, he was getting a lot better with that weapon. My brother turned and said, "When Buck pinpoints old Amos T. Blackburn just let me at him brother. He's a special case for me."

I told him I'd do my best to comply with his wishes, within the boundary of the law that is. I did know my brother had a longtime resentment for Amos that just wouldn't stop, nor did he want it to, not for a second.

seventeen

Stella Frank

My husband, Byron, and I lived in the southern section of the Wallowa Lake State Park. Although there were few houses allowed in there, we've somehow managed to reside there for several years. One of Byron's jobs was to patrol the park for several hours weekly during the high-summer season. During other times, Byron hardly knew there was a park. Our home was part of the park's historical section, where many years ago, only a few houses were allowed to be built. Those, in fact, were on their own lots. The area was cold and rainy most of the time, including the summer. The weather system created by the Wallowa seemed to jet out and glisten in whatever sun those rock shapes could catch. Even in the last parts of July, those ancient Wallowa peaks remained pillowed in snowcaps.

Our cabin was a home to many a lost child during the past years. Byron and I had lost our only daughter, Sylvia Sue, in a plane crash when she was just eleven. Our sweet child died on the day she returned from visiting her grandmother who lived in southwest Florida, not far from the edge of the Everglades National Park. It was a visit Sylvia Sue had taken every year since the age of six. Her last trip was experienced at age eleven. They say she died instantly in the crash, but that's the way those things are described. Don't you think?

I was a teacher of the eleventh and twelfth grades specializing in biology and science. I had a good relationship with all the students, but in particular, I was close to four of the best girls. In fact, Kaelin Jones and Tammy Bork were extremely fond of their teacher. The girls saw me off campus as the course evolved. Both girls came over to my house in the course of the spring semester and we went specimen hiking in the lower foothills of the Wallowa's. Byron was an old friend of Kaelin's mother and he'd invite her to go along on some of our bio-outings, well, that's what we called 'em, those great learning trips to the mountains.

Of course, my home was always filled with a variety of animals and plants, many of which we had saved or dried out

86

after our many hikes. No, we never killed and stuffed animals; I didn't' mean that. I was referring to the plant specimens only.

Tammy and Kaelin were two of the few students I taught the bio-art of pressing and saving specimens under glass. We worked mostly with the rare plants and flowers found off the various foothill trails of the lower Wallowa's. Our log cabin was large but we kept our home quite warm. People used to say it kind of glowed.

I had special feelings, which I dealt with about a few of the brighter kids who I worked with during my twelve years of teaching at Enterprise High. There was no doubt about it, I was convinced that I grew as much as any of the young people I worked with during my teaching years. I suppose I had a kind of unique closeness to some of my students, I just fostered that I guess.

Kaelin Jones and I became quite close before she disappeared, and a few people in the county knew this. She was one of those dedicated students behind me; anyway, I had a reputation, which I honored. It was said, "Once you were in one of Stella's classes, you had to learn to deal with Stella." With this type of reputation, I certainly wanted to live up to it, and through the years, I did all I could to maintain it.

Art Bell drove up to the cabin in his ancient dark blue-green Ford Mustang. He was a man uninterested in nature 'cause he perpetually yapped about people and I refused to be on his radio show. In fact, I refused to discuss Kaelin and our personal experiences openly.

Annabelle Mac Cruthers told me that Art would be coming down the glen to see me someday, especially if I refused his studio invitation. I had little time for the likes of reporters because I had students to guide, plant excavation trips to take, and specimens to preserve. Therefore, my time for his little interview had come; too bad I had just spotted an Aster Star or Bean Goose, mostly Eurasian, which is rarely found outside of the Bering Sea. I was so excited. No matter what, I couldn't imagine a worse time for old Art M. Bell to come up here a' calling. Still, this was the open schedule I chose, so one has to live with their own decisions, at least one has to around me.

"Do you mind if I use my recorder today, Stella, or would you prefer me to leave it off?" Art asked.

"Tell you what, Arthur; you can leave it on if you promise that nothing I say will be broadcast by you without my specific concession?"

"I'll promise that alright, as long as I can record and re-record later?"

The interview itself was fairly boring during the opening words about Tammy Bork and Kaelin. It was about the last time we were all together.

"Now, you're saying that you and the girls went off towards Chief Joseph Mountain about 1:00 p.m. on a Saturday in mid-November?"

"We did. I can remember the hike because we got lucky spotting a Euphagus Cynocephalus or Brewer's black bird, a light brown female sitting on a lower branch of a good sized conifer, eating something."

"Do all your experiences relate to animals, plants, and birds?"

"Most of the important ones I can mark or recall, either by spotting the species spotted or by being taken to dry; so the answer's yes."

Art Bell was somewhat of a thick thing when it came to biology. The man was like most men in this county, a bear-spotting, drinking, eating, and talking sportsman that is common to big-city newsrooms and other haunts such as that. Old Art wandered out here after his wife died of some rare bacteria while staying overnight in an Arkansas motel during a business trip. Apparently this bacteria, Chromobacteriosis, is usually found in the tropics or subtropics; it attacks the liver and skin and you're dead in two months. Art was devastated over his wife's death so he packed up what he could and moved to Wallowa from St. Louis in the early sixties. The county was his business by then and everybody knew Arthur M. Bell and his radio show; people were kind of proud of his local notoriety.

"Did you see anyone or anything unusual during the hike?" Bell inquired.

"Except for the brewer, I can't remember anything really unusual."

"Did you feel differently about this trip than some others, or perhaps one you've taken with some other students?"

"The only thing I did remember was that Kaelin and Tammy kept searching; they seemed to constantly peer in every possible direction."

"Did you ask them anything about what they were searching for and why they seemed to be so anxious that day?"

"Yes, I did actually ask them and after each question, the girls tossed it off in their own way. They acted as if it was nothing except a couple of strange out-of-town boys bothering them," I told him.

"What did these fellows want from the girls? Where were they from? What were they doing here?"

The boys admitted that they were from Le Grand and according to both girls, they were just looking for some 'chicken sex' with a couple of locals.

"Excuse me? What in the hell is chicken sex?"

"Well, according to the girls, it's when you meet someone new and immediately have sex with them without a lot of questions and nonsense."

"Is this a common thing? Is this chicken sex a normal teenaged occurrence?"

To answer that I'd have to say that at that stage of the conversation, old Art Bell looked stunned. He finally found himself placed somewhere that he couldn't relate to, not for a minute; not at all.

"Is there much of this kind of stuff going on here? Do you have any idea?"

"Honestly, Art, I don't know and I don't want to know, but again, according to the girls, for that day at least, the answer to your questions is 'yes', unfortunately."

"Where in this county does this chicken-sex thing occur?"

"I guess it happens in the parks, sometimes in empty rooms of the churches during certain evenings when they're closed."

"Could these boys have had anything to do with Kaelin's disappearance? Could they have had anything at all to do with that?"

"Maybe," I replied, "but I think you're chasing up the wrong tree. Someone she knew took Kaelin and it most likely wasn't for the chicken-sex thing or anything close to it.

"Are you positive about these boys? What's their names? Did the girls tell you?"

"No, well, yes; one was called Wolfman. Yes, that was the name the girls used."

"Wolfman. That's good! Have you told any of the sheriff's people about Mr. Wolfman? Stella, is this whole thing just your little secret?"

"Arthur Bell, don't take this thing for any more than it is. Please don't take it further than what I said already. Anyway, this young Wolfman had little or nothing to do with the girls. The girls were too country for them, they weren't citified enough for the boy's needs.

Now, Art, I want you to keep this chicken-sex thing to yourself. A leak about something like this would not be good. I'm afraid it could cause a few problems if leaked and we don't want any more problems."

"Yes, yes. Do you know the boy's last names? Can you remember? Were you ever told in the first place?"

"No, no last names just Wolfman and Ditter, but as I said, the two girls seemed anxious about them, real anxious."

"Did you hear anything else that night which might help us find Kaelin?"

"Yeah, find the man who connected them to the New Church and then you might find a lead on this thing."

Steve Dreben

Art's eyes rolled over his notepaper as I got up and walked over to my books and my incessant study of the illusive remnant Proghorn deer. How few of these gorgeous nap-haired creatures existed.

~~~

Eighteen

<u>Buck Parrish</u>

*Enterprise Gazette January 2, 1997. The El Nino weather
system has severely affected the mountain region by cutting into
every crag and subsection of Wallowa County. Rivers, streams,
creeks, gulches and ravines are swelled and overflowing. Every
water flow in the county is quite dangerous. Two professional
rafters were spotted by rangers smashed against the Hells
Canyon Summit Gorge near the Hat Point marker. The identity
of these Idaho residents will be withheld until next of kin are
notified. Further information on these flood victims can be
obtained by contacting the Wallowa County Sheriff's facility in
Enterprise. The Grande Ronde and Wanacha Rivers are
particularly hazardous. Travelers have been warned not to
cross-damaged bridges or enter any creek or river. Swamp and
Mud Creek are generally closed; banks have been overflowing
for two days. All volunteers are urged to call the county
emergency authority to aid where needed, or to help with the
sand bagging of specific areas. The rain continues to fall
sporadically with occasional snow spotted in higher elevations.
Again, travelers are warned to carry chains, fuel, food, and
effective outdoor wear in case of emergencies. (Art M. Belle,
Enterprise Gazette)*

Billy Onaben and Miles Carson sat across from each other
going over several maps of Mud Creek and Mt. Wallowa. They
additionally looked at areas east of Red Hill Summit, Sways Creek,
and Joseph Creek. I drank a large cup of good coffee while listening
to every word uttered by each man in pursuit of a real track. Next to
Judge Hamus A. Buchanan, these were the two men I most
respected in the county, period.

Miles was laid back in the conversation for quite a while
until that old heart inside him began pushing him to get serious.
Once he was really involved, Miles was noted for his human
bloodhound pursuit qualities. Law enforcement of one sort or
another had come to him for twenty-five years, particularly in the
Western states to help them with law and the art of tracking. Only
one man in his twenty-five years of law had escaped his web after
he had actually set the trap. That man was a veteran, a black man
named Freddie A. Walsh. Now that guy was one slippery old dog.

Miles pursued Freddie to the border of Baker County where he informed Sheriff Torrance C. Grumpt that he'd be coming into the county and he'd need some assistance. Miles was polite to most lawmen; he respected all of them with some suspicion, and with the specific exception of those on the take. Those, of course, he had little use for most of the time.

I recall that case in particular 'cause I was just getting started in law work at the time. Each day I read all the papers just to keep up on the case. The old local radio station KFRT kept us right up on the chase. Most of us would listen at the old post office in Joseph and make bets on the outcome. Miles rarely brought a gun along on the manhunt. Usually, he only used his dogs to run a suspect down. In the mountains, he'd use a mule and dogs in combination for a pursuit, or he'd use a horse taking it into the wilderness as far as he could with a trailer snapped to the hitch behind his Ford pickup.

Freddie Walsh was supposed to have killed a man named Vernon Peters, and then later, they said he raped and cut up Vernon's wife; sliced young Emily up pretty good, they said. Of course there were absolutely no witnesses to the assault except a half-breed shaggy old fool named James Corseen. James said he was a preacher of some sort in his early days and bragged about seeing Freddie come out of the Peter's place carrying a sack of potatoes. He described Freddie as nervous and looking in all directions making sure no one saw him leaving the house. Miles most probably would have done little regarding the case except Willa Shannon saw Freddie running in the back of her store; said he was running in desperate haste, moving like a scared rabbit pursued by a wolf.

Freddie Walsh was a good, hard working jack-of all-trades, who was used by nearly every citizen in Wallowa County at one time or another. Old Freddie came from somewhere outside of Macon Georgia and picked cotton with his share-cropping family until they lost their farm to the bigger farmers and the corporate farms with all their efficiencies and automated equipment. Round Wallowa County and surrounding areas it was the same story today; small farmers, orchards, and ranchers were getting knocked out of the economic game at a steady pace. Some of 'em got out by themselves; knew when the time was right. Some just took it too far and went broke. Others just packed it up together 'cause they loved that way of life so much and there didn't seem to be another way for them. In fact, many of them didn't want to see any other way of life; it was the only way they saw to live; period.

After Willa Shannon spotted old Freddie, she called Miles and told him to the best of her ability what she saw. Then old Miles would 'gut' on the subject for a while 'til he felt like it meant something. Afterward, he'd join the chase real serious like. At that point, Miles called or contacted every law enforcement man and deputy available in the area for the four-pronged chase of Freddie Walsh. At least a hundred men raced in to join the pack. They were all sworn in proper, and once again, the tracker tactics of old Miles impressed all those joining the sheriff's little brigade.

Few cases ever turned up as much interest and racism as Freddie's case did and Miles knew he would have a real problem holding some of the men back to stick to the law. This was one of the few times he packed a gun. He went into the old cattle room in the family lodge and loaded his father's 12-gauge long-barrel shotgun, which hadn't been fired for at least twenty years.

"Fires just as well today as it did twenty years ago. Damned thing was made better than most of today's shotguns," Miles had said.

The gun was dropped into a leather horse case and thrown over Miles' tracking mule. The gun had a cherry wood stock, which was one of the most beautiful pieces of that type of wood my eyes had ever seen. His mule was called Monkey Legs. It was probably the most famous tracking mule in all of the northwest counties from Oregon and eastern Washington to northwest Idaho.

The pursuit posse crossed the Powder River into Baker County not far from and just slightly north of Keating. Everyone in the whole of two counties followed the reports coming into town on the chase; that is everyone not dead and still standing. Freddie Walsh himself had to run 'cause he was afraid of the racism he knew from his past days as a 'working black man' in the old South. This combination of the past, plus his six-foot-five height and his 335-lb. weight, made him a formidable enemy, and a special pursuit prize.

Freddie was incidentally a former scout with the 3rd US Army Infantry who fought bravely in the Korean campaign, winning a Silver Star Medal and a Purple Heart. General Mac Arthur said that Freddie was one of the bravest men ever to fight in the cold hills of the Korean War' no matter. To twenty-five percent of the men in that posse, Freddie was just another 'gone wrong Nigra' who should have stayed in the South as a share copper, or been killed in action during the Korean War. There were many racists living in the hills and the mountains of Wallowa County Oregon, for sure then, and for sure now.

So in the final count, there were about one hundred men in that posse chasing old Freddie Walsh who was accused, or suspected of, murder, rape, and the slicing up of a white woman. Naturally nothing at all had been proved about the rape or anything else, but in those days, being black and big was suspicion enough. Those rural thoughts made Freddie run and run as far as fast as he could go. Would that be enough within the same circumstances to make a black man run today? Most likely it would. Not at all that much has really changed, except the gruesome parts of those kinds of stories.

Well, they chased old Freddie from four different directions down to Sunrise Creek near the far north end; and during that December of '74 there were some very heavy rains and snows, almost as much water as in today's El Nino driven cloudbursts. They were trying to catch old Freddie prior to his possible escape from Lookout Mountain where many a man over the years escaped or where one lost his life, or left there never to be seen again 'cept by the animals that devoured the bones.

There were quite a few strange stories surrounding Lookout Mountain told by Nez Perce who considered it sacred. Many of the other local area Indian tribes were also afraid of it. I'm here to tell you that no white man knew much about it except that it was extremely rugged and unforgiving.

Teddy Cochran was part of that posse. Old Teddy talked a lot, maybe because he was a lawyer, but if ever questioned about what happened out there during that Freddie Walsh chase, he was usually silent. Something was said and poorly described in the Baker Chronicle that indicated Teddy and four other men had confronted Freddie down a blind ravine off old Lawrence Creek. Freddie overpowered the men and then took them all off their horses. He tied them to four log pines and afterward, he headed east towards Durkee Creek. One of the men tied up like an old wart hog was old Teddy himself, and yes, old Teddy was ashamed for years over that incident.

Freddie now had a horse and a couple of guns, which caused him to suddenly become a 'dire' enemy. At this point in the chase, no one had been hurt in any way. However, that's not to say

Freddie himself might have changed the very basis of that statement.

Miles warned all the men in his part to absolutely wait for orders. The real problem was there were three other parties and he didn't directly control any of them. Somewhere near the southern section of Dally Creek, at the base of Lookout Mountain, a real battle took place. The battle could be seen and smelled everywhere near that party of men. Freddie fought for hours like the well-trained mountain commando he was until brother Will and Miles finally came up to where the fighting took place. Miles used all his negotiating skills to try and coerce Freddie out of the high jagged rock, but no matter what he said or did, Freddie absolutely refused to scale down through those rocks. Naturally, he moved fast enough and skillfully enough that no hunter or sharpshooter could take careful aim. Young Will and Miles let four of their dogs loose on the suspect in order to try their best at flushing him out. All the pursuit dogs were shot point blank or they were knife-gutted by one strong hand. When the yelping stopped it was like a Hollywood B movie. Only Freddie came out, and he kept moving up those slopes towards the south side of Daly Creek and the blind shadowed ridges of Lookout Mountain.

Old Freddie Walsh confronted young Amos Blackburn and his Papa, Henry, atop ancient Dark Crater Bulge. However, Old Papa Henry was killed in the fight and so was Freddie Walsh. They say Judge Buchanan was the man that pulled the trigger on Freddie. To me, it might have been a good thing Freddie was shot and killed, 'cause the posse wasn't looking too kindly towards him, not friendly at all by that time.

Judge Buchanan never said much about the whole thing. Only Miles and his brother knew the details of the confrontation. No one ever knew for sure who savagely killed Vernon and his wife. Naturally, everybody assumed it was Freddie but no proof was ever brought out to my knowledge. Some five years later, a white man, a country drifter named Sam Becker, admitted to the killings. Later, he was convicted and was hung in Union County for assorted other crimes. Old Miles and Will attended the hanging. This happened the same year that Hamus A. Buchanan became county judge; 1979, I believe it was; yes.

Watching Billy Onaben and Miles T. Carson go over various maps and ridge topography reminded me for a few seconds of the only pursuit Miles was involved in where a number of people got hurt, some got 'real' badly hurt and even two were killed.

"Buck, you look as if your mind's somewhere else thinking about something else?" suggested Miles.

"You're on it as usual, Miles. I was just thinking about the pursuit of Freddie Walsh, thinking about all I read and the way people felt about him and his case back in the 1970s."

Miles stared at me as if he'd seen a ghost coming from somewhere deep inside his body that he wanted to leave buried.

"My father Joe Diving Eagle was part of the posse, but he, like several others in the group were never part of the actual shootout. His bunch was on the Manning Creek side of the mountain waiting with guns fixed for old Freddie to appear," said Billy. "It sure was a hell of a chase from what I've read about it."

"The chase was surely more like hell itself, my friend. That fellow was smart and he could run and climb like a goat, and was one good damn solider. A desperate and frightened soldier on the run with nothing to lose and no one to jack with, but they naturally did screw with him, and old Papa Henry Blackburn was killed," said Miles. "Will could have prevented that shootout and the killing, but Judge Hamus fired first and kept on shooting. After it all started, there was absolutely no way to stop it 'til someone died."

"Maybe this time, no one in the posse will panic. No one'll shoot or fire first, then maybe no one will die," Billy suggested.

"That's a lot of maybe's, Billy; many too many ifs to even guess at, particularly this early. So at this point, the only thing we're chasing is shadows. There might be some concrete evidence, so let's all of us just go on with the planning here, stick to this case," Miles ordered, making it look more like a suggestion.

"Buck, I want you to take a party of four up to Lewis and head west. You take the dogs and sight for the upper part of Joseph and Swamp Creek Forks."

"I'll head up there with party number two. We'll be coming from the east side as well as the south side of Wallowa Mountain," said Billy.

"Right," agreed Miles. "You start there and head two miles east and then go straight north. Anything at all that looks like evidence, I want picked up and do it with a plastic glove please. Don't let anyone else handle the evidence."

"When do you want us to start, and should I take my brother along?" asked Billy.

"Absolutely. What's a damned chase without Frankie Onaben, second best tracker next to you and Will in two bloody counties? We'll head off 'round sunrise let's say 5:30 a.m. We can set our CB's at about twenty-five after to group it all on channel twenty. All right, boys, remember, our party will sweep in from south of Lewis. Again, we'll start at 5:30 and I'll control party three myself. I want Will to head party four. They'll come in from Flora and Mud Creek. I got a solid hunch we'll find something during that seven-hour track down we'll be hounding on, so keep sharp," said Miles. "Get it ready, Buck, and make damned sure you and Billy coordinate all activities through me. You're in charge, under me, along with Billy. No one besides the two of you can give an order without my full support, no one."

"So, what are you saying here, Miles? We'll continue to pursue how long?"

"If nothing is found, we'll still spend the next week heading east toward Hat Point. If we have to, we'll comb every object from beer cans to faded clothing to a broken piece of plastic 'atop any ridge. No object is too small or too meaningless to be eliminated from lab examination. Just find it; look for it and bring it back. Got it boys?" Miles spoke seriously, meaning every word spoken. Billy and I nodded to him as we folded up the maps and topography charts. Miles then followed by closing the door to the county court conference room. His movements were direct and even more determined than Miles' normally brutish physical demeanor.

nineteen

Tammy Bork Carson

I sat in my room for a long time thinking of Kaelin and Terrie Conson. I had no one like them, nobody really close to me to be with. I have to 'kind of be' with my own thoughts. My memories are of all the times spent together chasing some 'log' or another. Of course, I still have Tilly, but she's been pretty much out of sight since Terrie ran. Fact is, I even heard Terrie's living in another runaway shelter somewhere near Canyon City. Now, Canyon City that's a genuine boring place. No, maybe Burns is even more boring; yeah, a little duller or maybe, I'd call it a tossup. If I knew exactly where she was, I'd go get Tilly, Brady Thompson, and maybe even Willie Bradley, plus Tommy Boy Wenaha, and we'd all take a little trip. I always liked Tommy Boy, but he was afraid of my dad and Uncle Miles. They'd make it impossible for me to take up with a full blood and I'm just not that big a hero, not me anyway. Maybe I'm more like a Sentinel Chicken.

While I sat there thinking about all of the dumb thoughts coming up in my head, I suddenly heard the silence snap and the buzzer ring. It was Tilly coming up for a visit. "Come on up to my room, Tilly. I'm just pouring through thoughts and waiting for something to snap in my brain. Come on up and let's talk."

I really felt good about Tilly driving up that day. She couldn't have picked a better time. It was almost as if she'd read my thoughts. Tilly Wallis was both a friend of Kaelin's and a friend of mine for almost ten years, or at least since we all started kindergarten, or maybe even a little earlier. We played together for years. All of us shared all sorts of things and we rationed our most personal thoughts. At least that is what we did until Kaelin disappeared.

At that moment, a pre-spring pair of Nuthatch's landed on my windowsill. The male bird peeked in for a moment with its mate following right behind him. All of a sudden, the two of them quickly flew off southward.

"Well, what have you been doing, Tammy? Did 'ya hear any news 'bout the search party? Did you hear that they were heading towards Lewis next week?"

"No, all I know about Kaelin's disappearance is what I get from my Mom and Dad; that's about it. Uncle Miles, who knows something about everything that goes on in the county, never really talks about it," Tammy said.

"Listen to this, Tammy. Last week I heard Terrie Conson was in Canyon City living with some old half-breed named Jean Half-Horse."

I laughed inside. Some Indian names and nicknames just were so 'right on' that they just made me smile. "Are you really sure his name was Jean Half-Horse?"

"Yes, that was his name," Tilly replied. "That's what Tommy Boy Wenaha said, and when he says it one way, you can usually believe him, never knew a guy I believe as much as Tommy Boy."

"Have you seen old Tommy Boy lately, or are you talking about this happening some weeks ago?" asked Tammy.

"No, the last time I saw him was in Joseph at the ice-cream shop. It was day before yesterday, he looked fine and was happy to see me."

"Is he looking as fine as ever? Something 'bout that Tommy I'd always liked; you know that?"

"No, Tammy, I'm quite surprised, because I know your dad and uncle would not like a dating thing between the two of you and that's for sure!"

"Sometimes, you got to do what feels best for you, not what everybody else says. It's good to do what's right for you."

"Never heard you talk like that unless Terrie or Kaelin were around," Tilly said with a giggle.

Kaelin was real sweet on Tommy Boy Wenaha. In fact, she was more than just sweet on him. Fact is, I think the girl liked any young buck with a big bulge behind his zipper. She didn't seem to care who she chased during those last few months prior to her disappearance.

I watched Tilly snicker while turning an off-rose shade of pink thinking both about the words I was using and those bumpy jeans of Tommy Boy's always popping out at ya. I guess one of my favorite things always was shocking people with words; nothing much else shocked them.

"Tommy was telling me that his Uncle Billy and Frank are heading up two of the original search parties."

"Yeah, so when are they all going up Lewis way for the search?"

"Tommy says next Wednesday at 5:30 a.m., and old Tommy's uncle wants him to join them."

"That's kind of interesting. Is he going to ride along or is he just going to be 'a flapping' like most Indians do?"

"Most Indians talk a good deal less about things than whites when they talk. It's usually pretty straight; that much I can say for the Indians I've known."

I looked at Tilly for some time before I uttered any more about the local tribes. A few odd seconds of silence fell between us. "I hear there's some Nez Perce in you, Tilly. Is that why you're going in supporting them?"

"Yes, it's true from what the folks say; I got about a fifth Nez Perce in me and I can tell you I'm proud of every little blood cell," Tilly bragged.

"Got any other blood like that kind in you?" Tammy joked. "Possibly a little Polish?"

"No Polish, as you rightly know, I'm mostly French and German, with a fine cut of Nez Perce in there for looks," Tilly proudly replied, not the least bit ashamed of her background.

"My, oh my, Tilly, getting a little tight in the tooth with me aren't you? What's wrong, can't you take a little ribbing? It's not like we all sat around here talking about boys all the time and drinking up our gossip like a bunch of the Wallowa ladies clubs."

"Well, dare say, I'm getting a little touchy," Tilly shot back, "especially when it draws out the usual local racism about the Nez Perce. Yeah, it does bother me, I guess."

Racism isn't what this is about Tilly. It's all about Kaelin, Terrie, and bulging Indian jeans somewhere 'round the zipper of

Tommy Boy's tight pants. "You know, Tilly, I'm getting pretty tired. Would you mind if I get a little shuteye? We can continue our little reunion another day. Don't slam the screen door when you hit the streetlights. And, thanks for stopping by."

I rolled my body away from the face of the half-disbelieving Tilly as I chose to end the conversation. It had been a long day and I truly was tired; even more exhausted because of the tricky tongue plays between friends. That's why I always liked talking to Tommy Boy Wenaha. There was always room to say what we had to say freely and end it there. I did like him, not for the bulge, but I liked him for the young man he was. Fact is, he's the only boy in the area I respected. Yeah, Tommy and I were friends. Maybe I wanted to be more than just friends, but if it ever happened it could only be the right time.

The screen door slammed as Tilly closed it, or let it crash behind her. I listened for her steps as she headed down the street towards her car until there was no distance, until there was no sound. Yes, no doubt, old Tommy Boy Wenaha was someone I cared a lot about, someone for whom I felt something.

twenty

Jillian Douds
Jillian Douds' Diary

Diary entry January 9, 1998. It isn't easy to enter this kind of material in my journal, but I will try to replay much of what actually happened between Millie Roberts, Kaelin, and myself.

Millie Roberts and I walked across a dirt road not far from where Kaelin was last seen alive. A thousand yards maybe from this dirt road, which was unlit, was a field filled with old, dark stumps of once great ancient trees. On this particular day, there were only stumps of smaller great old-growth trees and not much else. These remaining wood idols made a strange cluster of shadows on a moonlit landscape. Additionally, shrubs of one sort or another further marked the pocked landscape on this moon-soaked field we entered. My bones were deeply frozen by the continuous rain and semi-frozen conditions and the snows, which continually fall in the mountain valleys around Enterprise. Millie and I chattered about Kaelin's quick disappearance and the upcoming massive search, knowing full well that very little would be uncovered of her remains.

Kaelin had told us where she was. The girl had told us exactly where she had been buried, and I had provided a way for us to hand in pieces of solid bone evidence. In fact, there were three pieces of foot bone. This evidence was given directly to Shawna Thore and Deputy Byron Frank; yet, I only passed on two of the actual bone fragments; one piece turned out to be that of a deer.

Both Millie and I were absolutely sure of the corrupt nature of Deputy Frank. It was known in the community that many times over the last few years, several pieces of evidence in other cases were passed to him, which never showed up again. Millie and I told Buck Parrish and Shawna Thore that we didn't trust old Byron Frank and in fact, never would trust this sort of a man. We said these precise words about trust to Buck Parrish and then we said it directly to Byron Frank, straight in the face. Byron just flipped our words away with his eyes, thinking I'm sure that both of us were just a couple of New-Age wackos. Of course, Byron was not the only person in the valley who thought that, and if this information got out, oh well!

So we came to a place at the northeast side of the field where Millie suddenly said she had the need to lay down. I tucked a blanket under her head to support it and handed her a special purple crystal from Brazil, which we both shared. In all of my life, I had never seen or encountered anything like the purple crystal. It was a solid mass of magenta and crystal frozen into natural glass; so pure to the center of its core. The crystal had a glowing diamond-like substance pulsating from its center. It was quite hot to the touch; in fact, so hot that it seemed to burn your hands. In the moonlight, the rock had a particular shape of its own. The crystal glow, its radiance was nearly overpowering. To me, this Brazilian crystal had a unique internal-like power, an energy and inter-energy; a cold energy, which magnified itself with human touch.

With the crystal in hand, both Millie and I knew we'd uncover or find something worth knowing about Kaelin's disappearance. Yet as I sat there that night pondering everything flowing through my head, I watched while Millie fell asleep. I began to wonder somewhere deep inside me if I hadn't lost my mind completely. Although these types of thoughts did pass through me once in a while, I never let myself dawdle on them for very long. I stared at the full moon for a while watching Millie fall deeper and deeper into her sleep clutching the purple crystal as she dreamed. Suddenly, a younger voice poured its way through Millie's lips and for a few faint seconds, I was afraid. Before long, I realized that the voice I was hearing was the voice of young Kaelin. At first, I just listened to her words; as I was unsure of whether to ask anything directly. Yet, she seemed to be talking to me directly. I felt chills go into every part of my body; plus, the excitement was both internal and external. The only time that I felt as excited was during my first year of nursing. In those days the genuine contact between patient and nurse was profound; now it seems like a trickle of that commitment for any nurse. It was easy to reflect all the thoughts passing through me, both from Millie's channeling that night, and other key times in my life when there were a couple of thrills left.

"I'm tired of being here. I'm so alone here I want to be with my friends. I'm so terribly alone," the voice said.

"Where did you go?" I inquired. "Many people have been looking for you for a long time." No longer apprehensive, I could talk directly to Kaelin even if it was just as though she were facing me; as if she were body and flesh in front of me. In fact, I was able to feel her in front of me and knew she was right there talking to me. This was the first time I was able to talk to her spirit. It was glorious and so was she.

"Have they found anymore of me? I told Millie where I was, both of you must go back to where they dumped me," the voice of Kaelin begged.

"Tell us where you want us to go and we'll go there," I promised her.

Kaelin insisted, "Higher, you must go higher. Go to the top of the ridge and climb downward, and there you'll find my neck and head bones."

Agreeing with her sad request, I said, "Okay, we'll go back there. We'll search the eastside of the road off of Finley Buttes."

"Yes. You must climb down from the top after you search the upper ridge for that plastic tarp. There you will find the plastic tarp they used to transport me. They carried me in it and then they dropped me down into the ravine." Changing the subject, she revealed to us, "I miss my friends; that's who I miss the most. I want to party. I miss the parties."

"Yes, Kaelin, but can you tell me more about the ravine? Which section of the ridge are you talking about?"

"There's a large gorge at the top or near the top of Buttes Ridge several hundred feet back from there. If you look closely, you'll find the brown tarp. It's there if you truly search for it," she begged.

She stopped speaking for a while as I studied Millie's forehead and face as it contorted with her neck turning back and forth. "Can you, can you, Kaelin, give me a better idea of where we can find your bones?"

"Yes, yes; follow the big ridge down about two hundred feet and behind a boulder; a jutting rock in the mud about five inches down, you'll find my skull."

"Are bones scattered in other places or are you mostly there?"

"No. Actually the skull and some of my fingers are there, but the hips and thigh bones are further down the ravine, much further down," Kaelin explained so we could find her body.

"Millie and I and some of the others tried to find more of you. We went there twice and I climbed up and down that chasm again and again and I never found more than the little I did."

Kaelin interrupted me with, "You will find more this time and you must turn whatever you find over to Buck or Shawna and no one else."

At that point, I could almost see her image coming through the moonlight. Her body seemed to take a form of some sort, and yet I could see her eyes and some of her facial features. It felt as if I was talking more directly to her than ever before.

"There will be a time when we will discuss things more directly and Millie will be here more than she is right now."

"Are you talking about the death of my friend?" I asked, somewhat confused. "What exactly are you suggesting?" I wasn't positive about the words. Maybe I didn't want to hear what Kaelin was telling me at that point.

"Millie will be gone in three years. Her heart has been weak from birth and her time on the earth plain is about up."

"Are people given exact periods of time here or something like that? Are we all handed some sort of different stacked deck?" I questioned.

"Yes, in a way that might be a good way of stating it. However, when a person's time is up, precisely up, it must come to conclusion; there is nothing beyond; time's up. So, in a way, you can describe your lifespan, such as mine, is determined to be given up at its conclusion; according to Master Wu."

"Who's Master Wu? Is he someone I should know; or are you the only voice privy to him?

Kaelin answered the question quickly. "No, Master Wu will be speaking to you, especially you. Actually he will tell you about the bones. You will 'heal' with these bones in the future at a another time. We don't' really deal with the future here."

I really didn't understand much of what she said about the bones and Master Wu; my brain just simply wouldn't take in the words.

"You'll know more about what I've said by direct contact from Master Wu. For right now, just receive my words as if they are coming from a recurrent dream," the girl instructed.

I tried with all my heart to listen to Kaelin but I felt very tired as if the full source of my body's energy was suddenly dissipating. For a few seconds, I stared at Millie, dreaming beneath my eyes. However, my pupils seemed to fog over, the tear ducts were overflowing. I was sleepy. This was a new sensation of sleep, which was almost overpowering as if I could do nothing about it coming over me.

"The only one I can see clearly now is the dark man. He was the one who stabbed me so many times. This was the one who raped my body, the one who tried to control and force out the very source of me with his constant raping of me. At that point, I was already gone and any control, especially his forced control, meant nothing."

When she spoke, when Kaelin spoke so abruptly, all of my powers of consciousness seemed to reawaken. "Who was the dark man you talk about, Kaelin? Was he your actual murderer?"

"Yes, he was one of the killers, but not the only one. There were two more men involved and one wife; yes, she was also involved."

"Perhaps all of these people played different roles?" I asked.

"Yes. They all played a part in the murder; in my murder. Again, Kaelin seemed to drift and bring up her loneliness. "I miss my friends you know. Most of all, I miss my friends and the good times we all spent together. I crave the parties."

"Are you frightened of the place you're in now, or does it make any difference to you where you are?"

"Time is different here. We share no present, no past, and certainly no future. All of us are just forever in-place."

I was quite confused by her statement but I still wanted to know who the killers were. Just as I was about to ask again, Millie mumbled something and came awake. Kaelin's voice was silenced and her image disappeared from view. I was surprised to see Mille get up and walk. She questioned me for nearly two hours regarding what was said and the event that transpired. Yet with all the time passing, I could tell her little which was in any way meaningful. I knew at that point quite well that I would be meeting Kaelin again, either with Millie, or without her. Of that I wasn't sure of; not at all. My little path to Kaelin's world suddenly opened up for me. This world opened wide as if I were silently standing in quicksand with no human help in sight. No way of touching anything substantial. It was as if I were floating somewhere myself.

twenty-one

Nathan Bork

I remember the day old Miles T. Carson and Buck Parrish walked into my office in the Wallowa County Court House. While I sat and stared at the old television set watching NFL playoffs, I smoked a fine thigh-rolled Havana cigar; sure as hell did enjoy those cigars the rare time I received a box for some holiday or another. To me, watching those games was the highlight of my year. I didn't really care for football except for those playoffs; they got or seemed to get my blood excited inside me. Yeah, there is just something about those intense playoffs- maybe it was 'cause I used to play high school ball for Enterprise. In those days, we didn't have to be six-foot-five and weigh three hundred pounds; a solid and strong normal physique would do very well thank you. Well shit, today they breed boys to be more like young bulls, some of 'em even snort and spit like bulls. The fact is, some of them even smell like 'em. I tried to organize inter-county jail ball for a while, but between the damned bureaucracy and the blood violence on the field, it is just got to be a little too much. I remember inviting old Miles T. Carson and A.T. Blackburn down to one of those convict football games in the early '80s. At that time, old A.T. was one of Miles' deputies. In fact, he was one of Miles' favorites until he was caught with his hands square in the till.

Anyway, the two of those boys came down to one of the games, which was between Union County Jailhouse, one of the toughest compounds in the northeast part of the state. This jail held crooks jailed just south of Walla Walla and was made up of Nez Perce, Cayuse, and a few odd but wayward Indian types. We had a few big Umatilla's on the team, but none of 'em was in any kind of shape except drunk, and none of them knew the first thing about discipline. The team was no fantasy Burt Reynolds type movie athletic group sworn to win under any circumstances like in the movie, 'The Last Yard.' No sir. Our team was not a fighting winner. Getting on with my story, that game was something else. I remember sitting in the box with old Miles T. and A.T. Blackburn. All of us were just as tight as could be and we were all concentrating on the game.

Right after the first few seconds of kickoff, one of those big Union County boys dropped one of our large Umatilla linemen dead in his tracks. He did it with some sort of an ice pick right up the Indian's nose, poking it right through to his brain. I've got to tell you, it took about four large guards to drag that old bull of a man off the field. In fact, the incidence reminded me of one of those bullfights that I saw in Nuevo Laredo, Mexico some years ago. Some of us watched as other guards got two mules and pulled the body behind the stands attempting to make it invisible to the crowd. The event wasn't a pleasant sight for the good women and children in that crowd. Yes sir; it sure was an ugly vision, seeing a human being dragged off that way.

"You ever see anything like that, Miles? There sure were two mean son-of-a-bitches butting heads down there," Blackburn commented.

"I'd say so; in fact, don't think I've ever been to a football game where one side used an ice pick on a player from the other side. No, can't say that I can remember a game like that," said Miles T.

"None of these boys are noted as being too friendly anyway; they weren't friendly before prison and believe you me, jail time does little to help 'em become friendlier," claimed Blackburn. "They fought like two mad grizzly bears on the tundra."

That A.T. had a certain way of smiling; just drove a wooden pick into your stomach muscles every damned time he spoke. A.T. usually meant nothing by it. It just was the way he was, and that angry mongrel ain't no different today.

During the next ten minutes of the game, another man from the Union side was stabbed in the left kidney and he had to be taken out by an emergency crew, right out of the middle of the field. The man who did the stabbing was Harry Montana. Harry was the drunkest Blackfoot Indian I'd ever met, and yet at the same time, he was certainly one of the smartest one's. His tested I.Q. is one hundred and fifty. Still, he drank and usually operated as one bad Indian. In fact, the man preferred being considered 'bad' but as so many bad Indians, he ended up hanging himself one night in a security cell within the closed block section of the prison.

That Indian was not alone in his depressions; there were many of those hangings in that prison, mostly Indians. Naturally, those hangings were considered suicide but many of us knew better. Some of those Indians were too drunk to get up on a bed or a chair to do that deed to themselves. Many local wardens told me that it (suicide) was an easy way out, but of course that way out was open to Anglo and black alike. But in most western prisons, I heard it was a majority percentage of wise Indians who hung themselves.

"Some Indians don't believe a spirit body will get to heaven if a man commits suicide," Miles T surmised.

We both sat there and stared at Miles T after hearing his statement. Unsure of anything else we could say, we sat in momentary silence.

The rest of the prison football game, Miles T. and A.T. Blackburn and I sat there. They never stopped the game even after two killings and a number of near killings, which followed. The truth is, by the time we got to the last quarter, there were four head bashing's, three more stabbings, four broken noses, two broken knees, and three broken shoulder injuries. Statistically that was considered the bloodiest football match in the history of prison football anywhere except down in southeast Texas. Some of those local Indians get pretty rough especially with each other.

After the games, the three of us went off to the 'Judges Club' in Lostine. At the time, it was known to be the best eating and dancing place in the whole damned county. The three of us sat there for awhile drinking and chatting while we watched the half-stripped old native women climb up those greased-up Go-Go dance poles coming down from the ceiling of the bar. That place was filled with noise, music and dancing from all directions, like you couldn't imagine. They were having a lot more honest fun than most of the places one goes to today, if one still goes. I sat there talking to Miles T. while old A.T. found himself a half-breed to dance and smooch with. They danced real cozy every time that mixed band played the right kind of tune.

"Seems like old A.T. stuck or maybe wanted to stick that little half-breed thing right there," said Miles T.

While waiting for his sirloin steak to come, Miles T. just rolled off that comment. He kept drinking that damned Jack Daniels and got real high, never before seen him that knocked on booze. Both of us kept watching him while he worked his way up that half-breed's dress. A.T. was trying to push his hands into her slot as they cuddled up together. I hear that woman's been floating the bars around here since she was fifteen years old. The only thing she's got going in life is a warm little pair of lips to warm a man's hard dick. Sometimes I hear she even gets paid for it.

"Sounds like one sad fucking life, so sad I'll have to swallow another shot of that good bourbon," said Miles T.

Well, those sorts of breeds don't have much of a choice. Most of 'em are whores or get beaten or just plain fucked over on the reservations; no life at all, way I figure.

"How do I know that you know what you're talking about, Nathan Bork? Where in the hell do you get your information from anyway," asked Miles T.

"Well you see, Miles, we all got a wing at the jailhouse which sections off about fifty of those little whores. So as warden, I get to see and talk about a lot of things with them all the time. A warden in these parts has his various rights and privileges; so it is he that properly screens every prisoner coming into his jailhouse."

"Must be some of the wardens getting a little greedy with the position they have. It's possible maybe they take advantage of their power?"

I smiled at him knowing full well he had some specific idea of the 'special screening' process some of the women went through before being placed in the general prison population. I swallowed my drink as I whipped the excess alcohol from the grin-creased corners of my mouth.

Miles and I watched old A.T. Blackburn slip his hands down the backside of the squaw's super short dress. One of those bouncers in the bar, who didn't know old A.T. was a deputy, came up to him and grabbed his arm and told him in plain English to lay off the girl. Naturally, the girl was too drunk to mind what was being done to her. She didn't seem to care nothing about what old Blackburn was doing with his hands. In the corner of the room the squaw-girl's pimp surely cared about what was happening to her. All of a sudden, one thing turned to another real fast. Old A.T. just spun around quick and slammed that pistol of his against the side of the bouncer's head. The bouncer cried out, actually wailing loudly, as he dropped near dead to the wooden dance floor. Miles T. got up fast and pulled A.T. from atop the man. He would have just beaten him to death if old Miles T hadn't been in the room. A.T. Blackburn was noted for having one bad temper, especially when it came to incidents involving women; that is, women that he'd taken any kind a fancy to of any sort.

That was about the last time I saw old A.T. Blackburn as a deputy. As everyone knows, he was caught taking bribes from a local merchant who blew the whistle on him after a deal went side-wards. Miles T. always said that he just appreciated a good crack shot like Blackburn. He was good in the field when and if the occasion arose, and it usually did, and that's when the A.T. Blackburn type usually proved worthwhile.

A.T. himself was far too wild. Most of the time he was a boiling steam engine. The man was too fierce; never even hired him as a guard. Fact is, about five years ago after that football game, old A.T. Blackburn came up to my office and asked me for a job.

"Think you can use an old professional like me, warden?" he' asked me. I told him as I visually recoiled from his warped smile. "Have to wait for the new warden to make that decision now, A.T."

Wasn't up to me anymore. My days of hiring guards were over. I was retiring at the end of the year. Now that was about November 1992 when he and I had our little conversation.

"I see, but if you will, I'd like a solid recommendation from you, warden, for the new warden's eyes; if you could do that," he said.

"Sure, I'll write you a letter of support right now and you can use the letter when you apply for the new job. If that's alright?"

Old A.T. Blackburn waited until I wrote the letter in long hand. However, something inside me said he'd never use it. If the new warden would have ever called me regarding A.T., I guess I'd be forced to take a middle road. A.T. was, is, for that matter, one tough son-of-a-bitch to recommend for anything. Met a bunch of men and women in my life, but something about that Blackburn turned my stomach muscles, just a twisting them into new knot arrangements. That boy always did that to me; he sure did. A.T. always drove some kind'a nails in my gut when around him. Generally, he'd be avoided. Didn't see him at all after I retired from law enforcement. That man was the type to play lawman, just play at it, that's about all.

twenty-two

Charles 'C' Marten

I had remained late at the Umatilla State Bank offices in Enterprise. We always kept a certain number of lights on within our offices, particularly at the second story level. Some of our people, including myself, would often work late and make up much of the work that was often missed during our busy days. When I left the field of architecture some ten earlier, I found myself spending countless hours learning the banking business, usually under the guiding arm of my mother's old friend Col. Cyrus F. Ford.

Old Cyrus groomed me for the job when I was hired. He was the one who taught me the true ins and outs of the local banking business from the president's point of view, naturally. The bank's board was usually in on every major decision old Cyrus made, and choosing me to be the future president was definitely one of those collaborated decisions.

It had actually taken four years for Cyrus to let me know the truth behind my grooming. I was chosen and cleared by the executive director's board to be the next president if old Cyrus solidly approved of the appointment or when he personally needed the support of my nomination.

Nearly four and a half years into the job, and I do mean actually into the position, old Cyrus F. Ford privately told me exactly why I was chosen for the role and by whom I was chosen. He explained how I was to be confirmed over all other long-term contenders for the job. Maybe that was the problem according to Cyrus 'cause Jerry Wicks knew his job well but lacked the specific 'roundness' which a local bank president needs.

"What do you mean by roundness?" asked Nathan Bork.

"Well, Nathan, you of all people should have a good grasp of 'roundness' because you're a perfect example of it. During your prison warden days, was anyone within your own staff capable of taking over for you?"

"When I really think about it, the kind of experience I had and the depth of it could only be accumulated by being a warden, nothing else would do."

"Dr. Oliveson, do you see anyone in the area who could take over in your key surgical position at County Hospital?"

"Not really, maybe a few," Dr. James Oliveson replied. "Still, only a medical doctor with fine surgical skills and a political scalpel would go along with it."

All of us laughed at James and the deep truth he uttered regarding capable people within the county limits. We sat there for nearly thirty minutes laughing, particularly at the whole concept of 'roundness' in a specific area of work.

"I never saw a man- fact is, never met a man who could operate a small prison better than Nathan A. Bork," bragged Nathan Bork.

"Nathan, I'd sure confirm that and the same can be said for Dr. Oliveson here, but getting away from the subject for the moment, we have other matters to discuss tonight. That's exactly why I called this meeting of the executive board of deacons."

I had asked the Jubilee Café to bring us over some late dinner. Yes, old Sally Caldwell made one hell of a pot roast. I kept a fine seasoned bottle of Bell's ten-year-old Scotch and three iced glasses for special occasions. Naturally this was brought up for me special from the bar of the Enterprise Cattlemen's Association. Yes, we were properly set for a night of important discussions and no disturbances. I could automatically secure the second floor of the bank at the push of three buttons, and so great privacy was quite possible. Nobody was able to get onto the second floor, and better still, no one could hear us. This was the one place in our local world, which could remain absolutely secure. For this conversation, it was supremely necessary that we had total privacy, full-blown privacy period. All of us sat there staring at one another fairly silent as we forked down the pot roast and greens.

"It's really great that we can gather confidentially as men and eat a real American meal instead of some Oriental garbage or that new Thai shit now floating through the countries' colons," said Bork.

"Few places left are open anymore which serve or make proper American meals, Western American food; you know, the kind we grew up eating. Yeah Calvin," said Oliveson.

"No you're right. Few places in the west, nor anywhere else, serve anything close to American food. The whole bastard country has been taken over by Chinese money and Mexican labor. Fact is, even the defense industry sold our damned secrets. Many of those executive type bloodhounds are on the take for Chinese money. Bastards bring in bags of illegal money and it's laundered by our finest banks and institutions; no, nothing's sacred anymore, only the little places like Enterprise can keep 'em from doing us in, with their boatloads of gold."

"That kind of shit's gonna come back someday and bite us in our soft fleshy asses, I can assure you 'a that, Cal!" Bork warned. Nathan always assured everyone of everything as soon as he got just one good belt down his throat. As he began swallowing his second double shot of booze, I instantly grabbed the free bottle.

"Nathan," I suggested, "let's just hold off here a while 'til we finish with the deacon's business at hand."

"Need to get my strength up, Cal, some of the subjects you boys are getting into need a couple of drinks to soften 'em up, prior to getting into the mood," Bork suggested.

I looked at him for several seconds and put the bottle back, placing it into the center of the table. "One more, Nathan my brother, then we'll get straight to the business at hand."

Nathan immediately grabbed the bottle and poured another drink for each of us. All the good food was fully eaten by this time as the pendulum on the old clock struck nine. We knew it was time to get to the meat of the evening. "The meat, sure can say that I love meat in almost every one of its forms, especially the one's got panties and bras," Bork crudely stated.

"In my opinion, you're loosening up just a little too much, Nathan. Must say, I'm glad at this point, we got this place shut down like one of your prisons," said Oliveson.

117

"So, gentlemen, what should we do about the young girls' rescue facility and the current snoopiness of our beloved Sheriff Carson and Trooper Buck Parrish? The board that governs the New Church is getting very nervous. Additionally, we have our good Pastor Chrisp answering questions that he shouldn't be answering. Do you get the drift here gentlemen?" Marten asked.

Dr. Oliveson inquired, "How far has the law penetrated the walls of our facility?"

This was the first time that Dr. Oliveson seemed interested in the conversation. There was always remoteness about him. I watched his face twist while he swallowed his drink, which was more like gulping his drink. To me, it seemed as if there was a new Dr. James Oliveson M.D., someone whose 'cool' was breaking down right within the walls of that room in front of Nathan Bork and myself.

"James, let me say this now. What we have here is an executive board of the church, which will look into the problem at hand and will solve it tonight with a plan. Do you understand exactly what I'm saying?" Bork asked.

"Yes, yes, I do but some of us have heard rumors about Mr. Bell, the reporter, and Pastor Chrisp, and some of us clearly don't like the implications," Oliveson replied.

"Well, he's purely right on that subject, Calvin. There are a great many people getting nervous when old Pastor Chrisp talks to the local press."

"By the way, Nathan, I want to remind you again not to call me Calvin, that's my middle name. I prefer 'Charles'."

"Yes, but I've been calling you that for thirty-five years; it's somewhat difficult to change now. But I'll try if it makes you feel better."

I remember slamming the Scotch bottle down on the wooden table; marking it deeply. "The first bastard votes here will be for ending all discussions between our good Pastor Chrisp and the press and damned near everyone else.

"How in the hell are you going to keep that man from talking?" inquired Bork.

For a second, I looked at Nathan in complete disdain for the complete drunken fool I knew he was. But I kept my perpetual banker's cool.

"We threaten him, we fine him, and cut his salary or we eliminate him on a permanent basis. Does it matter which one?"

Ignoring the fact he was asked not to call him by his first name, Bork continued his questioning, "Calvin, I didn't really hear what I thought you said, did I?"

"Yes, you did Nathan, and even more than that 'cause this man can put all of you perverts away for a very long time; every damned one of you. Do you fully grasp what I'm getting at here?"

"Now, Calvin, none of us has done anything which the church and the good bible hasn't dictated. It's right there; it's right there to follow the way it is!" Bork yelled.

At that moment, I took a few seconds and another drink before I spoke again. "It's in the book all right you idiot, but others might just interpret it differently. They might take those words to mean something entirely different and much of that interpretation is against us and for secular authority."

"Are we talking about the law as such? 'Cause much of the law around here is in on it as much we are, aren't they?" Oliveson asked.

"The law, my dear doctor, goes beyond who works for it. The codes when written took into account the possible corruption of men. Doctor, I will have you know that the law is pressured by disappearances and other possibilities, like fricken homicides traced to our care facility and us. Do you fully understand what I'm saying here?"

For several seconds, I watched Bork and Oliveson stare right at each other and then at the crystal, iced drinking glasses in their hands.

Oliveson answered, "We had nothing to do with the girl's disappearance, Calvin, nothing at all to do with it!"

That may be true my deacon brother, but her death and possible murder could be traced to the church and the 'fricken 'helping elders' or some of the stupid rag-sucking deacons of the same New Church.

119

"How's that possible Calvin? How in the hell is that kind of thing possible?" asked Oliveson.

It's possible 'cause a lot of you idiots out there got some very large mouths, and in this kind of situation, you want stone-shut mouths.

"Now, that ain't real nice of you to talk about your deacon brothers that way, Calvin," Bork said sarcastically.

Being chairman of this executive board gives me the right to say and lay dictates and things you don't like down on the table and as sure as sheep shit stinks, I'll do just that! Now, I will say this, that some of us understand some of your needs out there. We understand impulses to help, but when those good drives turn into teenage disappearances and possible finger-pointing murder, then it's just plain got to stop. So it's our job to tighten the whole damned son-of-a-bitch up! Do you hear what I'm saying? We vote tonight on our position, and here's what you boys will vote on, and this is what you'll bring to Selected Deacons. First, the two runaway shelters will be turned into one and that one will be the northern shelter, which is closest to Paradise.

"That's the facility which is most remote and of course, you realize, one needs a four-by-four truck to get to it," Bork reminded.

Your vote is accepted and Dr. Oliveson is of course for it. Am I right, James?

"Yes, yes of course; it's a damned good idea to consolidate," the doctor replied. "Pastor Chrisp and I said that two years ago, and now you're voting on it."

So that vote is passed and tabled, gentlemen. Now please move on to the next order of business, actually two lines of business.

"Wait a minute. Do we really have to close that northern runaway home? It's sure helped a lot of young ones?" Bork asked.

The item is now a tabled and closed issue, Nathan. Look at it as you would an injection into the veins of one of your condemned shit-killers. Start the injections and in a few sweet God-accepting seconds, it's over. It's simple. Not even the smell of the corpse gets in the way. The state has finally come up with a gentle plan of death and erasure that a good public citizen accepts, and with ease, it cleans and makes fragrant our society, at least for a couple of seconds.

I remembered a look of discomfort and a shutdown demeanor coming over Dr. Oliveson as I introduced the subject of lethal injections. For a man who worked with cancer and associated deaths on a daily basis, I saw a deep cowardice. This sense of cowardice in him was something to fear for all concerned.

"Next item, gentlemen. We will vote on closing all access to the runaway home, including an electronic gate set up at the site with television monitors set appropriately. Access to the facility will be privileged to specific members of the Special Deacons and no one else. Is that supported?

Bork and Oliveson nodded in automated agreement to the second voted-on-issue of the night, and I quickly penned in the results for the whole deacon committee.

All right then, the last item to be considered and voted on before this gala night ends is the subject that follows. This may be the most difficult decision and vote of the whole night. Let me pour us all another drink so a rational decision can come easier.

"This last decision will be final. Even the board itself cannot overturn it. Additionally, our position on this is supported by all financial concerns, especially those donors at the top of the church's list. Do you understand what I'm saying here?"

I wanted Oliveson in particular to understand his position and mine, and I wanted to know full well that he understood what I said, to acknowledge the full nature of my expression and viewpoint. For myself, Dr. Oliveson, the church hero, was a weak yellow-eyed man, a course mixture of Mexican and Swede, a balance of white-race and chicken-shit, where mostly the crap ruled. He was a man, pressed by frustration into five children of his own, supported by a 'clean' German-American wife, a Folk-Mama Hilda born to breed and smile, the kind Goring used in the Nazi-Brown Shirt youth breeding farms to future enable the master race, where legs stayed spread for all Arian semen.

Bork was a state prison warden assigned to Wallowa County for life. He was a rugged drunkard and was always pushed to extremes, or to the brink of expected extremes by the bottle. His view on life, his vote was always wrapped up.

"So, gentlemen, let's get to the last issue of the night. After the vote, we will finish up with a final celebratory drink or final toast, if you will?"

I watched as their eyes followed me. I could feel the power that I had over these weakened geese, these guarded masturbators who were afraid to ever make a decision without a leader. Tonight, I was their leader as I'd been a leader to many other groups. I was trained to lead and enjoyed the opportunity. The Ranger's had taught me a great lesson in Vietnam. I was taught how to lead by the connection to the men below me. Their own men shot so many officers, especially first lieutenants. Shot back in the rear because many of these officers were yellow rooster shit and were hated more than the enemy. Never ever did I fear the men under me, even the rough and brutal black bastards trusted me. I was the coach, their coach in war, and I'd get them to the finish line in one piece. Both the men and I believed that and so command came easy for me. Why was that so? They knew that I would get them out, so they understood that they needed me like a suckling calf needs its mother. I was their total support, their crutches, their priest; I was their master quarterback in the battlefield. Kill me, boy, and you kill yourself. Respect is what I had from those men and respect is what Bork and Oliveson lacked. People who can't respect themselves or other people create a fear in me; those sorts of people have always done that to me during the course of my life.

People were surprised at how quickly I climbed to the top level of the bank in two years. I owed it to genuine respect and solid leadership; no other explanation got me there. Numbers are easy but leadership and respect, now that's something hard, like a hot adult hard-on played with by a naked fourteen-year-old for two hours; that's stand up! Oliveson and Bork, they just never understood 'up'. Those boys never in their lives could stand up for anything and our last item on the agenda would support my position completely.

"Can we get on with the vote here, Calvin? I'm getting pretty drunk waiting for the finale," slurred Bork.

"That's the idea, old pal. We get you drunk and you vote our way."

"Isn't that the way it always is, Calvin?" Bork asked.

We all laughed as I got serious and stated my precise and disciplined stance. Using humor, one can usually voice his opinion even if it's contrary to all others at the decision table. This was a method I'd used both in Vietnam and within the structure of the banking system; it always seemed to work well.

"So the last item we'll work on tonight is the final and total dismissal of Pastor Chrisp!"

"Now, Calvin can't do that. I for one will not vote Pastor Parham Chrisp out of the New Church. In fact as you know, he was one of the five original founders," Bork informed him.

"I'll have to support Nathan on this. Pastor Chrisp is a 'God seed.' Besides, he's one of the best men of the 'Book' I've ever known," said Dr. Oliveson.

"Sure he's a good man; I never argued that. Maybe Mr. Chrisp is even a fine man of God, whatever that is. And let's not try to explain that either, not now. Let's just talk about the need here?" Calvin suggested.

"Go ahead, Calvin, but sure as I sit here, I'll not support this vote, not ever!"

I glared at Nathan's drunken face, looked straight into that pair of sloshed, over putrid yellow strewn eyes. "You listen here, Nathan Bork, and you too, good doctor. We will vote together tonight on the removal of Mr. Chrisp from church offices."

"Now, you tell me, Calvin, why you and those pushing you want Parham Chrisp fired?" Oliveson asked.

"Because the son-of-a-bitch talks openly to the media and he's too concerned with his own 'face' to be fully trusted by the board's authority. We got some rogue bastard deacon who probably murdered this girl Kaelin, and we don't need some face-saving, big-toothed, bastard, son-of-a- bitch speaking for the whole church, especially now. In fact, now is the time to shut him down and anyone else who implicates the church in any of these foul outside matters. Pastor Chrisp must be replaced by a smarter, maybe a younger man, who'll conform appropriately to the ultimate needs of the whole congregation and the Select Deacons."

"Conforms better, you mean. Some monkey on a string son-of-a-bitch who knows nothing except the 'Good Book' laid face-up on the pulpit in front of him," said Bork.

I watched Oliveson take another drink, but I was sure at that point that I had his little yellow bile vote.

"Now, Nathan, the whole purpose of a good pastor is knowing that the Good Book is there as part of him. Is there anything else he should know?"

"I guess not, but all the same, Chrisp's one of us from the beginning and he should remain where he is until the end," suggested Bork.

"The end of this may come like a surprise cancer, right the hell at all of us, if we as a collective body don't remove that old barking son-of-a-bitch. He's got a cannon-ball mouth and we can't have the likes of our good local reporter, Mr. Bell, squeezing those canned wrinkled balls out of our crispy little pastor. Do you get my meaning boys?"

At this point, I watched, and I knew Dr. Oliveson was in my palm, yet Nathan was still unsure and had to be persuaded further.

"Nathan, let's look at this logically if you're able to follow the words."

"I'm still able to follow, Calvin. Don't you use that pseudo undermining grammar of yours on me. I was the damned warden once. You remember that!"

"Dr. Oliveson, you with us here? Are you with us here?"

"Yes, I've heard every word spoken and I have to say I'm sorry, but I'm now being swayed toward your position, Charles. Yes, I'm now siding with your stand."

"Good. Now we're all beginning to see a little clearer here. So let's drive home, the final point for Nathan prior to our final vote. Pastor Chrisp must go, Nathan, because he exposes all of us to forces outside, forces that can destroy all of the good work accomplished by the deacons and the New Church for all these many years. Good work built on our blood, good work needed by the community at a reasonable price, just a few normal human indulgences coveted by our relationship and words understood within the 'Good Book.' One never is so important that he cannot be replaced either by removal or by the firing squad. Do you get my drift, Nathan?"

At that point, my view had penetrated even the drunken and thick head of Mr. Bork, our former warden of the county jail. The vote went forward regarding the dethroning of Pastor Chrisp, affording him a nice retirement and letting him remain in the church. Of course he must promote his first assistant, Rev. Filbert Buchanan, to be our next full-time pastor immediately.

We cast our votes unanimously for the removal of Pastor Chrisp and the installation of Rev. Filbert Buchanan as the new young pastor of our church. Pastor Buchanan is the son, as you know, of the Hon. Judge Buchanan, our fondest major founder. The vote was perfect and would be supported entirely by the other thirteen church deacons later in the week. That night I had accomplished my assigned task. The New Church would be greatly tightened and yet free to pursue the 'good work' it had a tradition of doing during all its years within the mountain ridges of our Wallowa community. Various leaky doors would now be closed and others shut completely. Big mouths would be nailed down and tucked in silent places and yet all accomplished with no violence beyond the soft words of drunkenness.

Later, I was congratulated by the senior deacons of the church, those of course with most of the power and clout and with large financial portfolios behind them. I led my way to success again for myself, and those entrusting me with the task. That night, I sat alone in front of the fireplace and finished the last drop of my personal twenty-five-year-old Chevis Regal Scotch. As a naturalized second generation Scotsman, I certainly deserved the last taste of fine whiskey, didn't I?

twenty-three

Millie Roberts' Truths

We arrived at Buck Parrish's office around three in the afternoon and each of us was as calm as we'd ever been, at least on the surface. Our trek to the Thorn Creek area was a success at least in our eyes. Jillian and I had been able to delicately connect with 'goddesses of nature' and the spirit form of Kaelin. Best of all, we found evidence. Of course this wasn't the first time evidence had been found. Millie and I had collected just three bones: two were handed over to the authorities. The other bone, a finger bone, we had kept hidden.

At this point, in the search for Kaelin, and with the evidence discovered, Buck Parrish was one of the few county officials we trust. The other man who we had some confidence in was Will Carson who had been stabbed by old Amos Blackburn and was himself in half-critical condition. Billy Onaben was another man who we also had a great deal of faith in it was hard for a white woman to get close to him, with the exception of Jillian, who he regarded as a sister. Yet Billy's basic influence on law enforcement was nil because he was a local Indian and could be hired for what he did and no more. Sure, the county boys had made some accommodations with the local natives recently; but still, deep in the gut, the general resentments were there and probably would always be there.

"Millie, how are you going to present these metacarpal's to Buck?" asked Jillian.

"Just take the little things out of my protected sack and drop 'em in his lap," Millie replied.

"Better be careful with that dropping stuff. We got to protect what little we have of a man around here."

I snickered at Jillian's lewd comment. She and I'd been kinky with words between each other for a long time, seems like more women should share things like that with their friends. Women should exchange intimate humor with one another. It's part of a healthy relationship. The whole jaunt to Thorn Creek and the upper Inmaha River sort of wore me out for nearly three days. My heart's not very strong and my weight holds burden even on these big bones of mine. Jillian could move and foray far easier than I could, and she alone should be credited with discovering the new bone evidence. In fact, it was Jillian who led to 'em' by a spirit-force far greater than anything either of us had ever encountered anywhere. To me, in my opinion that spirit-force was Kaelin, but that force was far greater than Kaelin alone. There was something extremely powerful about those two eagles leading Jillian to those bones. It all sounded somewhat strange but nevertheless that's how Jillian got there, and damn it, that's how she uncovered the bones. This time there's no doubting Kaelin's force. This time there's no doubting the power of those eagles. To the natives in the area, especially the Nez Perce, the eagle is the ultimate sacred bird. It is the towering force of nature in animal form. Eagles are the living image of the purity in both animal power and magical power that surrounds them. No white man will ever be allowed to legally hold or kill eagles. If a man or woman kills an eagle then the Nez Perce believe they will be damned in the deepest parts of their souls for a thousand years. That's a high price to pay even for a bad man; few would pay that price if they knew what price they were actually paying.

Well, we sat in Buck's office for about fifteen minutes before a young female assistant deputy came in with two cups of hot coffee and said, "Buck said he'd be delayed. If you wait ten more minutes, he'll be right in to talk to you."

I asked her, "Do you have enough time, Jillian?"

"Yes," she agreed and we both decided to wait.

"Do you have any strange feelings about coming here? If you do, we can leave immediately."

"No, no, I'm quite determined to help get this disappearance resolved. You and I both know the truth. It's proving it to the outside world that's always difficult."

"After rambling through miles of that rugged wilderness to find these bones, you can bet your life I believe in what we're doing. The magical unearthing of Kaelin's evidence and the killers surrounding it."

"How do you know for sure there's more than one of 'em?"

"Millie, I don't know anything for sure but I've experienced the same spirit talk as you have. I feel that it's all perfectly truthful and right there!"

"Good afternoon, ladies. Sorry about the delay, but it's looking as though we've got a new lead on Kaelin's disappearance." While Buck entered the room he removed his coat and pulled up a chair.

Jillian asked, "Can I ask you what the new lead is? Can you say anything at all about it?"

"Well, Jillian, I can't say much except that Jeb Hirsch, the FBI Special Agent in Charge, got himself a telephone call from Sheriff Pete Moss of Grant County. A friend of Kaelin Jones was taken in on drug charges, drunk and disorderly, down around Canyon City."

"Who was it Buck? Was it Tilly Wallis or Terrie Conson?"

"From the description I'd say it was Tilly Wallis, but Sheriff Moss said she wouldn't talk to anyone but me. The deputy sheriff reported that the girl was extremely frightened, half-frozen and dehydrated, yet basically sound."

"That's really great news, Buck. Are you going down there to question her, or are you and Miles bringing her up north?"

"Don't know yet. We haven't worked out the details, but this, my dears, is the first real break in the case we've had in two years."

"That's real good news, Buck, but I'd guard that girl real close if you bring her here," Jillian insisted.

I remember watching Buck's expression as Jillian said those words. Buck was noticeably stricken and his wrinkled forehead turned flat and ashen.

"If we make the decision to bring her up here, I can assure you, Jillian, she'll be as guarded as our US President. No one'll get to that girl; I can assure you. Damn it, yes, I can absolutely attest to that!"

"Presidents have been guarded in the past and if you want to kill 'em bad enough, somebody always does, don't they, Buck? We got a history of it!" said Jillian.

Buck was obviously disturbed by Jillian's statement. He was acting almost ashamed and protective of something. It seemed that Buck rarely reacted to anything, yet here was an overreaction.

"So let's get to the quick of it ladies; what can I do for you today?"

"Well, Buck, we got a couple of presents here for you. Maybe this is the second real break in the case," answered Jillian. "Of course Buck, you had another real break in the case recently but according to Byron Frank, that evidence turned into animal bones like most evidence turns into-"

"Now, you listen, Millie, if you came here to run poles up Byron's nose then you'd better stop talking 'cause I don't have time for that sort of thing."

"No time for it, Buck? Maybe you have time for what we have for you and maybe you don't, but as a good lawman, maybe you should take a look at it."

"Jillian, you're a good, sound-thinking woman, but even you aren't making straight sense. So get to the point."

I looked directly into Buck's red and worn eyes and I was sure he felt dog-tired about the investigation, but I said nothing for a few seconds and just looked directly into his eyes. For a couple of more seconds, I waited for Jillian to speak. "You remember how your search party went into the Dougherty Springs' back country and all you came up with was two sad bones?" I asked her.

"Yes, of course I remember. I was right there when we uncovered the second piece of bone," Jillian answered.

"Did either of 'em look like animal bones to you?"

Buck searched his mind to see exactly how he wanted to answer the question. "Well, Millie, I will admit that my unprofessional pathology eyes did see a human's leg bone. I'll admit that and my opinion turned out wrong. My personal unscientific assumption was definitely incorrect as you know."

Seems to me, any bones that go to Byron, stays with him for days. Later, he ships them off and they turn out to be animal, maybe vegetable or mineral?

"Millie I want you to keep your comments to yourself regarding Byron. Even if I support part of what you say, there's absolutely no proof and so the bones are not human. Understand?"

"I understand, Buck, understand well. The bones sent to the Pendleton Lab were not the same bones that were found and you know it."

"I sure as hell don't know it. In fact, I know nothing about it, Millie, and neither you, nor anyone else can prove otherwise."

Buck was brewing under his collar, which he unbuttoned slightly and opened his shirt, pulling down his tie. "Again, Millie, other than speculation on animal bones and maybe on human bones, tell me what brings the two of you here."

Jillian gently dropped the new metacarpal bones covered in a plastic bag on the table directly under old Buck's nose. "Don't send 'em for testing through either Byron Frank nor Shawna Thore. Buck, please promise me that as an old friend," begged Jillian.

"Looks to me like a human finger bone."

"It's Kaelin's metacarpal bone, Buck. I can assure you of that. Therefore, you should test it yourself, maybe even in another county; like Grant?"

"I can't do that, Jillian. It's out-of-county policy and you've got police regulations."

"Damn it, Buck, if you want her killers, you're going to have to break regulations. Get the bones tested on your own. People trust you, Buck; not the system you work for and sometimes protect."

Buck looked across at each of us. He pulled the plastic bag to him, put it in his upper right pocket and buttoned that pocket. "We'll see, ladies. We'll see precisely when the objects get tested and I'll try to keep you informed on the progress."

"Do your best, Buck. You got two good people standing in front of you here and many others standing behind us counting on you, don't put it in another's hands."

Buck slowly stood, looked down at us, and shared some sort of a silent calm. It was a cross feeling of belief that transpired between the three of us. Also, it was as if he was saying 'it's time to get this case down, ladies.'

Jillian and I sat silently looking at the door for a while as Buck rushed out into the main hall of the Justice Building. Buck was a man completely possessed by this case, cursed by the evasive disappearance and likely death of a young girl, one whom he'd known all her life.

twenty-four

<u>Jillian Douds</u>

After leaving Millie near the creek, I hiked up several jagged granite formations just above Corral Creek, slightly east to Thorn Creek. The climb was steep, yet the view of the magnificent snow-covered peaks was pure and spectacular. I could feel the hard sweat oozing from every pore in both my upper body and lower torso. It was the type of strain that made one feel both exhausted and exhilarated.

I knew Millie would be waiting for me at the base of Dodson Creek Fork. This particular climb needed a hiker, but Millie was in no shape to attempt it; so I thought, 'why push her'?

As I moved upward against the ridge, I was cut at the upper section of my eyebrow by a sharp willow shrub. In some of the rocky places, this shrub and the Manzanita spread itself out over the mountain-like wild fire, which is of course what usually ate it.

At times, blood, especially a woman's blood, attracted bears. Still, I knew that the sort of blood they liked best was 'period blood' which of course naturally oozed from a healthy woman's body every month. Therefore, I stopped and took the mirror out of my pack and treated the head wound as well as I could; my main objective was to stop the bleeding. Finally, I was able to stop the flow of red by using my husband's simple shaving nick-stick, which I always carried in my daypack. Near the upper edges of the hill leading down to Thorn Creek, which eventually crossed the Inmaha River, I spotted two Bald Eagles.

The two birds circled around a large Ponderosa Pine, which had lost a few branches at its peak. Eagles had always fascinated me and for some reason; generally one would show up somewhere in the woods during spring and fall when I hiked the most.

My climb continued as I made my way down the steep rim. Occasionally, I looked toward the higher trees at the edge of the next ridge. Looking in that direction, I noticed the continually circling two eagles. Finally, I made it to the far western side of the Inmaha where Thorn Creek runs directly into it. There's a dirt

132

road that was cut by the forest service many years earlier called 4260, where they've built a large conduit to handle the excess water in rainy season or during the annual snow melt. There was something about the fragrance of the air in this wild place. It 'fired of purity.' From this height, in this area, many of the gulches, glades, canyons, riverbeds and creeks started flowing eastward and down towards Hell's Canyon. The northeast wind began cranking up and I looked straight upward at the eagles that were lowering themselves just above me. The two giant raptors actually began circling above me while gliding no more than twenty-five feet from my body.

The two wondrously mated eagles were trying in some way to communicate something to me. Hence, I followed them while they moved. I pursued the diving and soaring birds to a churning and twisted bank a quarter of a mile up from Inmaha River, or from the confluence of Thorn Creek and the bigger river. I couldn't help gulping in the crisp air. The smell of it seemed like some kind of an aphrodisiac. In fact, everything about those moments seemed somewhat ethereal. Not for a moment was I frightened, not for a second did I feel any fear, for the two Bald Eagles were calming to me. Again, the wind picked up and clouds formed at higher elevations. Very quickly the sky turned somewhat grayer. I chased the eagles to another marked break in the Inmaha River. While searching up and down that bank quite thoroughly, I jumped across the narrow break in the river and my feet slid beneath me because of all the accumulated mud. I eventually landed against a pointy sand rock.

There was a shallow sandbank at river's edge. It was covered in red-white pebbles, which were coarse and grainy and filled with newly washed-up and rough-sand rocks. I looked above and noticed that the eagles were soaring around my head moving further and further upward into the clouded sky. As I watched them flying so gently and directly above the tree tops, my internal instincts said, 'look below'.

At that point, I spotted a small white object, peering out of the coarse sand as if it were a rare ocean shell. Carefully, I bent down to see what it was, and then I began digging the object out with my knife. The discovered bone was the phalange from the left hand, possibly the finger next to the pinky. I searched the area around the sand pocket and after digging a little deeper, discovered two additional bones. The second bone was a carpal, and the third bone was a metacarpal looking as if they had come from the same left hand. Not having a microscope, it was quite hard to be certain. Hence, I carefully took each bone section and slipped each of them in a plastic sandwich bag. Afterward, they were placed inside a zippered pouch in my daypack. I was overwhelmed with my discovery. In fact, at that moment, I was convinced that I'd found Kaelin's actual hand bones. Again, this was a feeling passed indirectly to me by the two hovering Bald Eagles.

My search continued and I spent at least another twenty minutes covering one area of sandy space after another on both sides of the riverbank. Since I ended up empty-handed, I knew at that point that it was important to return to Millie. After all, she might need me and she'd probably be frightened of some of the forest noises that normally sounded at the end of the day. As soon as I tightened up all of my gear, tied my left boot, pulled the hat string under my jaw, I took off down river as fast as possible.

The day quickly grew darker. I moved twice as fast, yet not quite as carefully as I normally would have stepped. About three quarters of a mile down the Inmaha, I slipped on a smooth, but mossy rock and cut the hell out of my right knee. Again, I stopped the bleeding almost instantly and used a small bottle of peroxide to clean the wound. I bandaged the cuts with a square type bandage and then quickly moved on with my hike.

Two distant sounds of Spotted Owls echoed through the forest, and yet, I never saw a visual sign of either calling bird. I jaunted faster than I'd ever moved to get to where Dodson Fork Creek, Corral Creek, and the Inmaha River crossed.

My eyes searched to locate Millie, but she was nowhere to be found. Changing my tactics, I hiked another quarter mile west to where Corral Creek and Dodson Creek first crisscrossed. It was there that I found Millie peacefully sleeping under a giant Ponderosa. Leaning against a rock across from her, I watched the girl sleep tranquilly for another ten minutes, letting each of us rest, but the dark was rapidly coming down on us.

Right before I woke her, she began speaking, or a voice began coming out of her mouth, which actually wasn't Millie's. "I'm pleased you found my left hand and some of the bones, some of my finger bones," she said.

"Who am I talking to here? It sure looks like Millie Roberts but she sounds different, and the Millie I know, seems to be sound asleep?"

"Millie is sleeping, Jillian. You are the one I'm chatting with now," the voice whispered.

"What and who are you? Or, am I so tired and achy that I'm imagining this discussion?"

"No. You have felt the flight of eagles and I was the female Bald Eagle, the one that flew lower," she said.

"So you're the Bald Eagle, the great femme eagle that soared twenty feet above my head?

"Yes, Jillian, but you've found me, or part of me anyway. You must look deeper for the other part."

Millie was still sleeping. I just wasn't sure I'd recovered from the meeting of the three waterways and my crashing fall over the mossy rock. "I'll still do my best to help you find the other parts, but for now, we'd better get moving. But to indulge myself for a few seconds, please allow me to ask you a couple of questions. Can you tell me where the other parts will be? If so, what parts they will be?"

"Part of me will be found by the search party, but my general body and most of its parts have been scattered all over the area. It's been two hard winters now since my death. My hip and neck bones can be found up Tully Creek just west of Spain Saddle. Please look around there as hard as you can."

Who in the living hell was I speaking to? I was certain it wasn't Millie Roberts. At that precise time, an acorn fell and then a pinecone dropped near me. They were all driven by wind. And then Millie woke up.

"Millie, all I can say is that you sure sleep deep. You were so sound asleep I didn't want to wake you, so I just listened."

"You listened to what? To my loud snoring? My husband says I snore real loud sometimes."

"No, I'm pretty sure I was talking to Kaelin. It was at least her voice."

"Oh, so she came right out at you did she? Kaelin did say that she wanted to discuss some things with you directly. That's what she told me."

"Well, I guess that is what she did. Plus Kaelin, or maybe it was those two Bald Eagles, but one of them led me to these three bones."

Millie took the bones and examined them carefully. She then smiled and we hugged each other gently in a soft special friendship kind of manner. From somewhere in the breeze, I heard Kaelin's words, words that seemed to get fainter and fainter. "You'll find more, Jillian. They'll find more. I love you, Jillian. I love you for listening. Love you for listening."

It took us almost three hours at a very slow and near-mechanical pace to get back to our jump-off place. As we hiked back, the two of us talked of the next trip to the upper woods, and our plans to speak to Shawna Thore and Buck Parrish. We spoke of Kaelin's voice and the road we'd both chosen. Both of us spoke about finding her killer, or killers, and exposing them. It was a path chosen out of deep empathy and personal ties, maybe a little love even entered into it. But it was all we had and it was all that was left of our sense of kinship, just our local feel of real community.

~~~~~

twenty-five

Will Carson

An article appeared in the *Enterprise Gazette* describing a fight between Will Carson and Amos T. Blackburn. It was all to have happened according to witnesses in the Long Tongue Bar and Grill. The article surfaced under the by-line of Roger T. Townsend who was the actual and sworn true pen name of Mr. Arthur F. Bell of KFWC Radio out of Enterprise.

Enterprise Gazette January 1998: According to several witnesses, Amos T. Blackburn, former deputy sheriff, and Deputy Sheriff Will Carson, were directly involved in a serious matter of fist-de-cuffs inside the Long Tongue Bar and Grill. According to the bar's owner Mr. Myron E. O'Donnell, Mr. Blackburn turned on Sheriff Carson with a small knife inflicting stab wounds in Carson's neck and ribs.

"Will Carson had beaten the tar out of old Amos when he drew a small knife from somewhere. He dropped Will immediately to the bar floor."

Another witness, Mr. Graham, recalled, "Well, I saw Will beating him to a pulp in the corner. His face was all bloody and his tired body dropped down when a small knife flashed as if the thing had come from nowhere."

Other witnesses blamed the fight on Will Carson who knowingly provoked Amos Blackburn with various insults regarding his religious convictions, the New Wallowa Church of Christ, and the Hon. Pastor Chrisp. Mr. Blackburn is a noted deacon, woodsmen, and freight hauler. Few people in the community had ever involved themselves with this quiet and humble self-contained backwoodsman.

Deputy Will Carson is currently hospitalized at Mid-County Hospital Critical Care Unit under the wing of Dr. Simon Thorp. Information and questions regarding the incident can be addressed to the County Sheriff's Department at 824-6700. Will Carson will recover from wounds inflicted by Mr. Blackburn and will not file a complaint against Mr. Blackburn at this time.

It was one of those low days in my life. Maybe it was because I had stopped drinking on a regular basis, but that had been six or seven years earlier. Therefore, there was no excuse. I made a pact with my brother, Miles T. that I'd stop or slow down on my whiskey drinking if he did. We both pledged to the pact. However, Kaelin Jones' disappearance caused me to pick some drink up, a little bit anyway in the aftermath. Yeah, it sure did bother me, not because I knew the girl directly; actually, it was more than that. Fact was that she was both a friend of the family and my daughter's closest schoolmate. The girl was like another daughter to me and I was convinced that foul play was involved in her disappearance. I was additionally quite aware that she had stumbled into something stinky within the New Church, something quite secret that she wasn't ever supposed to know.

In a county as large as Wallowa, my brother Miles and I had seen many strange disappearances. Usually, they were out-of-county people who'd been murdered. In this instance, this pretty young child, this beautiful and innocent babe in the woods was crudely taken from us and I've prayed deeply about it on a daily basis. I've gone down to the First Presbyterian Church and prayed about her death and I prayed about her being found alive. Still, there was little real hope of that, very little hope.

As the investigation continued under Chief Deputy Buck Parrish, some of the things I'd known about The New Church started to surface. Yes, we'd been watching the Solid Brick Café, the Homeless Help Center, and the Recovery Center, for wayward female teens for about a year since Kaelin's disappearance. It seemed that Pastor Chrisp and his self-anointed Christian clan were actually doing some good around here. At least it seemed that way.

Both Miles T. and several other locals watched the New Church grow from a park-side bible-reading group holding meetings in Wallowa Lake State Park, to an enormous congregational church of four thousand members. There were followers from all around the county and beyond.

It was Pastor Chrisp and a group of wealthy deacons who first formed the Recovery Center for Teens in the early 1990s. Buck Parrish and I watched this group go out and spread its word all over the county. In point of fact, almost every town in the county has a Recovery Call Box set up by the Deacon's

Club for young females who were lost in the county needing help. There was help for wayward teens no matter where in the United States they came from, anywhere. The deacons had put together a solid charity and a teen-help network. They were doing the sort of thing we thought every pureblooded person that calls himself a Christian should do. Yes, should do to help others; that's Christ's way.

In the gut, Buck and I felt something wrong about all this teen charity stuff. The two of us shared many a drink over it, but neither of us could put a finger on any solid evidence regarding any wrongdoing related to those deacons. I'd talk to Miles T. about what we felt, but he admired Chrisp and some of the deacons and could see nothing at all wrong with their charitable activities.

We all sat back and watched as the new church's money base grew, 'cause each member had to sign a tithing contract which gave from ten to fifteen percent of the family's annual income to the church. In the county, their outward notoriety regarding all of these activities seemed to suddenly cease. The reasons for this happenstance were few. The most restrictive information of all stayed within the church; or at least any information related to the wayward teens and the Recovery Center did. The church structure closed and all voices remained inside.

Miles T. liked to let things roll on by the church's own power unless there was some reason to get involved. He believed in the long objective arm of the law all the way. "Why don't you leave it alone, Will? If every group I had in the county did as much as those good deacons have, then it'd be a far better county," explained Miles T.

The only people who felt something gut-wise like myself about the Recovery Center for Teens was Buck Parrish and Willa Shannon. Maybe that was how Willa and I first got close to one another. It was over our mutual suspicion of the New Church's various charitable activities around the county.

"Amos T. Blackburn was never a religious man; that is not 'til the deacons sucked him in and baptized him. He became re-born. A convert he certainly was, and that was all he talked about!" shouted Willa Shannon.

Willa and I'd sit around drinking those 'healthy malts' couple times a week. We talked about the church and the silence related to it all through the county, especially during the last year. At the beginning, the deacons just poured as much information out as possible; but after time, it all just slammed shut. Everything pounded down like two-inch metal nails on an oak casket.

At the Long Tongue Bar and Grill, I did have a little too much to drink and I said something foul about The New Church to Frank Forman, one of the stewards up at the Dougherty Spring's Coal & Composite Mine. Amos T. Blackburn and Byron Frank were sitting about two tables from us and they were able to hear every word spoken. I mentioned something about a report I'd read having something to do with a short fourteen-year-old female yapping about local sex clubs, fornication, strip dancing and pass-the-young-pussy slave-sex games. I told Frank Foreman that this information came directly from the robbery confession after a Seven-Eleven convenience store was robbed down in Baker City, Baker County Oregon. The gal's name was Sally Withers.

"I'd have to read that report myself. She was staying at the Wayward House you say?" Frank asked.

Yes, that's what the report said. Actually it said a lot more. However, the county sheriff down in Baker didn't believe a word she and her boyfriend confessed. Still, that nearly killed the whole thing regarding the New Church with both Parrish and Miles T.

So, my friend, as you know, I got a pretty loud mouth about most everything, especially when I have three or four shooters in me! I watched Foreman smile as he downed his fifth or sixth shooter. Both he and I were pretty gone by that time.

Low and behold, Blackburn and old Byron Frank picked up our conversation. I remember Blackburn looking over at me with those puss-filled yellow snake eyes of his squinting some of their usual hatred. That man's been full of hatred since I first knew him, full of the same twistedness I recall growing up with during our times shared at Enterprise High. Son-of-a-bitch always got into fights over nothing, and he hurt a lot of guys pretty bad as I recall. He always got away with it 'cause of his kin's relationship with Judge Buchanan. Plus, the son-of-a-bitch got away with everything and some of it was pretty awful. Well, when he got up and walked over to me with a schooner of Butte Porter in his hand; stood right next to me. I can tell you this, I did flex for his next move. Yes, I quietly got myself set for that schooner to come crashing into my face. However, old Blackburn just stood there staring me in the eyes and I just stared back.

As a kid, I saw the bastard do this same thing. It was like some kind of torture waiting for the right moment to slam somebody in complete surprise. I watched Blackburn intently and stiffened up while grabbing the wood trim at the edge of the bar getting myself prepared for Amos T's 'quick shot.'

Instead, this sneaky pompous bastard said, "Been talking too much as usual 'bout things which I surely consider none of your fucking business."

"Listen, Amos, my conversation was purely between the bar man and me. It was between me and Mr. O'Donnell, between the two of us, and not you and old Byron Frank there!"

"So you think you can sit in this place and say things out loud about good church people that's a full out lie and have nobody get up and say something to you about it? Is that what you think you can do, Will? Is that what you think?" Blackburn asked.

"Amos T., I'm a man who says what he wants to say, when he wants to say it, drunk or sober. Get my drift?"

"Well then, Will, I'd say you're a man who needs a lesson in proper USA manners," Amos T. warned.

"So who do you think is going to teach me those types of manners? You tried to teach me once and I recall it was me who did the teaching?"

"Me. It's me gonna teach you 'cause you see, I'm a man. I'm a deacon in the church, a brother among holy men, and you're a nothing law-boy. That's all you are is a negra law-boy, a damn Indian-sucking bent-squaw-squealing law-boy!"

In the next moment, I saw his hand twitch towards me. As it moved, he stabbed me in the ribs with his other hand. I hit the bastard with my clenched fist in the nose and I felt it collapse. I felt the bones in his face crack and smash with my punch. In fact, I put as much power as I could into it before I went down. I watched old Amos T fall back against the table. Blood poured down his face and ran over the front of his pretty, sparkled cowboy shirt. He quickly passed the knife to his other hand. At that point, it came straight into me and I knew I was stabbed in the lower back just below the ribs. After his blow, I hit him twice more, once in the cheek, and again in the solar plexus with a powerful uppercut.

Blackburn fell back against the table. He stared outward, so I picked up a chair to come down on him direct, and as I did, he swung around quickly managing to put his knife in the muscle of my neck. I backed out almost instantly. People say he somehow managed to slither weakly through the door. Blood poured from every possible facial pore. I remember, for a second waking up as Byron and O'Donnell picked me up like a half-slaughtered bleeding pig. Yes, I recall them taking me over and laying me down backside on the pool table. Someone phoned 911, and I was pretty much in the black from there.

Next thing I knew, I was in a hospital bed down on my back laying there with more puncture wounds than a mad dog sniffing a female porcupine in heat! Dr. Gibson said I was lucky that the wound in my neck just missed the Carotid artery. I guess I was just lucky 'cause two millimeters more to the front and I'd be flat dead right now. I wasn't sure while lying there who got the worst of the beating, but I was surely gleeful about the way Blackburn's nose cracked down beneath my right fist knuckles.

twenty-six

Millie Roberts

I had another one of my dreams the other night, and I called Jillian asking her to come down to my place and help me search for Kaelin on Saturday. Also I told her we'd bring a bunch of concerned close locals.

We took old Highway 46 up to Conner's Cabin, passing the old Zumwalt Shack as we drove through the Ponderosa-lined road, always something special about those big trees, especially their bark – always loved the color and the coarseness of them. There were only four cars in our entire party. It was a very bright day, and some tiny flakes of snow fell, as we kept moving north. We parked around or near Conner's cabin and decided to take off following the old path down Thorn's Creek toward the Inmaha River. The hike was a little over three miles with some real elevations to overcome. Parts of the group headed up towards Buckhorn Springs and the others took the opposite side of Thorn Creek. Jillian and I stayed on the south side of the creek while heading due south towards Dodson Fork Creek.

While moving forward there was so little sound, it was almost as if the birds were aware of a big cat. All of 'em took off and waited in some dark cave for the danger to pass. It was an eerie feeling to be without the sounds of birds. That by itself, almost scared us. This feeling was uncomfortable at first but after listening to the silence for a while, it all seemed natural and calm.

"What is it you sense out here? Does it feel any different to you this time?"

No, not really. Actually I can only remember the dream, the dream of the Bald Eagles, the eagles leading us to a spot where we could find her. We walked until we could get to the place where Coral Creek intersects with Thorn Creek. A sudden rush of water came out of nowhere and then it all spilt somewhere leading to another crashing murky place and intermixed into water sounds, which were spectacular. The cold mist from this rock-pounding water filled the air and it covered the fern vegetation, which surrounded us.

The rushing water and the absence of other natural sounds made the place somewhat creepy, and yet there was a silent joy in being within this forest. The trees and the woods around us were real tall and it was like that all up and down Thorn Creek. There was a solid blackness to the woods. Far above us, a very blue sky and sunlight crept in with its warm rays stretching gently down upon this thick shadowy forest. I had come to this place once before, but I wasn't positive if it had been when I was conscious or if it was me being in a dream but both times I seemed to be with Jillian. In fact, I asked her if she had been there before, said to her, "Can you remember anything about this spot?"

Jillian replied, "No, this is the first time I've stood at this exact spot; first time ever with you or without you."

"I'm going to walk down to Dodson Fork," I told her. "It'll let me shortcut the upward climb to Thorn Creek and Inmaha; it's quite steep. I'll search my area and then wait for you where Corral and Dodson Fork meet."

"Now, don't get lost out there. You wait for me or some of the others," said Jillian.

"Sure, I'll wait down there and I'll be looking for a sign, and maybe the eagles will point the way for me again."

She and I separated and I took off towards Dodson Fork. Jillian began her sharp ascent over the hills to Inmaha. I walked in a forest-kind-of silence that I'd not known before, which was almost as if I'd been drugged. Every step was heavier than the next one. I watched for a while as Jillian disappeared over some sharp and large outstretching boulders. It was only three quarters of a mile to Inmaha and I knew Jillian would get there much faster without my overweight body dragging behind her.

As I approached the confluence of the two creeks, I definitely felt something in the cold hush around me, which was impossible to explain even to myself. All of a sudden, a voice that I thought was directly inside me began speaking to me. I turned my head around and there was nothing in sight, nor did I hear anything from any identifiable direction. At first, I was somewhat frightened, but after a few moments, my body calmed down as if I were instantly tranquilized. There was a large grouping of rocks near the bend adjacent to Corral Creek, so I made my way to it. While sitting against a smooth boulder, I took a tiny bit of pot out of my satchel and rolled a small, thin joint. I lit it and flipped my head back facing upward and flattened my body against the large rock. The day seemed so peaceful and full of wonder, but I couldn't help thinking of Jillian and what she would find and how long she would stay up there before circling back to me. I guess the smoke had temporarily eased my mind and I was able to relax enough to listen to the voices coming at me from inside.

Looking up toward the upper branches of the trees, I saw a pair of Bald Eagles circling. I wasn't sure what they were at first, as the bigger of the two, with a greater head, landed on an outstretched dead branch. Soon, the smaller eagle landed to the right side of the first one, just as each of them looked down at me bridged against the rocks. The first great bird peered down at me hard as my eyes caught his eyes, which transfixed me somewhere inside the animal's head. At first, I was convinced that it was the pot causing me to see things. I thought the pot must have had something in it 'cause I was sure I was hallucinating and/or dreaming during every part of my experience. The two eagles stayed perched above me for a long time or what seemed to be a long time. Anyway, it was as if they were somehow glued to their branches. The smaller eagle, or the female, dove down and landed on the rock across from me. We sat there, each of us and stared at one another for what seemed to be an extreme amount of time. Then as if by some spell or magic, the eagle spoke to me, not in words, but in what could only be described as thought patterns. I knew exactly what she was saying to me. Just before she flew away, the eagle told me about the murdered girl being dumped off at the upper section of Thorn Creek. Three men were described: one who watched from a car and two others who tossed the naked body in the creek. The eagle's eye penetrated into my brain and I became convinced of the truth of the story, absolutely persuaded. As I listened, the two eagles told me of a bone that was stuck between two rocks in an off-creek wash twenty yards from where I was propped up.

After those words, I didn't remember much, only Jillian's lovely face posturing over me. Yet the feeling remained that I had in a very strange way been to places never before entered. Plus, I'd gone there with a consciousness, which I had never before understood or opened into. The soft sound of the breeze blowing through the crackling branches was the only sound that at that moment remained clear. This moment was as poignant as brass steeple bells.

twenty-seven

<u>Jillian Douds</u>
"Personal Journal Belonging to Jillian Douds"

Kaelin's disappearance was looking more like murder than a single runaway teen problem as the papers described it. All authority involved in Kaelin's eclipse seemed to want to end it all, to finalize the case by condemning it to a very narrow US Legal definition of 'missing person.' They all seemed to want to put it on the Wallowa post office wall and let the damned thing hang until it shriveled. To me, this has seemed to be the way or actually the best way, our law enforcement was in cahoots with all the laws in the systems responsible for burying all of the similar 'teen runaways' cases forever. It is a literal scandal across the country and the world regarding the wholesale out-casting of most teen-runaway police cases. The number of vanished teens is so massive and the interest in it far too little – both unprepared and underdeveloped for any effective action via the problem. The way I see it and have read about it, teen disappearance is happening at pandemic levels and yet the response is little, but murmurs and those dull sounds come mostly on local-concerned levels.

We had now found more evidence of 'darkness', of 'foul play' regarding the total absence of this young beauty in our community. Since her flight, our whole locality has changed. It has passed into something else, not necessarily better or worse, just something different. I recall a movie once about a scientist who was finally given his freedom from Baden-Baden Concentration Camp. He looked through the barbed wire and wasn't any longer certain what freedom was. In the end, often through the miracle of survival and his fighting his way back to Italy, he finally found home. Naturally for him, and for the European countries, home wasn't the same. All the dynamics were changed and in his particular case, many of the hometown people weren't sure who he really was, he had lost God. In the end of the film, and within the actual story, this man lived for many years and wrote fine books about his love of science and his love of the earth itself. This man of science was a genius of peace swallowed up by the horrors of the most devastating war and cruelty ever encountered in the history of mankind. A war fought on a world scale where the end was the predestined outcome of the evil the war itself presented to sane minds. The scientist in the film was free to live with the memories of Baden-Baden and the deeper atrocities he was forced to endure on an everyday basis. Ah to breathe! Ah to escape from his knot! This man, in his 'real' life, had no choice but to find and escape even after forty-five years of relative freedom. Naturally that escape was suicide and the shock of this event sent waves of anxiety through his family and extended to worldwide friends and associates.

Few things in my life moved me as the story of this brave scientist caught in such brutal circumstances of political horror. Much of his story comes back to me as we search for evidence of Kaelin's body. Yes, both Millie and I have spoken to her spirit and I truly believe that the voice and the energy, which I confronted in that field was the dead or dynamic spirit of Kaelin. She spoke of the details of the murder, and she gave Millie the names of two of the killers. Millie, at least to this point, can't remember, or she's not willing to exhume the secrets to me. I can't wait. I need to know. I want to know! The sooner I find out the better. People may question me and what do I say? I just don't have an answer to that question. Don't know something when I do know, when I believe in the sanctuary of life and the power of living. I condemn all killing and the destruction of life in whatever form it justifies it's ugliness.

While tramping the Thorn Creek wilderness area, something unnatural, something undefined, led me to the truth and those two metacarpals are the in-your-eye raw truth. Kaelin was forcibly brought to Thorn Creek and killed either before or after she was taken there. The child was probably raped and then dumped along the banks of the fast-flowing Inmaha River just above Thorn Creek. For two years since that day, animals have scourged the earth for food, and of course the natural decomposition makes quick work of flesh, muscles, and organs. I recall coming across a female cougar, which looked as if it weighed maybe one hundred and forty pounds that found itself a comfortable place and then died on a hill right above my cabin. I studied the deterioration, the animals and the bugs. Yes, I watched the decomposers tear that body apart in six months. At

148

the end of one hundred and eighty days, nothing was left except a few scattered bones. There were maybe two paws and the skull with about half the hair still holding onto some skin. In the wild, decomposition happens very quickly and the forest is the silent 'seer', the silent observer of everything.

So the bones were the key for me. The metacarpals, they came from a young female without a doubt. My years of experience in botany, biology, zoology and chemistry support my personal but practical views. I don't understand how Buck Parrish can't see or accept what I do. Maybe the test results on the bones this second time will expose the murder, and murder of this young sweetness. It was indeed a life so beautiful and way too shortly lived. This time it seemed as if we got to Buck 'cause he was as shocked by the new find as anyone else was. It's those times when the eagles led me to those bones. After I communicated with Kaelin's spirit and she told me generally where to look, I began to believe even more. Yet the most solid belief came when I felt her bones in my hand. It was then that I knew those bones were hers. I knew without any scientific proof that these bones were the true remains of this slain child. Tears came to my eyes and rolled down my cheeks, for Kaelin was one of those sweet-enchanters who the good Lord blesses us with, all of us. Her mother will never accept the loss; what mother could? Yet this good mother needs to uncover the truth, the truth itself is dynamic which has the power to start the healing and the heart needs healing. It surely does.

The meeting with Buck Parrish will bring him to the right side and this time, it'll bring him fully there. Buck Parrish is a man who follows the gut of his own truth. He'll follow that gut to his own demise. There are powers here that can and will kill in order to keep Kaelin's dark secret buried forever, and many may vanish as a result of a proper investigation into Kaelin's death or reason behind it. Even Buck Parrish must take care. Already one of the Carson's has been stabbed, Will. He's just one of the future victims of the battles over Kaelin. I have believed for a long time that our county has both a good and a very corrupt core. We are all soon to face the vengeance and extreme darkness of this corruption.

I will speak to Millie again about the evidence when it shows positive, which I'm convinced it will. At that time, I will return by myself to the Thorn Creek area and this next time, I'll follow the gulches, glades, and land dynamics of Corral Creek where I believe some larger bones can be found, maybe even the poor child's skull.

Talking to Kaelin's spirit image myself turned this case into a search for stripped-down truth for myself, for Kaelin, as well as for the good people of Wallowa County. I have kept one of the original metacarpals in a small bag hidden beneath the floorboards in my bedroom right under my four post Green-Oak bed. There is a scent to the bones, a silent smell of roughed bones, something that is hard to describe. One has to live with them for a while to know something about them. I revel in silent moments to be in that four-poster bed where there is a connection to what I feel around it and the bones entrusted to me.

Oftentimes, sleep is the answer to many of the questions we have about living; just sleep and dream.

twenty-eight

<u>Rev. Parham A. Chrisp</u>

I can remember the three of us sitting across the table from one another while discussing the girl's shelter and the gripping need for such a place. I looked at it in the same way any man of the cloth looks at anything Christian, anything that can bring a positive influence on the community and the ministry. We are all chosen as children of God and Jesus Christ; a good Pastor is just a guide with a few more references. That's really all he is; isn't it? Sure, we're picked at birth in some way to follow 'his Word' to take the path of earthly choice; that path can only be referred to by our Lord and his son, Jesus Christ. Naturally it's hard for a pastor to speak about the extended needs of his extended flock without any reference to God or Jesus Christ. So forgive me, will you please, if I, as a pastor, slip into it for a moment, or on occasion. My concern here is for the girl who's been snatched from 'our whole' and led by force to some unknown Hades. We fear she has been taken somewhere very distant from her church and from Jesus.

I have given my adult life in service of the church. I have been there for my people, and the New Church of Christ Wallowa is no exception to any rule by which I've ever lived. In fact, I helped erect this church, which is a house chosen by the deacons and myself to worship the Lord and his blessed son, Jesus Christ. This house is sacred and was built with our own hands to know the connected walls of this sacredness, and these minor barriers are swallowed by the purity of our worship and the sanctity of our warm brotherly church. I am a man of simple tastes, simple ways, easy ways of worship and a full heart.

Mr. Bell sat across the table, along with one of the key deacons of the church, Charles C. Marten. Mr. Marten had demanded a place at the news interview that had been granted to Mr. Bell. Naturally him being the Chief Deacon and head of the board, I had no choice but to allow him his right at the news conference. So we all continued to converse on my positions, on my various duties and on my visions for the New Church. For the first fifteen minutes or so, Mr. Bell steadily took notes while I rambled; Mr. Marten sat across from Mr. Bell with his great eyebrows rolled forward and a very stern look on his large head. Sometimes I wondered what sort of information Charles C. Marten allowed to travel through that giant head of his. I stopped wondering about Marten's thinking process many years ago. Instead, I just trusted him as a man and a deacon who followed biblical dictates to a perfect T.

"Can you tell me, Mr. Marten, the exact purpose the deacons had in building such a large facility for runaway young female adults?" Bell inquired.

"We, or maybe even all of the original deacons, had made that choice almost at the foundation of the New Church itself when a few of us got together in the early seventies and formed it," Marten replied.

"I recall us all getting together praying at South Wallowa State Park at the Boy Scout Camp right down from Adam's Creek. It was a pretty; almost a holy sight, for the originators to come together, I'd say."

"The young woman's protective center was to be an integral part of the church and our Christian good-will activities," suggested Marten.

"Yes, and how many young women between the ages of thirteen and eighteen did you people plan for at the beginning?" asked Bell.

"I'd say about fifty. We never planned to handle or go beyond fifty girls. Most of us thought it would be too difficult to have much more than that."

"Did you meet those goals, Mr. Marten?"

"Yes, we met them. In fact, today we have exceeded those goals by fifty girls in the pre- and the post-formative units of the shelter."

Bell jotted Marten's answers in his notebook, and continued. "May I ask; what are these pre-and post-units you talk about and why have they been closed to public scrutiny?"

Marten replied, "They are closed to the public because they're private church issues. The shelter is charity-owned and is completely operated and funded by our church. More than that, we have chosen to isolate these areas or units for the young ones' own benefit."

"It has been rumored, sir, that certain sexual activities do take place at the post-unit in particular." Charles Marten and myself looked astounded as our eyes crossed each other's in utter amazement while trying to fully take in Art Bell's accusations.

"Mr. Bell, let me tell you and anyone else who reads your trash, in this church, there has never ever been any sexual activity by any of our church supervisors and the young girls. Never!"

I personally confirmed Mr. Marten's exact views and told Mr. Bell that this interview was very close to ended if he continued asking questions in this manner.

"Pastor Chrisp, my readers demand truth. Therefore, I must continue 'in this manner' as you call it, or until that very truth is revealed. You see, Pastor Chrisp, the truth for me as a journalist, and as a man, is prominent. My truth is very much like your Jesus and his truth, and it too must also be followed to the letter."

"Yes, it should be followed, sir, but not to the point of personal insult with associated deviate insinuations."

My internal and external demeanor had changed and I knew that I was on the defensive, as was Mr. Marten and the foundations of the church itself.

Marten spoke in defense. "Let me say this, Mr. Bell; we are people who believe in the will of God and Jesus. We believe what was written in the Holy Bible and that we should follow it to the letter of the word!"

"Well spoken, Mr. Marten," I added in support. "I support your words and 'the Word' itself. It is God's holy Word that moves us; the Word motivates us to be the good people we are; and without it, we are far less than what we are. You do understand that, don't you, Mr. Bell?"

"I understand perfectly, thank you," Bell replied. "Let me put it this way; you cannot answer truthfully, because 'the Word' as you call it, shields me from understanding it for myself and the rest of the public who are not one of you. Am I right?"

"You might put it in those terms, but your description of it might be somewhat harsh and closed," said Marten.

"So, Mr. Marten, if I asked you or Pastor Chrisp or anyone at the church a direct question about deviant sexual behavior on the part of certain church brothers at the pre- and post-units, would you will defend them and shield them under all circumstances? Yes, would you?"

"There is no way that we can go on with this interview if you as an honest journalist insult us with insinuation and rumor as your sources?" Marten shot back.

"I insist only on truth, and my sources are far more comprehensive than rumor, sir!"

"Your sources are nothing but the restricted mumblings of false accusers and you are the servant of those accusers!" Pastor Chrisp yelled.

"I'm insulted, sir. Still, I will take my concerns to the people. I hope you're aware of that."

There was a rehearsed type of silence that fell between us for several moments.

"You can take care, Mr. Bell. In fact, you may go too far with your version of the truth and so the wrath of heaven may just befall you!" Marten warned.

"Are you trying to intimidate me, Mr. Marten? Is this a personal threat?"

"No, it's just a way people of the church look at falsifiers and propagators, Mr. Bell."

"We'll see who's looking at whom, Mr. Marten. It's time you religious bigots and fornicator's are exposed for what you are and what you hide behind. I stand here with witnesses, evidence and recorded material. We'll see!"

"Yes, we will see, Mr. Bell. Let's just see if you report anything blasphemous in your pages or through your microphone," warned Marten.

Mr. Bell's face turned bright red and his teeth turned from cigarette yellow to a shade of bluish white as he quietly gathered his paraphernalia and exited the church's committee room. Charles C. Marten and I stayed for a while discussing natural church business just as if no one had been there. It was as if it had been all a quiet afternoon. Charles was as always a humble man. He never mentioned the rudeness of Mr. Bell's words or his insinuations. The church was run this way by the deacon committee and they were men who knew 'the Word' and knew how to make decisions, judgments that required certain risks and yet had to be made. That day did bring a lot of tension to my understanding of the press and the outsider's views of our church. Yes it did.

twenty-nine

Charles 'C' Marten

Note: Prior to any shootout at the lodge, a small gathering commences within the walls of the New Wallowa Church of Christ.

One of the Onaben sons is dead, not both Onaben boys, unfortunately, just Frankie. Remember, 'A good Nez Perce is a dead Nez Perce'. We will destroy Billy Onaben and his white henchman Buck Parrish. That guy's a dead man too; that Indian-loving bastard. Take everything; take every weapon available as your own. Please take all your ammunition and prepare to protect what's yours now! Gather all you need for the 'transgression to come' and we'll all meet up at Robert's Butte where plans have been implemented and fortifications are in place. If necessary, we can hold out for weeks. At that position, we could keep a small army at bay, if we must, or at least until this country and this state understand true Christian priorities. This is our land, this is our county and state, and in point of fact, dear Christians, this is our country. It was always meant to be so as designed by our Christian forefathers. All others, all heathens: black, brown, Indians, Chinese, all others are interlopers/intruders and falsifiers of our space. I recall looking down at those pure Christians below me; those sanctified children of our sacred church.

"It's just like Waco here. It's just like Waco, isn't it Deacon Marten? Isn't it exactly like Waco," Byron Frank begged.

"Yes, it's all very similar, Byron, and yet we in this church and in this county are fighting for more, more perhaps for the sinless source of both Christian and white rights. We have given to our children. In fact, we have fed, clothed, and taken care of many poor and wayward potential young whores. These ladies were taken in from out of a cold night and we saved them from the savageness of the streets. Some of us taught them the values of good Christian wives so that they could understand their place at the lower end of a husband's bed. We have freely given them the pleasures of their desires, which of course serves his or her higher needs, and we have had them serve God and Jesus Christ through those needs. In all of those ways, we have served the church and those young orphans and

156

helped them 'decontaminate' for our Lord Jesus Christ. We have tamed them into good Christian white women. Then, there were the girls who we 'purged them of sin' for future wives perfectly suited for solid Christian fathers and sons. Stand there my brothers and let it be known that you are exemplary; you are the 'good ones' who have pleased our Savior. Now is the time for the guns of the system to be placed on you. Still, you need to freely acknowledge your beliefs, because your actual lives are nothing in this cursed world 'cause you have already shared space with God in heaven. You are not unpurified; you are not 'painted men'. The fact of the matter is that you are exactly what Christian white men should be; so be proud, my brothers, be very proud!"

The air was filled with so much joyous willpower it was hard at that moment not to jump down and join the men in celebration of our connected Christian energies and goodwill.

"Shall we meet at dawn at the preplanned positions near Robert's Butte? Is that our destination, Deacon Marten?" Byron Frank inquired.

"The plan is already well-established. If anyone has forgotten, he can refer to the appropriate paperwork and associated map. Deacon Frank will hand copies out to all requesting it. Our long-term goal is appropriate recognition regarding who we are, and some of course, will fall here. Maybe all shall vanish. Yet be prepared for 'a road to a righteous Lord' and a purity of place. Pastors Chrisp and Buchanan fell for us; others within the congregation have fallen for us, including Amos Blackburn and Miles T. Carson, our beloved sheriff who's one of us at his very core.

"Yes, dear brothers and then there's Nathan Bork, our beloved senior deacon who was struck down by the consistent harassment of Deputy Buck Parrish. Parrish must die. We shall all make a pact between us that, whoever remains, we'll eliminate Mr. Parrish. This man, this Indian-loving beast-coward must die. He has hunted down too many of our good Christian souls over the would-be-innocent disappearance of a local runaway whore named Kaelin Jones. It is this incident, which has turned this county upside down, upside down, brothers, over the measly disappearance of a local slut, a stupid local slut!

"Today, several good Christian men are dead. Others are dead, or near dead, because of this missing little vagabond. And several others have paid the price and then some for the slut's lack of training; and what do we have here? We have an uncontrolled non-Christian text, a text that is not of the gospel. It's one we have no part in and it is, my brothers, a context of misguided folks in search of one positive and real Christian soul. It is you, deacon brothers, that have this soul; and it is you who possess this large Christian heart I talk about. I want you to know, it is you and only you who can come with me on 'the bus'. You can come with me as we rise up to heaven on that judgment ahead, rising – rising up proud of what we are and what we've accomplished. So, I want you to take as many of the sinful souls with you as you can, my brothers. Take them out of this world to a place more suited than this one for their rotted souls. Like the Christian Crusaders of the twelfth century it is our duty to rid the world of this non-Christian heathen. Our duty is to take them out and believe me, it will lead you to the kingdom of heaven. By committing yourself to the Lord's way, it will lead you more directly to heaven, because all of you are the key servants of our Lord! Protect Robert's Butte at the cost of everything we believe in. It's time to take a hard stand. Now, it's time to show your power. It's time to release your 'clean' Christian power, and you will do that, I assure you my brothers, you will accomplish that!"

"Shall we fight to the last? Shall we refuse surrender like Waco did? Should we ignore surrender under all circumstances?" asked Byron Frank.

"Absolutely, my brothers. Never give an inch to a pagan under any circumstances. By all means, let's hold our holy ground to the last man! The non-Christians, the atheists, the rest of the non-believers, these are the corrupt of the corrupt; these are the horrid infidels who despoil our children. We are few but we must fight hard to uphold what we believe in. Do not give in whatsoever, brothers, not an inch. It's the martyrs of Waco who must be remembered, and you, my brothers, if the need arises, will become the martyr's of Robert's Butte. Hold your ground and fight in place for the Lord. He will protect you and take you to where all good Christian souls must go."

Steve Dreben

Looking down from the pulpit, I recall how the ten main deacons behind Byron Frank screamed at the top of their lungs in unison. "Kill Parrish!" Some yelled, "Kill Billy Onaben, and all non-believers around them! Kill all the heathen anti-Christian skeptics!"

At that point, I yelled directly towards my brothers, "Fight to the last man! Battle for who you are and fight for Jesus. Kill them for the rights of white Christians. Heaven is yours, my good brothers. You're already on the bus!"

I felt an internal kind of divinity come over me. Yes, I was with them and we were true Christian brothers finding our way to the Lord; Glory! Tears filled my eyes as men marched out of New Church joyous in their own solid Christian 'stuff,' and a weapon at their sides. Yes, this was a day of Glory, and what a day it was!

thirty

Jillian Douds
'Entering the Journal'

December 8, 1998. We were sitting close together, beside each other, as I watched Millie gasp at every breath. It seemed increasingly harder for her to talk about the murders, particularly the murder of Kaelin and the spirit discussions, which Millie had with Kaelin. It was hard to relate to anything serious watching Millie's nostrils clasp for more air. As the young girl fell into a very deadly or quiet sleep, I felt something different than before; some-thing about the situation was most altered. There was a musty smell, an odor something like thick layers of moist dust or mites in an old mattress. I could easily describe it as a smell of impending death. The first time I smelled it, I was a child and my grandfather was putting on his old woolen overcoat. My grandfather was a strong and stout man. Even in his eighties, he was proud and stubborn. Many described him as an old fighting bull. My father and my grandfather had just finished arguing about something, I don't even remember what it was, when all of a sudden, the old man put on his musty overcoat, turned, and stormed out the front door heading into a very harsh, icy Mid-West winter day. I never forgot that smell. Yes, and that was the first time I truly sniffed that particular type of musk. It was also the first time I connected that odor with imminent death; in fact, ensuing death; might be a better term.

We were good friends, Millie and I, for many years; perhaps I can confess that was the tightest personal relationship I'd ever had. Feelings deep inside me began busting out, for one senses the scents, the musk, and she knows, well, she really knows. It was a month or so after the argument when I first smelled the musk that I knew, like an animal knows, that my grandfather was going to die. The old man did die soon thereafter. He died of a broken old heart and the loss of my gentle grandmother. She was the passing wind, the mellow Condor blown across his shattered mind after an obligatory fifty-year marriage.

That night I talked to Kaelin about Millie; we spoke to each other the way friends speak to one another. Our talk was casual, and her spirit image was very much there. Truth is, I almost forgot about her being dead.

"Henry says that Millie will be with us soon," Kaelin reported to Jillian.

"Who's Henry? Is he someone with you out there? Is he someone close to you?"

Kaelin's voice answered, "Yes, I love Henry. He's very close to me. He's an old and wise Chinese man; very old in fact, he might even be a sage."

"Are there sages around you? Sages who talk to you?" Jillian asked.

"Sure, plus- Henry knows things about time. He knows a lot about time and space and he actually discusses many things with me. We have so much time here, yet I do miss my friends. I miss the parties and the times of laughing and smoking."

"Yes, Kaelin, but did Henry tell you about Millie? Did he say something to you about Millie or her time?"

"Yes, he told me that Millie will have a heart attack soon and she'll then be with us."

I sat there for a moment somewhat rationally thinking that I was just dreaming the whole episode and the discourse with Kaelin. Yet, no matter how much I tried to rationalize it, I knew we were truly discussing Millie's coming death. What made it all worse was the musk fragrance around us; I had denied the odor while Millie and I shared dinner some weeks earlier, but my memory could never forget. In fact, I wrote my feelings down within a journal. My emotions were very clear, and cellular memory left a deep very clear and lasting impression. Somehow, I had to refocus Kaelin's attention back to Millie. "So, Kaelin, you're not telling me exactly when Millie will be with you and Henry?"

"No, I don't know exactly when that will occur. Time is very different here, it's not at all the same as when one's in the body."

"So, let me see if I understand this. You say that Millie will die of a heart attack soon?"

"Yes, she'll soon be here sharing our time, but she will only be here with us, for a short time."

"Why is it that she will only be with you for a short time?"

"Henry told me that that's the case with only those who die suddenly; it is only those who share this space with us, not all, not everyone."

Kaelin mumbled many things to me sounding more like a lost teenager than a wise ghostly spirit. I listened to her losses and her impenetrable sadness regarding association with lost friends, but all I could do was to think of Millie. It was only through a semi-conscious Millie that I was able to talk to Kaelin face-to-face. She then told me how gentle Millie's death would be compared to hers, and compared to the way that she died, by strangulation, rape, and stabbing. She told me how she hovered above her body, how she remained above her flesh while a man's knife stabbed her body over and over again.

One of the killers, one of the rapists was Amos T. Blackburn, a man tied into the local law, and a man protected by that same legal force. Kaelin told me about Blackburn and another man, a doctor, a name, which couldn't quite come to her, she said. She knew the doctor and Blackburn from the New Church and its runaway home. In fact, all of us in the town who knew the girl also knew that she had good friends at the runaway house. In fact, Kaelin made several trips there a month. According to her, Amos T. Blackburn drove her there on occasion and it was during those trips that she got to know him. As a matter of fact, I could see that he might be able to get close to Kaelin that he might have been trying to obtain her trust before some eventual attack, setting her and other young girls up similarly.

The unbelievable truth was that Kaelin wanted to live, and they took her life so young. She most wanted to spend time with her friends. When listening to her, it was most clear that she seemed more saddened about lost friendships than anything else. My thoughts and tears flowed continuously as I peered down at my semi-conscious friend. And only this journal knows the truth about Kaelin's forced death and the projected natural death of my friend Millie. Each word in this journal becomes more difficult as I think of life in Wallowa County without Millie.

So, all I could honestly do was to promise Kaelin that we'd somehow try to identify the killers, and more than that, somehow persuade the authorities to believe our stories. Trying to create belief in murder cases was as difficult as playing the first violin for the New York Symphony. In total, it was a major task.

Kaelin begged me to work with Millie and Buck Parrish to uncover evidence of her, which would convince the authorities of her slaying. I made the promise to Kaelin and additionally swore that I'd talk to Millie about it after she revived from her 'state'. We were each determined to expose the killers and anyone else involved no matter how long it took, no matter who tried to stop us.

My very bones were cold that night and the last journal entry of the week was directly about Kaelin and what she told me about Millie. Deeply inside me, I knew what she said was true; so true, it frightened me.

thirty-one

<u>Shawna Thore</u>

I can remember the shots coming from two different directions not one, and I recall the way the Onaben brothers moved with such confidence and grace, always in control…in balance even as one of them took a flesh hit. I've prepared a full report for you and the bureau regarding the incident at 'Downey Gulch'. Parrish is a far better lawman than we ever gave him credit for, he never stops the pursuit crisscross – crisscross sets a plan and executes the agenda the old way. "Sometimes the old ways are a great deal better than modern tactics," said Hirsh. Maybe a combination of the two ways is best, maybe something altogether different but I'll never forget how the Onaben boys saved me by pushing me into the dry half of the canyon where no one could get a clear shot at me.

"So one can see that you are impressed by the Onaben brothers. The best part is no one's really been hurt by the incident except for a bullet hole or two; nothing permanent."

"Have you been hit before Jeb? Have you been hit by a high caliber rifle slug somewhere in your body?"

"No; never hit by a rifle slug, just a small hand gun. Damned thing did put a real hole right through my thigh, and I bled a bunch but not much else. It didn't hurt."

I watched Jeb as he read the report that I prepared and had already submitted to the bureau. His face remained perfectly still and he never smiled while his eyes danced through the words many of which were technical. "You've been trained quite well in chemical forensics. I remember reading that in your record. It was your minor in college and you almost went into the specialty, again, that is according to personnel."

"Yes, even today, I've still got a real keen interest in it but now I just use it as an adjunct to my investigative work. It's more or less like a professional scientific hobby forensics is – that's what I call it…a hobby."

"Yes, well, it's an interesting report especially the conclusion; let's talk about that for a moment."

I watched Jeb's eyes as he re-read the last paragraph of the report. We were getting close to something solid; something to bite into and all of us who were working on the case could smell it. It was like a long fishing trip in deep waters; you just move to the right spot 'til you find the big school.

"Looks like we traced the hair and blood you picked up to an upright citizen. In fact, the boy's a hardened veteran of the Viet Nam heir. Yep, the boy's a real hero."

"Hero or no hero; if he's one of those shooters out there plus an upper level deacon of the first church, then we got ourselves a 'supportable' suspect."

"Blood and hair that's pretty hard evidence to avoid…just waiting for a possible match-up relating to the skull and elbow corroboration."

"Sounds like you guessed it pretty well boss. If there's no match, we still got that red wool that was found snagged on a branch by the other shooter. If the other shooter hasn't noticed and therefore hasn't gotten rid of the coat or jacket, we have him."

"Got another report from Willa Shannon which states that she saw a man who looked exactly like Amos T. Blackburn. Furthermore, it says that precise person threw a red jacket into the steel garbage bin behind her store. All of this happened just after dark. She was there quite late and reported it…so it's on the record even though she admits never liking Mr. Blackburn, Willa still remains a quality witness."

I watched Jeb as he finished reading the report. He walked over to my refrigerator and pulled out a cold beer. "Want one?"

"No, it'll just get me nervous- always get the jitters when we get this close to tagging a case."

"Well, we'll tag it alright but not until we tie a few of our upstanding church elders to these girls…to the runaway's."

"How's that part of the investigation going Jeb? Have you cracked any of it yet?"

"Just about, here's my report which I just sent into the bureau. It pretty well defines the son's a bitches."

"This thing does get you doesn't it, Jeb? I never did see anything quite hassle with your guts like this case and I've seen you pretty put upon with a lot of different kinds of shit."

"Nothing's a lot of shit when you're dealing with vicious racism, rape, even serial rape, slavery and finally murder. You add twisted religious zealots and you have a real New York freaky party."

"Looks like we're ready to arrest Oliveson, Cochran and Blackburn. Can we move on it soon?"

"No. We'll wait for Buck Parrish to discuss it with Sheriff Carson then Buck will report the results of the discussion with me. I got a gut hunch about Carson."

"So you believe Carson's involved? All part of that old boy town web yeah?" I watched Jeb's eyes. I kind of knew when he felt like I was putting him on and this time, he wasn't really sure.

"Maybe bonehead or that brother of his, maybe both of 'em; it's all too damned early anyway. Can you believe we've traced old State Senator Cochran down as a shooter out there in Downey Gulch wilderness?"

I watched as Jeb switched on the local television to see what the NBA score was. He was absolutely mad about basketball. I also recalled how he turned to me that afternoon with some fire in his eyes, emotions seldom exhibited by him.

"We'll nail that son-of-a-bitch Senator Cochran on conspiracy charges and attempted murder at a minimum but there are other higher-ups in the church that I really want to burn. So, my dear, understand this: we're not quite ready for a full fish fry. Also, I want Parrish to arrest the good doctor and Blackburn. It may just frighten some of the others. We might even get a new one to rise from the grave?"

He smiled in an unusual way for Jeb. I can only describe it as a gloat or a deeply engrained sense of self-confidence. Senator Cochran was a real surprise to me, a rich man and a state legislator, a famous farmer-rancher-builder. He seemed like a real waste. As for Mr. Amos T. Blackburn and Dr. Oliveson, we'd been following them for a year. We were fairly certain that each of the men were involved with Kaelin's

166

disappearance but we couldn't prove anything until now. The next move would be led by Parrish and a well directed flush-out, but we had to set up a full watch on all the men involved just in case of possible *massive run* in many directions. The trap was being set and all aspects of the 'drum beating to target' or prey had to be well-coordinated, which was our job. I sat down after grabbing a beer and watched the ball game with Jeb, but my mind certainly wasn't on the score or the game's outcome. Sometimes television has a way of numbing your mind into 'thinking off' somewhere else, sometimes.

thirty-two

<u>Buck Parrish</u>

I decided to take another search party up country road forty-six to Wildhorse Springs to cover Deadhorse, Cold Springs, Old Cold Springs, Frog Pond and in particular, Downey Gulch. I believed Tommy-Boy Wenaha was old enough and had learned from Billy Onaben how to track right along with us. Also I took or recruited the Onaben brothers, Nathan Bork, and Shawna Thore. We had the best dogs in the county plus a tip from a major source.

"Who was that major source you've talked about Buck? Can you tell me who that source was?" asked Art F. Bell.

"Art, as you already know. You can ask me many questions for public consumption. But you can never ask me 'bout a source!"

"What in the hell made you invite Tommy-Boy on the trip. Wasn't he a bit young for this kind of hunt?"

"He loved Kaelin. He loved her like a young boy can only love a girl her age. To me, he deserved and desired a place within our party."

"Tag along then. Didn't you think the thing was a little dangerous for a boy his age especially with what probably happened to the girl?"

"Art, I had absolutely no idea there'd be any danger during those three days of searching. Turns out, I was dead wrong. I watched Art take notes and record my words in his micro-recorder. Also, I watched his eyes grope over those gray metal glasses of his somehow giving a tangled self-impression which questioned my very sanity."

"All right then, you went up country road forty-six to Frog Pond and Downey Gulch, which is probably the coldest place in the county either winter or summer."

"We pretty well searched the area five miles in every direction up from Wildhorse Springs. First, we camped out at Cow Camp and the next day, camped at Cold Springs. Got to admit there was something eerie about the place. No individual one of us could quite put a finger on it but we were all on edge. Well on the third day, I told the Onaben boys we'd meet them down around the middle of Downey Gulch. I wanted Billy and Frankie to approach with hounds from east gulch running a set 'a those beasts along each side of the water's edge. I also included Shawna Thore in the Onaben party because I knew the boys would take care of her unless she got a little too friendly with Frankie. Then of course, I figured we'd have some real trouble."

I watched Art take some short breaths before he asked the next question, wasn't quite sure about which way to take this…yet, he moved right along regardless.

"What 'ya referring to here, Buck? You gave me the impression that Shawna was all professional FBI and all the shit that goes with that?"

"Women like her have always fallen hard for men like Frankie especially when they watch the way he works his horse and dogs. Frankie's a kind of Indian man's man, for that matter, so is Billy. There's not many men, Indian or white, left around here can match those boys in most anything?"

"So as the story goes, Nathan and me went up one side of the western gulch together and Tommy-Boy came up the north gully just inside of the gulch right across from us. I kept my eyes on that boy most of the time but at that point, I pulled my thirty-thirty Marlin out from my saddle pouch and held it tight across my lap."

"Tell me something; why'd you do that? You've never been known for using a gun of any sort 'less you had to?"

"Precisely the point Art; something just startled and pushed the hairs up on that wrinkled old neck a mine, wasn't sure just felt something coming."

"Can I quote a 'gut feeling' on that or am I taking 'rational' law enforcement too far?"

"No; you go ahead. In fact, I'd appreciate that kind of quote 'cause there's times that the best and basically 'only way' to operate is from the gut. A man gets too limited by all the set rules and regulations, even a lawman. It was the end of the third day and the sun was fast falling; yet brilliant old mountain rays were still stretching their dazzling orange shadows across the wooded terrain. We moved quickly from the flat upper ridges of old Cold Springs across the dry grass of Dry Creek Ridge, and then we doubled back to the north flank of Cold Springs once again."

"Why'd you do that? What was the point of crossing Dry Creek Ridge?"

"At that time, or about six in the evening, we could see particularly well and nothing on that ridge could evade any of us. Maybe that's why I brought young Tommy-Boy Wenaha along. He had those powerful youthful eyes and a driving need, which is an absolutely unbeatable combination!"

"Buck, nobody could ever say you're a poor lawman. You always seem to have something up your sleeve, every inch of the way up there?"

"You know, you've said nothing about Nathan Bork. You didn't ask why'd I bring him, or what purpose could he possibly have in the group?"

"No, Mr. Buck Parrish- Nathan Bork is an excellent choice for he represents the 'perfectly acceptable witness' doesn't he?"

"Yes, he does. Plus, old Nathan's a crack shot when he's sober and was a central part of that 'other posse', which chased the black man some ten plus years ago now. That episode was a disaster, not on my watch Mr. Bell, not on old Buck's watch I can assure you!"

"As we moved the horses down a shallow creek bed to Downey Gulch, we all had the pleasure of seeing a regal mated pair of Golden Eagles soaring and weaving overhead. Each of us managed to garner a long and intense look at those graceful Raptors as our full-footed Appaloosa's moved down both sides of Downey Gulch."

"I hear Downey Gulch up on that gorge is as big as a small wild river cut canyon?"

"Downey could have easily been named 'Full Horse Canyon' or something like that. A lot of water feeds into that gulch both summer and winter. It's pretty wide on both sides of the bank with each edge capable of supporting two horses and

Steve Dreben

riders. It's a wide place with a lot of large rocks coming down in the spring months. Now old Downey Gulch pours down pretty rapidly at times almost straight into 'Cooks Creek'."

"How long a run is this Downey Creek, would you say?"

"Downey from Cold Springs cross over is about three miles to the front edge of Cooks Creek."

I watched still-like as old Bell crafted my words into his copious notes. He knew exactly what he wanted and knew how to get it.

"So, with a rifle across my saddle horn, we trotted down the banks of the gulch towards mid-center where we were to meet with the Onaben boys and Shawna Thore."

"Did you see anything unusual as you all rode to the mid-point of the gulch?"

"No, not at that point, but like I said, something in the air got my neck hairs up, something I could feel just wasn't quite right. There's a high ridge, which breaks out from Downey Saddle, where it cascades out. It's like a jagged ridge atop mid-point. It was just about there, when we saw Shawna come around the eastern break of the gulch."

"What precisely happened then? What did you see or hear that surprised you?"

"I heard several large twigs crack above us and I could feel some movement down the upper ridge to the north. Several shots rung out from both directions and at that point, I saw Frankie Onaben hit twice with the second shot that snapped him right off his mount."

"Were other shots zinging towards anyone else?"

"Yes, Billy was shot at directly. They missed him but his horse was hit in the rump. The horse smashed against some rocks and Billy was damned quick enough to dismount before the horse fell. He wasn't hurt and the horse lived through both the wound and the rocks. As Billy dismounted, he grabbed his rifle from its leather pouch and pulled it out above his head just before his feet hit the ground. I never saw a man move with such grace and balance, plus the son-of-a-gun was so fast. He moved so damned fast as his horse fell-out from under him, and it was one hell of a sight."

"At least three more bullets flew at him from a southeast direction, two of them pinging off the ground rocks echoing into the canyons. For a blink of a second, I saw some movement near a sturdy Ponderosa Pine. A man had a rope strapped around the tree and a gun barrel was jutting straight out aiming at God knows what. Not seeing very clearly, I took a quick shot at the barrel hoping to stop the shot. My bullet zinged into the tree bark splintering it in several directions. Some of the bark material splintered and it must have hit the shooter in the nose 'cause he cried out 'my nose' as the barrel of the rifle hung up in its rope cradle. I fired another shot at the shooter as he mounted a chestnut mare. The bullet jammed into the tissue just above his knee and that son-of-a-bitch yelped out like a wild hot shot in the upper flank."

"Did the man get away? You said nothing about the other shooter, did he get away?"

"Both of the shooters got away even after Nathan Bork fired at one of 'em from the ridge where he stopped. Nathan later said he never really got a clean enough shot to wing 'em. Good marksmen try to wing a target 'cause one never knows who he's shooting at, unless of course it's a direct life and death confrontation…that's another story."

"So, at the end of all this shooting, the two culprits got away and Frankie Onaben was clipped twice non-serious and his horse was wounded?"

"Yes, that's correct, except that Shawna run her horse up an incline dry ravine and dismounted. She took aim but never fired a shot."

"Did she see anything clear to fire at…anything?"

"No. According to her story, she didn't clearly see anyone. By the time Shawna came from behind the rockslide at the side of the ravine, all the shooters had disappeared. She claimed that she did hear the pounding of horse hooves but even that was somewhat unclear because of the thumping sound of occasional falling rocks."

"So, Buck, I got to say, that's one exciting story, but do we know who or why anyone would shoot and try to kill either one of the Onaben brothers?"

"Yes, old Frankie and Billy were both shot at and obviously followed after they discovered some critical evidence regarding the girl's remains down Downey Gulch 'bout two hundred yards from where it meets Cooks Creek."

"What's this evidence you talk about? What kind of 'remains' are we speaking about here? I never heard anything about the girl's remains?"

"Well, we've had the specimen analyzed and it's definitely the skull and elbow joint of a fifteen-year-old female newly deceased."

"Was the skull cracked or mutilated in any way?"

"No. The skull and the elbow were perfectly in tack. The discovered evidence is exactly what brought the shooters out."

"And you claim there were two shooters not just one?"

I watched Art's face. He knew how I hated repeating stupid questions and he understood how I completely despised them.

"Art, I won't tell you this again. There were definitely two shooters up there and I hit one. We found shells from two rifles and some blood on the tree bark and more on the ground several yards away. Later, we had the forensic boys up there to take prints of the shooter's horses' hooves and pick up on the blood samples. The fresh blood specimens were gathered by Shawna Thore right there at the scene of it. She carried specimen bags in her saddlebags just for this kind of event. All agents are well trained in fresh evidence collecting and some forensics and she did a hell of a job for us up there searching and gathering everywhere 'til night fell."

"Can I quote you on all of this? Do you mind if I also interview agent Thore?"

"No. Quote me all you want, Art. But don't say anything more in extrapolation than I've reported to you already; do you agree Mr. Bell?"

"Oh yes, yes, I agree. We have one hell of a story now especially after Billy Onaben told his own tale."

"Now, you do remember the fact that Billy sometimes exaggerates his stories a little bit? In general though, he's always just about right."

"Right. Can I quote you on most of this, Buck. Or is there anything you personally want deleted?"

"Tell it like I told it, Art, please. Just add this- the evidence is clear; Kaelin Jones was killed and more…the killers will be *flushed out* no matter how long it takes. Quote me on that, Art, will 'ya?"

Again, I watched Art's face and noticed how anxious he was to finish his writing and get the story down to the pressroom. It was evident he wanted to get the story written and on the radio show. In fact, Art was a willing pawn in the game and for a change, the press was the lever. Finally, we had some evidence regarding the killing and the shooters. Some horsemen-shooters were definitely involved or paid to get involved, so the chase was on and the goal was clear. It was important that I let the killers and the community know where county law stood.

thirty-three

<u>Billy Onaben</u>

It wasn't easy to track Filbert down 'cause he knew the country as well as any of us did. As a child, Judge Buchanan had paid me to show the boy how to track prey, pursue, and kill it. Filbert had learned well. On that particular Saturday, Filbert himself was the prey. He was accused of shooting at a posse from a rocky ledge off Dobson Canyon. FBI agent Shawna Thore was the only eyewitness, and she gathered evidence that was somewhat conclusive on Filbert. He disappeared as soon as he heard we were onto him.

I drove the Ford 350 truck up towards Jim Creek Road, turned at Downey Saddle, and then pulled off at Hollow Road onto Old 169. Afterward, I stopped the car and unhitched the horse trailer. My five-year-old Appaloosa mare, Caspian, shook her head, eager to get out. She was one of the best trail animals I'd ever ridden. Danny and Creek, my two finely mixed black and chocolate bloodhounds, jumped out of the truck bed at my signal. The dogs sniffed around, starting to pick up a faint scent. My experience told me that the horseshoes marking the wet soil were that of a large powerful paint horse used for uphill canyon rides.

After a few seconds, the two dogs snapped at a strong odor and took off running while Caspian and I quickly followed. We found ourselves backtracking to Jim Creek and circling upward, heading north, towards Coin Creek and the high country above Snake River Rapids and Cougar Rapids. We ran hard for nearly twenty minutes, weaving through the rocks and cliffs where the tracks began and heading downwards into upper Snake River Canyon.

The weather got intense as it usually does in that part of the canyon's rim. I slowed my fine steed and watched the dogs run into a ledge cave just at the edge of a massive drop-off into the canyon. The tracks of the paint led downwards into a semi-dark canyon falling directly into a blind area near Frenchy Rapids. Instinct told me the horse was alone and the tracks were slightly lighter than the ones on Hollow Road. I figured the rider dismounted and slapped the horse out into the blind area on its own.

I pulled my thirty-thirty Winchester from its weathered leather saddle holster and checked the load. There were six shots with extra ammunition in one of my rear saddlebags. Filbert was a crack shot and was certainly no one to fool with, so I backed off into the boulders above the cave and waited for Buck Parrish and my brother, Frank, to catch up.

A shot echoed way down in the canyon, the retort coming from Gailord Gulch. From there, the canyon flooded and went off into the difficult terrain of Nez Perce County, Idaho. The rain started slapping against the rocks and my large-brimmed black hat. My hat, which I always wore while tracking, was my good luck charm, but the best thing about that was that my hat kept the rain out, keeping most of my body dry even in the most severe downpour.

Pushing against the rocks while holding my rifle tight against my body, I waited silently. I strained my ears to hear something; but all I could make out was the dogs' rustling at least twenty feet inside the canyon's cave entrance, just near Cougar Rapids. It began raining hard, and I knew that I'd have to find shelter soon. In the meantime, I hoped that my hat and canvas duster would do its job and keep me somewhat dry.

In a true pursuit, the hunter often feels as if they are the prey. When I was a child, this feeling created the only true fear I ever felt, for the Nez Perce trackers are raised as traditional warriors and fear is something we're taught not to feel.

Without warning, there was a rifle shot from inside the cave and one of the dogs yelped out in pain. I was pretty sure that Filbert shot him before the barking could give his position away. Well, the rifle shot and resultant whimpering gave me all the information I needed, the pain I felt for my hound had to be dismissed.

A truck slowly drove up Hollow Road, and eventually, Buck and my brother, Frank, came into view. I raised my rifle in the air, signaling them with the reddish-brown kerchief tied to the barrel sight. Buck and my brother silently approached the area from different directions. The wounded dog kept yelping near the cave, and the other hound kept barking in response. Buck crept to my side and pressed himself flat against the boulder. Frank found cover among the branches of a nearby oak tree to get a better view of things.

"Heard a shot and quite a bit of hound commotion," Buck whispered to me. "What's the situation like here, Billy?"

"Pretty sure old Filbert's got himself pinned down in old Cougar Cave," I answered. "And, at any time, he's about to swing down Gailord Gulch towards Nez Perce and Lolo country."

"Think it's now or a very long pursuit, do ya?"

"Yes. Best thing we can do is flush the man out now. We could try to wing him before he escapes down the canyon," I said.

"So, we move in now and then we circle behind the cave entrance. Billy, Frankie will stay where he is so he can cover for me. If we can, let's pull the scared bastard out alive. You understand what I mean here, don't ya, Billy?"

I watched Buck's face as his words blistered off his tongue. He gazed off onto space, knowing full well that Filbert was one enraged son-of-a-bitch, like a Kootenay grizzly wounded and angered. We, along with most of the other people in Enterprise, knew Filbert and his family well.

The raindrops burst against the boulders as if they were missiles falling through the clouds. It was cold, wet, and getting darker. Sudden changes in the weather such as these are typical for this part of the high country.

We tensed up because of a sound coming from the cave. Filbert shot three times at Buck and Frank; however, the bullets ricocheted off two massive boulders, their echoes ringing for what seemed like forever. Both men quickly took cover behind the boulders. There's no other sound like a thirty-aught-six zinging and ricocheting off solid rock. Those sounds could be heard in the canyons for at least ten miles. Filbert emerged from the cave as the sun went down against Zigzag Rapids. He began running like a cougar towards Lower Bar Rapids where it was far easier to get lost.

I was in an excellent position to take a wounding shot. The bullet hit Filbert in the fat muscle of the left calf. I watched him go down, tumbling into some mesquite shrubs on the side of the trail. Buck and Frank moved down towards the Nez Perce River Crossing in an attempt to cut him off. Men who trapped and footed northeast Wallowa County knew how to track fast and to surround. It was the same game against any prey, man or beast, except a man on the lam was far more dangerous than any other mammal.

Night had fully fallen. Darkness had taken over, except for an occasional shot of light from a silver half-moon sometimes hidden by clouds. The sound of shoes scuffling came from the edge of Lower Bar behind some large Ponderosas. I spotted Filbert's fresh blood on the side bark of a birch and followed the splotches to the side of the trail, which led down to Bar Rapids. Frank and Buck were closely moving in on Filbert. I had my doubts about his ability to escape from this 'gill net' we'd prepared.

From his safe position behind a tree, Buck called out, "Throw your weapon down, Filbert. We have no intention of shooting you again."

"Listen, you Indian-loving son-of-a-bitch. You've already shot me, so I'll make sure my next one goes either through your head or into one of those tin-pan Indians you keep around you."

His voice was not that of the boy I'd known growing up; nor that of an ordained minister, not any longer.

"Billy, cover me!" Buck yelled. I could barely see him dive behind an old Douglas fir. He wasn't in the open for more than a split second, yet Filbert took his shot regardless. His exploding barrel flashed in the dark and it gave me just enough brightness to pinpoint the target. I fired. Filbert moaned, and I heard the sound of his body and the rifle hit the ground. A rare silence fell over the dark, wet, wind-blown night. As Buck switched on his magnum flashlight, a blinding stream of white light filled the black vacuum. Again, the hush in the Lower Bar area was deadly.

I'd been other places- both in the woods and the mountains, many times. Each time, when something dies, there is an utter stillness, one that creeps into your veins causing an ever-deepened shivering. Before Buck could get to Filbert, I knew he was dead. The moist air stank of death. Still, I covered

Buck and Frank as they approached the body from different directions. Buck told us to come forward, and we switched on our flashlights, thereby illuminating Buck standing next to Filbert's corpse on the frigid ground.

My shot had gone straight through Filbert's neck, breaking one of his vertebrae into fine pieces. One of the sections had split and wedged through the skin. It wasn't a pretty sight.

"This man didn't want to be caught," Buck said. "He knew too much. Plus, what he knew, killed him just as sure as the bullet did."

"I'll get the mule down here and try to pack the body to the truck," Frank said. "Best thing to do at this point, I guess."

I remained perfectly speechless, looking down at Filbert's body.

"You knew this man well didn't you, Billy?" Buck asked.

"Yes, like many of us 'round here, we grew up together. He and I did some hunting together with his pa; sad day when a man has to kill his friend's son!"

"You had no choice, Billy," Buck said quietly. "He'd never give up and would've shot each of us if given half a chance."

I sat on the truck seat next to Buck, both of us saying little as we drove back to Enterprise. There was a great silence in the truck, a muteness that cut to the bone. This whole thing in this county had been getting bad ever since Kaelin's disappearance. The closer we got to the core, the worse it got, and I knew this was not the last of the spilled blood. Buck looked over at me as I stared out into the darkness of the woods with the rifle on my lap.

"Hold on, old friend. I need you in one piece," he advised me. I knew that all of us would need each other badly before this whole thing ended. His words helped, a show of support. Silence always got to me, reminding me of the end of spirit ceremonies. Buck gently put his hand on my left shoulder and squeezed with a great deal of brotherly kindness. It was the first time in years I'd felt something like that come out of old Buck Parrish. This touch from a friend was very warm and very

179

close. The truck hit a large bump in the road, and we were jolted upwards, but only the upper part of my hat was crushed from the impact. The jarring brought a slight smile to all the faces in the truck. It was a break in the silence and pain.

thirty-four

<u>Frank Onaben</u>

A week after Filbert Buchanan was killed, we slowly began closing in on Amos T. Blackburn. Lucinda Bork was filled in on who and what Amos was, and the way he specifically exploited young female teenagers at the New Church for his own dark personal needs. When the news of the six bodies found at Wildhorse Springs Reservoir emerged, the whole county descended into a peculiar type of fright. It seemed as if neighbors lost contact with neighbors, brothers mistrusted brothers and all the 'righteous' people looked to someone for guidance. Most of us had on the subject rumor and innuendo. Some people even began to leave the New Church, it was said that during the last two Sunday services only about one-half of the usual congregation attended.

Everyone in the county talked about 'things' and they talked about the New Church and the lost teens coming from their own sanctified teen-refuge shelter. Citizens all over the county were yapping and the pressure was mounting on the 'law' to do something to find out who killed and systematically dumped six, fifteen-year-old girls in old Wildhorse Springs Reservoir.

I well remember the days before Blackburn ran for office; I recall how people looked hard at anyone strange or who acted different. Even the bars were different after the girls were found in the reservoir, they were quiet; people barely spoke above a whisper. The funny thing was that all the bars were the same way. It was like some kind a secret virus spread around the county.

My brother Billy worked with various tracking teams, which took off in all possible directions from some of the rough clues we were able to gather at Wildhorse Springs. He worked closely with Buck Parrish, Shawna Thore, Jeb Hirsch and Miles T. Carson. It was about the second week in a cold November when something quite bewildering happened. Miles T. Carson asked Judge Buchanan to put him on an extended leave and appoint Buck Parrish in his stead. The Judge who was himself caught in his own grief did exactly what old Miles T. asked, never even once asking any questions or questioning Miles' motives. So it was done and Buck Parrish became acting Sheriff of Wallowa County. Now, old Miles T. did precisely the best thing he could under the circumstances, he just wasn't ready for another chase, or at least that's the impression he left on all of us. Will Carson had come back to work, and he'd be under Buck. Will had been out recuperating long enough from his wounds and was gasping for some action. Old Will was a good hand, never lazy and always ready to make a solid move in some direction. In other words, he had a lawman's brain and he wasn't afraid to use it, was never afraid!

It was just about three weeks, maybe sixteen days from the start of the Wildhorse Springs episode and body count that old Amos T. Blackburn broke from sight. The boy had a good motorized fishing boat, which he kept down at Mountain Sheep Rapids right in the historic heart of Hell's Canyon. Some big Steelhead still struck down there in season and old Amos used to catch and eat those lovely tasting fish while they were real fresh. Amos had a reputation for being one of the best fish fry cooks in the county, and that honor, he deserved. Not far from the spot where Amos moored his boat, a man could quickly disappear down the Snake River towards Baker County and a breakaway into Idaho. Old Buck had both myself, and Will, watching Amos Blackburn both day and night as he expected him to flee. In fact, there was a lot of evidence on Amos at that particular point in these cases, plus a vast personal record of violence and physical abuse associated with this 'knife-like' skinny man. Blackburn was the sort of man who came to hard angles all over his body and face from his knees to his bonnie cheeks including his tightly chiseled bird nose. The local 'Breeds' had a nickname for Amos Blackburn; they called him 'Crow eyes'. Everyone talked about his black deep eye pools that had a way of drawing you in and never letting you out once he teased you in or drew you inside of 'em.

Blackburn was a man who moved during the night. He rarely was spotted during the middle part of the day or any part of the day for that matter. It was almost as if the man refused to let people 'ever' see him clearly. Most of his jobs were usually at nightshift from the second shift to the 'graveyard'. From Enterprise, he took off on about the fourteenth day of the investigation and headed up O.K. Gulch to Old Zumwalt Shaft zigzagging from dirt road to dirt road heading directly towards Mountain Springs Rapids.

Will and I pursued him from a safe distance unless he stopped and looked back from a given mountaintop, but there was no way he could have spotted us, no way. Amos T. Blackburn was a 'natural killer' and a crack shot. He had worked on his gun skills from the time he was eleven and was an extremely dangerous person to follow. Billy would call ahead to Buck on many occasions as he traveled north to Wild Horse Springs and up north again to Lent. Some of the time, it was damned difficult to get the digital signal through to him. Buck told us to follow him wherever he went, but to keep ourselves pretty far back unless of course Amos tried to spring his boat down the Snake towards southern Idaho. As we bounced in the Jeep, Will loaded three handguns: two automatics, and one revolver; and his thirty-thirty lever-action Winchester with seven-hundred-fifty-power scope mounted on the barrel.

Blackburn reached Cemetery Ridge Pass Road, a shadow-logging trail not far from Mountain Sheep Rapids. He was a determined man trying to flee down towards the Snake River. As soon as Will and I understood what he was doing and his direction, we phoned back to Buck for orders. Buck and Shawna were searching up Cottonwood Creek north of Wild-Horse Springs when I received an emergency call. I could usually second-guess old Buck and he needed my brother Billy to keep the search energized. More than that, he needed him in charge with Byron Frank right there in everybody's face. So old Buck Parrish himself put Billy in immediate charge of the situation at hand. Old Byron put up a fight about being under some Indian, but Buck put him in his place as Buck usually did.

Shawna and Buck headed for Cochran Islands where the Sheriff kept his river patrol boats. Will and I kept on close tail of Blackburn but the order was for me to pick up a commercial 'fast' boat at River Landing and head straight up river. Will followed Blackburn like a tick on a Squirrel's tail. He followed Amos wherever he went like some kind of extended appendage he couldn't lose. Blackburn was an extremely good hunter and tracker. He knew the county in the same way he knew the short hairs on his arm, in the county except for him there was just Will, two matched men in many ways. It was a contest between the two best Anglo outdoorsmen in the county.

"Frankie, I'll stick to Amos like a mosquito grabs on the ear of an Elk. If he has a boat down from Mountain Sheep Rapids, I'll try to take him, but I won't do it physically." I don't know exactly what you mean but don't do anything until you hear from Buck. Just follow by boat and we'll plan to trap the bastard 'bout Five Point Rapids.

"Good idea. It's tight there, hard to move a boat in any direction, difficult to manipulate even in the water."

If he shoots at you, stay far enough behind; do not proceed. Wait for orders and wait for Buck and the woman.

"Frankie, if I get a clear shot at him, believe me, I'd love to end this thing now; no point in prolonging the story?" Will there's no clear evidence here. You're the law. We can wait for the courts to decide.

"Right! This bastard was directly involved in child rape, murders, molestation and probable sex-farming and you say he's a prime candidate for a soft legal trial?"

Again, you're a lawman and have been one for over twenty years. Don't let this case get that deep into your crawl!

"Six to seven local fifteen year olds were slaughtered and raped and you're worried about my crawl?"

There's more involved in this thing than just Blackburn. Buck needs a *live being* to question. We're getting too many dead suspects and witnesses, too many.

"Then my brother, one more sour deceased bastard would hurt no one. A little justice needs to be done. This piece of garbage deserves a painful death; one bullet like Filbert got is far too easy."

The Jeep jumped a rock near the center of the road and nearly threw me right out of its canvass top.

"Drop me off at Bark Gulch and you can find your own way down to River Landing. Remember to pick up that commercial boat."

184

Best thing we could do is trap the dork before he gets to Robertson Ridge.

I'll see you soon, Will. Just try real hard to keep out of his site. He's too good a shot.

"Frankie, whoever gets the first shot in wins this one hands down; maybe him and maybe me but this one won't end easy!"

As I dropped Will off next to Nez Perce Crossing, I was quite sure that Blackburn had to vanish before the day was out. In my heart I hoped the 'dead man coming' wasn't going to be Will, but for me, the odds were too close to call between these two hunters.

I drove the roads like a man heading for the emergency room after a child was hit by a car and had some minutes to survive. Turning a blind corner, I hit a large Elk on the hip knocked him over and tore up the right side of the Jeep. The Elk got up and marched away a little stunned maybe, bruised from the impact but recovered just the same. The wet-cold wind picked up as I reached the top part of the road at the end of the landing. All the ridges at the crest of Hell's Canyon were real rough. The weather always turned bitter about late day. The rain filled and bloated Cumulous clouds would hang over high ridges and sure as night falling the rain would come. On the river below the canyon's ridges, the air temperatures were thirty to forty degrees warmer, and occasionally, the sun would break through on the Idaho side.

Years before, I worked with old Ben Ross at Rivers Commercial Boathouse, so he naturally loaned me the best and fastest boat he had. He did wish me luck knowing all to well who we were chasing.

"Blackburn's a tough cookie, Frankie. I don't think I'd want to be in his sites if he got mad?"

I calculated that anyone who knew Amos Blackburn would have a similar opinion, but I thanked old Ben just the same and took off. Now it did seem like anyone who wanted out of the county territory usually headed towards the river in order to leave. The men who ran knew that if they made it past a certain point in the river. However, it was unlikely that they'd be found easily and most likely, they'd get out. The Snake River at that point had too many places to escape unnoticed and of those hidden coves and inlets, old Blackburn had been down most of 'em. I pointed the bow of the boat towards Wolf Creek Rapids not knowing anything at that time about what took place on the river north of my position. I didn't know how long it would take Buck and the woman to get down to this area from Cochran Islands, but Buck had the powerboat and that made his time downstream slightly faster than any of ours. If Blackburn had a boat at all, we knew it had to be his steel fishing trawler. Amos loved to fish and that was the boat he was able to afford. So the law it seemed was creeping fast at both ends of the river. We had the speed advantage, yet old Amos knew the waters and the sub-canyons better than any man on the chase. There was definitely a Ferret in our bare hands.

Not being right there to watch the goings on, the story evolved more or less like a give or take of some minor events. Will was moving right behind old Amos, staying on him like the Romans on Achilles heel when a shot rang out atop Zigzag Rapids Ridge. That shot tore in about an eighth of an inch on the side of Will's head tearing a good part of his left ear off. He fell immediately, totally unconscious bleeding pretty badly. The man lay there for quite some time before old Buck was able to pick him up. Buck said he was quite unconscious when he found him, yet he was still breathing soundly. Buck was the kind of a man who often calculated pretty well what people would usually do. He was the best lawman I'd ever known. Billy and I had a great deal of respect for Mr. Parrish; we revered that man to his core. Buck was most likely the only Anglo either of us really trusted. Shawna stayed with Will and did her paramedic training/work on his head injury, because old Will at that point, got his funny looking ear sewed onto his funny looking head. That's the best a man can hope for when he gets his damned left ear half shot off. The next best thing is a pretty competent woman to wake up to, after she does what's needed?

Buck took his big county-owned speedboat to the chase and from the opposite direction I was coming up river to pin Amos in like a winged Grouse trapped by a pack of hungry Coyote's. Pushing that boat full throttle all the way down the river 'til Boulder Rapids, Buck caught the small wake of a boat edging the rapids. Near Five Pines Rapids, I saw Blackburn's boat heading directly towards me but I saw no driver, anywhere? Instantly a streak of blasting light crossed my eyes; lucky for me I had dropped my small bullet-pack and moved to the left. A bullet immediately split the windshield of the boat exactly where I was standing. It looked like Blackburn was firing at me from a crest of boulders about two hundred fifty yards above Five Point. The next shot hit my arm, the arm holding my rifle. My next move while bleeding all over the place was to swing the boat into a protected cove where no one could draw a beat on me. I immediately jumped from the boat and slid behind two large granite rocks. At that point, Buck had arrived and he'd heard the series of shots. He took out his seven-by-fifty binoculars and searched the upper brush for Blackburn knowing full well that I may have been wounded or dead. If Blackburn took two shots it was likely one had hit the target. He was just that good a rifleman and Buck surely knew it. At the exact time Amos made a mistake, he kept shooting in my direction not seeing or paying attention to anything else. Quickly, he fired five shots in rapid succession. Immediately after the shots stopped, I could hear him cranking up the boat to run down towards my floating craft and me. I was less than two hundred yards from the edge of the Five Point Ridge water marker. From the surrounding Silence of 'birdless air', a single rifle shot sounded. It rang out into and through the canyon walls and from it, a morbid silence arose.

I could feel the pronounced silence of death as Blackburn's boat drifted down the river. Next, I then spotted a man slung over the windshield his face soaked in new blood and the glass-shield penetrated and cracked from one side to the next. Buck Parrish had put a bullet right above Amos T. Blackburn's right eye and he was quite dead upon initial impact. Few men could shoot like Buck from a moving position. He was the absolute perfect weapons man when it came to velocity and movement. In my life- both in the Army and outside, I'd never known a man who could shoot more accurately than Buck and here was a man who hated guns. For Buck, guns were just tools of a final resort. They were never any more than that and he tried not to use them pretty much throughout his twenty some year law career. As the boat drifted by, I couldn't help but wonder what the county folks would see before this whole damned thing ended, before the killing stopped?

At the hospital in Enterprise that day, I was treated; or, I should say: my wound was treated by Dr. Oliveson and May Pierce R.N., a woman I had always admired even as a teenager. It was said that she had half-Blackfoot blood in her, but that made no difference. Nurse Pierce was a thorough beauty inside and out. The way her hands treated the wound somehow made it all feel that much better. Funny thing was, Dr. Oliveson seemed both blind and innocent to his own involvement in 'local conditions'. Oliveson, I observed, was a man unconscious of his own connection to the community's horrors. He seemed only to act out his function without cognizance or concern.

thirty-five

<u>Charles C. Marten</u>
Sunday, November 18, 1998

It wasn't easy to prepare myself for my speech to our fellow deacons and the New Wallowa Church of Christ assembly. It was 10:00 a.m., Sunday morning, November 18. The air was crisp outside and the dribble was entering our sacred church. I watched carefully while many members of the assembly walked up the stairs from different sides of our beautiful circular structure. Never in the history of the county had anyone ever seen a church structure like ours, a site to bring both the rabble and the good citizens in, bring them in under the solid beamed roof of Jesus Christ and all that He means. We had an assembly here to be proud of, and no one or nothing was ever going to change the impact of good works this church had on our total community. My eyes teared as I thought of our beloved Reverend Chrisp and our wondrous newly ordained pastor, Reverend Filbert Buchanan. The core shock of their sudden deaths had taken the community by storm, it was by no uncertain terms a shocking disturbance, and here was I in front of all to fulfill my fellow churchgoers fulfilling their needs. At the bottom of it all, our community was a family of people, an assembly of Christ connection who followed the bible and the exact word of God as it was written. We were a united flock, no matter what else we were in Jesus Christ's arms, floating in temporary space because our leaders were taken in an untimely way, in a series of sudden violent departures, unexpected.

So as the last body (a child) walked head down to the front of the church, I watched her and at the same time raised my eyes toward the great wooden and iron arches above us all. From the door, I watched the faces. I viewed the gathering as various profiles turned to examine me, dressed for the first time in Reverend Filbert's gown, a fine adornment filled with the pride and hope of a good Christian man like Reverend Filbert. He single handedly showed us all what we were, and what we could be from his entering of the church divinity school to his devotion as a child of the Lord. This service that I was to preach was for a memorial and from my personal heart. For myself, as for many in that day's audience, it was an honor to celebrate the passing of these two religious men. I was particularly proud that I was chosen by the deacons to speak on this important occasion. This round chamber as I viewed down the isles was filled to capacity; it was standing room only for that day, and one speech would be made to celebrate and honor, only one. As I climbed to the pulpit stairs I saw expressions, I saw old faces from the community, old faces never in the assembly before, and I was proud. I stood at the pulpit for several minutes before speaking, a lump in my throat, tears beginning to run down my cheeks, watching an assemblage that was quite silent. This profound silence in my eyes was a respect due for the loss, a respect for the dead buried in the rapture of our collective belief, and the absolute melding of our congregation's silence.

I looked around before I spoke. My throat clogged, and then I spotted Buck Parrish in the assemblage sitting next to Linda Bork in the third isle directly within the center of my vision. Quickly, I overcame my anguish for Parrish, and delivered a direct sermon as powerful as I could render. All the sounds in the hall and within the audience had ceased. Even the rustling was muted, all seemingly waiting for my words. And I began.

"Today, I speak to you from my chest, the blood beating a kind of drum chant for two who have fallen, two of our best, yes, two of our finest have leaped into God's arms. These two grand men have been taken from us unexpectedly, yet we know that they live in a better world in a truly rapturous place. We know that death isn't the end, it isn't the end, it's only the new beginning and we understand these words, don't we?"

The mass of people generally nodded in support, I could feel the center of this throng totally within me. I was aroused genuinely by the joy I felt looking out at them. "Yes, today I speak to you of the tragic passing of two of our very own. These were surprising and sudden departures in this new world of ours, a world of constant and rapid change. There are some of us in the audience who wish to remain in place, but all of us must confront death when it comes in a way similar to our acceptance of the cries of a newborn. Death is the last cry we hear, not the first cry!"

Again, I peered out at the mass and heard their silence, I heard their pain and I was with them, yes, I was one with their pain and muteness. "Today, I speak of two special men, two blessed reverends, pastors departed, taken from us each in swiftness and totality. Neither of these fine men, the Hon. Reverend Parham A. Chrisp, nor the Hon. Reverend Filbert Buchanan, were ever married to anyone or really to anything but this church. Their loss is our loss, and it is both a loss to the larger community and to the holiness of this social assemblage itself.

"As you may or may not know, nearly one week ago, two of our finest deacons found Reverend Chrisp hanging from the sacred rafters of our bell tower. Never mind what brings a man to this place, to a space that life itself has no value, let us for the moment look beyond that aspect here. The two deacons said that Reverend Chrisp's face was divinely at peace. Yes, Mr. Chrisp was at rest because our beloved pastor saw Jesus directly, and that was his joy before he passed on, passed on into the loving arms of our holy Lord. You too will comfort in Jesus when you're deceased. Yes, that is exactly who Reverend Chrisp confronted prior to his passing on. You all will attend Jesus and you will also become part of the will of Christ's deepest spirit. You too can achieve his power and become part of his will. Christ gives his love to those who take him in, and Parham A. Chrisp, our beloved reverend, is one who potently did just that. The proof is Reverend Chrisp died at repose. Yes, he took his life for reasons unknown and I'm sure, for many reasons we'll never know, but his face, my brothers and sisters, his face was tranquil!

"Who among us is to say, brothers and sisters, if that calmness, that blessed peace, isn't what we all hope to achieve passing through this dark tunnel called life? We can get there if we follow Jesus and his teachings, and the good words of the Hon. Reverend Parham A. Chrisp and this church. We can still reach that wonderful peace; yes, all of us here in this place can do this. Yes, we can! So, for one moment let us all bow our heads in silent prayer for our departed pastor, the Hon. Reverend Parham A. Chrisp."

While watching the whole congregation bow, I noticed that a deep sense of inner and outer quiet ran within each of us in that holy hall that day. "Let us pray for the kind of good man Reverend Chrisp was, let us remember what he brought to each of us personally during our many years together. Let us honor this fine man's memory no matter the circumstances of his recent departure, no matter the circumstances!"

I watched still-like as that crowd of people prayed silently for about five minutes honoring the memory of Reverend Chrisp. I can say now that I was proud to be on that pulpit watching those many faces during those special moments

"Next, let us honor as we may, Reverend Filbert Buchanan, the son of our great county's founder pioneer lineage, and the dear son of the Hon. Judge Hamus A. Buchanan."

I viewed Buck Parrish glancing over at Judge Buchanan, knowing full well what he'd done, or better, allowed the squaw-man do to an innocent man. I watched Buck and Willa Shannon sit there and stare at the judge and me as I spoke, as I opened the wounds yet again of the final eulogy. Sheriff Miles T. Carson was also there sitting in the back of the amphitheater with his head down. Probably was the first time in my life, I'd ever seen Miles with his head down. The parish of five hundred or more people had come from all over the county, maybe even a few people coming from some of the adjacent counties. Who knew for sure? There was quietude, calmness over that crowd as something important was happening, and I was speaking it for many a solemn ears.

"So, my brothers and sisters, with finality we have all come to honor the passing of the Hon. Reverend Filbert T. Buchanan, a man I'd known and loved since I was a boy, a man many of you had known personally for several years. With the resignation of Reverend Chrisp, we appointed Reverend Buchanan with enormous esteem and all that goes with it, to replace our fine Reverend Chrisp. We brought Reverend Buchanan in as a 'lion' devoted to attend the flock within our new community. Reverend Filbert had come to us as a fully ordained preacher, schooled in Texas at Baylor University, and then he went on to Oral Roberts University where he was the prized special student of the founder himself, and of course the honors and the awards were showered on our beloved county son.

"Yes, does one ever doubt that Reverend Filbert T. Buchanan was the kind of man all of us could be proud of everyday of our lives. Yes, this man is in my heart as he is in your hearts, and he's there every day of our lives! I recall a time when Filbert and I traveled across the south Wallowa's to Bonneville Mountain near East Peak. We climbed for a day and a half. The Reverend Filbert was tireless. Finally as the struggle became all too much, we camped near the bowl of old Bonneville. It was June and that particular night in June was beautiful with no rain, and few breezes. Except for the massive beauty of God's own sky and stars there was little else which had a place. Filbert and I talked at length about Jesus. We talked about the wonder of God's creation which seemed to dance like dew on the ice tips still dripping and sparkling in many a surrounding pine. Right there, right there, I knew the power that Filbert had. He was a natural preacher from birth with all the energy and spirit our creator can give to a human being. There was a unique twinkling in his eye that night and I stood there right in front of him staring at it, but I wasn't afraid. Filbert had a softness, plus an inner assuredness that took my fear away, even the fear of the dark night, sure did!

"My friends, the next day I fell directly into an ice drain, plunging twenty feet down, gashing my head against a rock and going totally unconscious. Somehow Reverend Filbert found me the next day hidden in the rocks under all that snow and blackness. Like a fallen angel had descended on his rope, he tied my body in a perfect Indian-hoop chair and pulled me by his strong-arms twenty feet to the hard-ridge surface. I owed this man my life; I owed him my life in many, many ways. Yes I did! Now, dear brothers and sisters, this man, this hero, has sadly departed from this earth. He has left us for God's world, and I can vision him in my dreams every time I shut my eyes.

"What Reverend Filbert T. Buchanan was running from, we'll never, never know. But, dear people, he did run and the consequences of that chase are what we now honor here today. We are here to honor Filbert Buchanan, not to degrade his image and his works in any way. Let us remember Filbert as the good son of our beloved county. Let us further remember him as the reverend of honor that he was in life, as the pure man of Jesus that he was. Praise Filbert Buchanan and praise Jesus Christ! Let us all bow our heads in sincere prayer to honor a good life taken, and replaced by God with another. Because whether you believe it or not, a baby was born in Enterprise at our own hospital-clinic that very night Filbert died. The boy child was named Filbert. Yes, this bright red-haired baby boy, ten-pounds-five, was named Filbert. He's right there in the back of the church next to the second pillar. Mrs. Anne Marten Cochran, my daughter, will you please stand up and show the congregation our beloved little Filbert Cochran?"

I watched intensely every twitch of the crowd as my daughter and grandson stood proudly, tears flowing from both my daughter's eyes and mine. It was a moment of great exaltation and triumph and a personal glitch in time I shall never forget, never!

"Now let us bow our heads and pay our final respects to a man we all knew and loved, Reverend Filbert T. Buchanan, son of Judge Hamus Buchanan, a proud father of a great man our blessed church and community. Let us now drift our thoughts into sympathetic prayer."

Every head in the amphitheater was bowed in silence, deeply bowed, giving last respects to our slain reverend. Our pastor and native son brutally shot down like a running animal in the prime of his life. These were the thoughts in my head trying to justify Filbert's early death brought on by our 'local heathens'.

"Now, let's sing 'Shall We Gather at the River', and know that it's to be sung like a prayer with all our hearts for the fallen 'goodly man' of our community church."

While the song went on, through my head, words kept pounding, 'Vengeance is mine, says the Lord', but sometimes men must do the Lord's bidding. Sometimes men must do His work. This was one of the glory days of my life where numbers of good Christians heard my words and prayed, with me

Steve Dreben

honoring a blessed son of our own Wallowa church, yes, it truly was a day to remember.

~

thirty-six

<u>Tammy Bork</u>

I'd been waiting a long time to open up, but there was too much involved, too many people whom I loved, too many who would be hurt. My mother and father were the last people who I could talk to; therefore, I made a decision and commitment to talk to Sister Mary Espinoza. For years, I'd known Sister Mary but rarely talked to her for any length of time. Kaelin had been extremely close to her and had shared most of the personal stuff she was involved in with the Sister. Sister Mary was like the topsoil, rich in nutritional quality, but too dry at times to fully stay on the ground. I recall a day when Kaelin and I came into the Inmaha Mission for Lost Girls established by Sister Mary and her grandmother, Angelina Espinoza, a matron of the oldest frontier family in all of Wallowa County. Sister Mary currently ran the mission but her roots drew way back into the original culture of our wonderful county.

Some weeks ago, I asked for a time to set up a private meeting with Sister Mary, and of course, it was granted. On many occasions, sister and I had watched each other through our eyes. This contact was made particularly sharp during the last two years, since Kaelin's disappearance. The sister's office was a warm place filled with a number of bleak religious items, limited that is for a nun. Still, it was cramped with an assortment of photos of young runaways, both male and female, who the sister had both come to know and help through the years. I recall the words so clearly now which seemed to pour through her soft heart regarding the hanging photos.

"These, dear Tamara, are the images of souls, just those souls passing my way, souls God had honored with me, souls he has allowed me to aide through the years."

I looked at the walls in amazement, astonished to see so many faces, so many kindred spirits facing me, most of them my own age or older. "Why the devotion to the girls, Sister? What possessed you to connect so much with runaway girls?"

"They were simply part of something I found deep inside me to serve. Every human being needs someone to give to or his or her lives will not become whole. Perhaps my concept of 'the whole' comes from Buddhism mixed with proper Jesuit teachings, yet each at a varied spectrum of life and spirit are equally the same: balanced."

"I'm not sure I fully understand what you're saying, Sister?"

"What one has within herself is what one can give. We are only what we give. It's a Christ concept but it dominates my whole life."

"I've come here, Sister, to talk to you. I'd like to discuss something stuck in my mind. There is something glued down in my thoughts regarding our friend Kaelin, and the last night of her life."

"I know my dear, and the time for you to give me all that has come; the words can be spoken now."

Her eyes shined like a small star, so bright that I almost felt my pupils burn as I stared into her face. I studied the fullness of her fleshy lips, their softness, and the little bump at the ridge of her wondrous nose, and her soft thick black eyebrows. My mother, Lucinda, had known Sister Mary since the two of them had been children and they had been very close. According to my mother, Mary was the most sought after teenager at Enterprise High. My mother said she carried a tinge jealous toward her, yet no man but one would ever have her in any way. Still, that story was a closed secret all locked up in the vault of the Enterprise Bank, or should have been. Sister Mary and Buck Parrish were young lovers and as devoted as anyone can imagine. Nonetheless, the surprise death of her loving brother changed her. At that point, she pledged her life to something better, something 'lofty' she said, beyond her own basic needs. That's when she fled to Sister Holly's Catholic Mission in the high country of Western Colorado, where she stayed and studied for five hard years. My mother recounted the story of the sister and Buck many times, but in all the time I'd known Sister Mary, I'd never broached the subject, at least not until my private appointment in her mission study.

I asked her several questions that I'd never asked before, possibly to throw her off, possibly to renew my sense of trust.

"Does your spiritual view of giving come from the church, or a personal Holly's Mission, or some other place you've been?"

"It comes from somewhere in the heart zone, someplace above the skirt line, an area between the belly and the heart muscle. I felt it in my gut and that's where it stayed all these years."

I remember clearly how lost I felt in her presence. It was far more than just being twenty years younger, no, it more of an awe which I felt for her. I felt a strong reverence just in her beautiful presence as one human being to another; somehow, she was able to capitalize all parts of my being with hers. As I sat and talked to her, my words and my thoughts got clearer; it was almost as if just being there took me to another zone of human connection. Sister Mary had counseled many of my friends and peers; none of them had ever said anything negative about her, ever!

I seemed to flash on the way Sister Mary walked to the side of the room. She stopped near the mantle next to many of the framed photos and gently poured her red wine. "Tamara, why, have you not come to talk about Kaelin before today? Why have you waited so long?"

"I don't know why, Sister. Maybe it's my secretive nature, possibly the fear of my family, maybe fear of the town's reaction. Who really knows?"

"I can surely understand that, but here is your place of honor and peace. Not a word ever leaves this place unless you say it does. Do you clearly understand what I'm saying, Tamara?"

"Yes, I understand, Sister Mary, and your assurance is exactly what I needed."

My eyes wondered to a painting of the Virgin, by Modigliani, hanging adjacent to the sister's large study window. It was within its simplicity and was one of the most attractive faces I'd ever seen. As a matter of fact, there was a similarity of expressions crisscrossing the virgin's face with that of Sister Mary's; it was an irksome sort of thing and yet wondrous. Never before in all the times in the study had I noticed the facial likeness of the two women. Nevertheless, to me, Sister Mary's faces was more beautiful than a picture of the virgin. Everything about Sister Mary shined. She was the bright star of the county, yet she was a nun, a sister of the church; too bad.

"What happened that night, two years ago? Can you bring it clearly to mind? Can you put it together in some kind of logical detail?" I watched the question come from the sister's mouth as if the sounds somehow poured out into the air. In fact, her words seemed to slow down as if I was watching a bad movie or a kind of distorted dream.

"It's not easy for me to talk about her, Sister. I've made a hard move to come here tonight and this is where I'll speak my truths."

"You know that I was not always Sister Mary, and there were young men and old men in my life, and so I have experiences beyond most women in the church. I do understand a great deal about secular things."

I stared at her because she was talking subtly about old times. Reminiscing about the times she spent as a wild young countrywoman, she somehow tried to convey her accepted knowledge of sexual experiences.

"Sister, my mother has told me about you and Buck Parrish. As you probably know, mother has been like a sister to Buck since all of you were far younger."

"Ah, then she told you about Buck and I, did she? So be it, but note, my dear, there are many thoughts involved in experiences, many words that should pass privately between a mother and a daughter. I can easily say this because your mother is one of the true woman left in these parts, she is part of the past as I am, and I respect her head to toe."

"Yes, Sister, my mother talked to me for hours about your love affair with Buck Parrish, but it was always something I respected, so did Kaelin. It was a great something we hoped for in our lives, instead of what we found."

Sister Mary watched my lips as I spoke. She said very little and instead sipped her wine and walked toward the roaring fireplace, which was blazing enthusiastically to her right.

"Tamara, I want you to tell me what you truly know about Kaelin. Tell me about the men she was involved with before her precipitous disappearance."

"Tommy Wenaha was her beau. There was no one else really, except the various men from the New Church."

"Yes, the New Church. Now tell me what it was between you, Kaelin, Tilly, and Terrie Conson. What motivated all of you to directly help all those deacons at the New Church's shelter?"

"There are a lot of things that happened at the runaway shelter. It was something to do. Actually it was fun at first plus, all of us could use the money."

"What money?"

"We were paid well for the work we did. We were paid for our 'task performance.'

"Task performance? What was that?"

"Well, we all dressed in all these elaborate costumes, and then we'd dance for several of the deacons."

"What kind of dance did you do? Can you be more specific?"

"We danced at first using some Turkish style dance, like belly dancing from the Middle East, but we were completely naked under the beaded clothing."

"Who asked you to perform that way? Can you name them all?"

"Sure I can. But you already know most of them; Nathan Bork, C.C. Marten, Amos T. Blackburn, Dr. Oliveson, Byron Frank, Filbert Buchanan, and occasionally, even Sheriff Carson."

"Sheriff Miles T. Carson, you say? Are you sure he was there, are you absolutely positive?"

"Yes. Even Reverend Chrisp was there at times, but he was always less enthusiastic than the others."

"What was the reason for nude bodies under the beaded clothing? Didn't you think something was wrong?"

"No, it really didn't matter. At first, we all had some fun with it. The dancing was somewhat different, maybe stimulating at the beginning. We were all treated well. It was like it were all part of a school play. In fact Dr. Oliveson said that dancing that way created a lot of body heat. He believed that freely open and nude bodies would relieve most of it. So he was a doctor, you know, and we kind of believed him."

"A play they told you? It was all part of a play did they say? And all of you automatically played the roles as they demanded?"

"Yes. We all talked about it between each other and were thrilled with the excitement of it. We enjoyed the dancing and role play until it all changed."

"How did it change? What exactly was their next move, or at least next request demanded of you?"

"They weren't ever really demands; well, at least at first, they weren't looked at as demands. Instead, they requested certain things and we pretty much followed what they requested."

"Why, may I ask, did you do all that? What pressed you onward? Was it the money? Was it all the money involved?"

"No. At first, it really wasn't the money. The thing that motivated us was the kicks involved. You know, older men wanting us, desiring us, it just juiced up our sensations. The audience consisted of married men, upstanding men in the community, and they were at our feet. It was powerful."

"Sounds like they might have wanted more than your feet?"

"Sure they did. But at first, they just wanted to gawk like little birds. Eventually, the gawking bird behavior stopped and they wanted us to play with them, unzip their pants and lick them openly. It all started like a game, a game we played as if we were the tainted painted Parisian women, Turks to them. On the other hand, the men were the servants of purity. They were the direct servants of God. The men were the pure men of Christ and we were there to be cleansed, to serve their needs."

"Sounds like an orgy in which all the men you mentioned were directly involved. Is there more that you can remember, anyone else?"

"No, no one else that we ever saw. But it did seem at times that all the men in the retreat were controlled by someone else."

Sister watched me rubbing my hands together trying to say as much as I could. The retreat ritual had been a closed secret inside me for so very long that it was difficult expressing myself.

"Was Mr. C. C. Marten the leader of the church group, or was it someone else?"

"Mr. Marten usually called the shots. He was usually the one who paid us afterwards, and he always thanked us for helping do Christ's work. He repeatedly said that it was the duty of the Turkish women to satisfy Christ's servants. He explained that they had to be stimulated by young Turkish women so that they could go on doing the good work."

"Doing the good work by molesting and raping young innocent girls?"

"Maybe not so innocent, Sister, and there was no rape, no one ever raped us. All was freely given through the will of Christ and by mutual consent."

"Do you not realize that it was in fact rape? You were all underage and therefore, it would have been considered statutory rape?"

"We wanted to do it, Sister. It was never any kind of rape. The men were always kind and gentle with us; at least they were very careful to be gentle with the girls they knew."

"The ones they knew you say? What about the ones they didn't know so well, like those stray girls coming to a runaway shelter?"

Sister Mary put her wine glass down and approached my eyes very directly. She actually confronted me, speaking point blank in my face nose to nose. "Tamara, what about the others? The other girls who came into the shelter monthly? Like the girls that come to Inmaha's Shelter right here; what about those kind of girls what happened to them?"

"I wasn't there for that part of it; I can only tell you what I heard about it from Dr. Oliveson."

"Dr. Oliveson, the obstetrician who works at Enterprise Hospital in the clinic? Is that the man to whom you are you're referring to?"

"Yes. He and I got real close. I was his favorite Turkish dancer, and so, he'd tell me things. He'd confess things about their safe-house. One of the girls mentioned Terrie Conson was used many times in tough ways by several of the deacons."

"So the treatment of some of the girls, particularly the ones who were referred to as strays, were treated very differently than the known girls."

"Yes. In fact, she often told me how they would take her into a dark room and all the men would pray together in candlelight. Afterwards, they'd have at her."

"Have at her? What do you mean? Are you saying they'd all have intercourse with her? That they'd rape her in a mass?"

"Yes, I guess. She said that she was raped multiple times all over her body. They forced her to have two men in her at the same time while a third man put his dick in her mouth. She became a kind of sex slave she said, just for room and board, no real extra money. Terrie wasn't the only one."

"Let me understand this. You say that Terrie and many others were forced to engage in multiple sexual acts with the New Church of Christ's Deacons? They forced them to perform these many lewd acts under threat?"

"Yes, and according to Terrie, the physical threats got more severe, more severe as long as they were interested in specific girls."

"What happened to the girls they lost interest in?"

"Don't really know, but no one ever actually saw them again. It was said that they were all shipped to other runaway shelters where they could be watched better."

"What happened to Terrie Conson? Where did she go after Kaelin disappeared?"

"She ran off to Union County. Terrie said that she was afraid for her life. The girl believed she was the next target to be shipped out. She had become convinced the deacons were beginning to get tired of her 'cause she kept complaining about the multiple rapes."

"No one knows anything about this stuff. All the girls who were there for months were continually molested and raped. To this day, no one has ever said anything. No one ever did anything?" Sister Mary's eyes questioned silently with a piercing kind of astonishment.

"No one, Sister? The deacon's were powerful and they threatened all of us with horrible retribution if we ever spoke of these things, terrible reprisals, they said."

"What about the fresh runaways at their shelter? What in the living hell were they threatened with to keep quiet?"

At that point I looked out through Sister Mary's large window, looked out at a car fast approaching. Only the lights on the front of the vehicle could be seen clearly, only the beams. A tall man with facial hair and a large hat opened the door. He was a solid sized man and he walked deliberately but slowly towards the study. Suddenly, I recognized Buck Parrish. I kind of knew it was time to discuss things with Buck, my mother always loved and trusted Buck Parrish, and most of the quality women in town did. Just about the time the lights from the truck got my head spinning, I couldn't be sure of much of what I'd already said, and yet I said a great deal and I'd be speaking about it all a lot more, and I knew it. Buck was a plain-talking man that I could speak to, always could speak to. It wasn't at all easy but I knew deep inside me that it all had to come out, had to.

As Buck entered the study, Sister Mary greeted her old friend and lover warmly. She hugged him for some time acting as if relief had somehow entered the room.

"I can remember times in the past when I'd wait days for you to hug me like that. I detect it's quite novel now, quite altered isn't it?" Buck greeted with a wide grin.

Sister Mary cajoled and gently grinned. In fact, she almost blushed at Buck's comments, but held the pose, as many a teen expression goes, 'she held the pose'. There was silence as Buck turned in my direction waiting for someone to say something. 'Mr. Parrish,' I said, 'I'd like to tell you something new about Kaelin, or at best what I personally know about the last night anyone saw her, and how she got to where she was that night. Sister Mary can fill you in about the rest of the stuff. I don't want to go over that, at least not tonight.

"I'll go through as much as I can about our earlier conversation. With your permission, I'll relate to Buck at another time. But go on and finish what you've got to say."

Buck Parrish sat down on a sofa right across from me, and the sister sat on the edges of her armchair, all intent and waiting for my next few words.

"You were about to tell me who was with her that final night. In fact, it would be appreciated if you told me how in the hell she got there that night, sure would be important to know that."

"Actually, the girl who was supposed to be there that night was Terrie Conson, but Terrie was real scared of Mr. Blackburn and that's the night she took off to Grant County somewhere."

"We know where Terrie is now. In fact, Tammy... she's quite safe; the girl's in the custody of Sheriff Pete Moss. No one dare bother her while he's in charge."

"Tamara, go on with the story. Tell us all about that night; drag it from your consciousness. Lift that rock from your soul. End it," said Sister Mary.

"It was Tommy Boy Wenaha, and me, and of course Tilly Willis, who came to church that night along with Kaelin. Dr. Oliveson and Mr. Blackburn were scheduled to drive all of us up to the runaway shelter that night. Naturally, Tommy Boy was not included in the plans."

Buck looked somewhat puzzled, but he waited patiently as I gathered more of my thoughts. "Why exclude Tommy Boy? What made them want to exclude Tommy?"

"Sister Mary, should I tell Mr. Parrish the exact words used that night by Mr. Blackburn?"

"Yes, my dear, use his exact words. Don't hold back, don't ever hold a thing back from Buck; he can be trusted."

"Okay," he said, "don't need no dirty, red-skinned pock-eaten peckerheads spoiling all that pretty white-meat, laid and

205

dressed out on the tables.' Tommy Boy was real hurt by Mr. Blackburn. I walked with him up to the New Church, and we never got to go up to the runaway shelter that night, not at all."

Buck took out a little notebook from his back pocket and wrote down part of what I'd said. "I can recall how we watched Mr. Blackburn's faded green Buick pull out, moving down the road quickly, with Kaelin and Tilly Wallis in the back seat. You see Tilly was a regular at the shelter entertainings. The girl told us how well she was paid to play hard. She was paid to screw 'em all hard too. She kind'a liked being part of it. Tilly was always some kind of a thrill-seeker, which I knew from the time she and I were five; always loved the stir."

"What happened that night? Did you ever hear about the goings-on that particular evening?" said, Buck.

"Sure I did. Tilly was proud of her body, real proud and not afraid to show it off. She loved to play with men; it gave her some enormous sense of power. She told me she loved it and the filthy money paid for it. Now remember, to Tilly, the whole awful thing was just a lot of fun, the whole debauchery scene was just for kicks, stimulation, thrills; a way to rid herself of the boredom of this place, at least for a few hours."

"Now, you claim that sex and games were just so much enjoyment for many of the girls. It was their work that's what they were required to do to pay for their stay? Plus, the tips of course? How much were the usual tips, or did it depend on the man and the activity?"

"Oh, I guess maybe fifty dollars if a girl was good and she put herself out openly and freely to the crowd."

"So what happened that night? Tell me exactly what happened; tell me what you know right now."

I watched Buck and Sister Mary. Both of them seemed anxious to get at the truth, at least the truth coming from my mouth. "Well in fact, Kaelin kind of balked, she flipped at the actual sight of it, it was depraved to her, and that's the exact word she used to describe it to Tilly. And, of course, she also used the word perverted."

I watched Sister Mary's face at the use of those two words. She was definitely affected by what was said in that

206

room. "No matter how stoned she got, and no matter what drug she took, Kaelin said she never wanted to be there again, especially after Dr. Oliveson put his hand directly up her dress. She told me how he prodded her clitoris, how he pressed the inside of her vagina with his fingers like he was doing some kind of examination on her opened cavity. She told Tilly how she froze and let him run his hands up and deep inside her wet vagina, how she let him pull her panties off on the great couch, exposing her crotch to all."

"So, Oliveson exposed her to the group and played with her openly to all in attendance?" asked Buck.

"Sure, that's exactly what happened, 'cause all of 'em were looking on or playing with other girls. But Kaelin was new to it, and some of the deacons just stood there and gawked at her and her fully exposed body. Tilly explained how she just laid there with her legs opened, for five minutes while Dr. Oliveson and Mr. Blackburn played with her from both sides of her thighs. They spread her legs wide and licked her from two sides, right there in the open as if she was a toy to be jerked with."

Again, Buck Parrish took down several notes as the sister drank two or three more sips of her dark wine.

"You've been there yourself haven't you, Tamara? You've been there at that spot standing nude while those men gawked and paid you for it, and they played with your vitals too, didn't they?" Buck inquired.

"Yes, I was there too, but during my time, I did enjoy it. Kaelin never did, like some of the girls. Some of 'em really got off on it and they loved both the money and attention. Then there was the other group of girls who were forced to do it, and they hated it. Some said they went into a kind of shock as the sex just continued."

"What happened next, and what really changed the scene for you?"

"Well, Kaelin and Brandy Thompson started to scream, busting out in some kind of pain. After that, the group of deacons dressed them like painted dolls and took them away somewhere."

"Did you hear anything more about where they took them? Did Tilly Wallis say anything to you about it?"

"No, not really. They just drove them both away somewhere after Mr. Marten gave some kind of hand signal to Amos Blackburn."

"A hand signal? Tell me if you can exactly what kind of hand signal he used?"

"He put two middle fingers up and bent them downwards. Next, he pointed at the central building exit door."

"So it was Blackburn and Dr. Oliveson who escorted both Kaelin and Brandy Thompson out of the building that night, and to your knowledge they've never been seen again by anyone?"

"I guess so, 'cause I've never seen either of 'em again after that evening, and the same may be true of Tilly who was also there that night."

"We'll just have to talk to Tilly. But for now, you and the sister will keep all of this to yourselves, until I can get you to make sworn statements on your best knowledge of that night. Right?"

"Right!"

I do remember the relief I felt watching Mr. Parrish and Sister Mary's eyes meet, with a sort of mutual satisfaction garnered between them, a look of appeasement somehow transmitted between each of 'em. For me, I did achieve an inner comfort and knew that I'd gotten to the two of 'em, two of the people in the county I most trusted. We all talked for another forty-five minutes, going over the meaning of some of my words, Mr. Parrish writing down five more of my statements, asking me only to repeat a couple of 'em.

Later, I told my mother that I felt some contentment regarding my personal confession to both Buck Parrish and Sister Mary. My mother said nothing, she just turned and nodded, moving across the living room to her bedroom, tears falling from her cheeks as her eyes reddened and washed in moisture. I slept easier that night; it was the first really solid sleep I had in about two years. My brain never filled with the awful thoughts I usually went to sleep with, instead there was an ease to my immediate slumber, as if tensions had been lifted for some important moments prior to sleep and dream. My body felt more like its old self as I narrowed myself in a comfortable groove, shaped to the mattress indentation. I fell off quickly that night and the morning seemed to come within minutes, not the usual and continuous waking bouts fought at least four or five times a night.

thirty-seven

Billy Onaben

I can recall my brother and me scaling the walls of the upper Snake River Canyon, climbing north eastward into Idaho, following the wild creeks and river rapids of the old Nez Perce war trial. We'd hunt long hours up the hollows and through the flowering meadows above Cochran Islands, so many of the four-legged ones still grazed there even in the mid-sixties up to the early seventies. My brother, Frank, was a fine shot, as well known as Buck, and he was specifically known as the best tracker, white or Indian, in three states, next of course to me, and I'm getting kind'a old. My father and my father's father, they were trackers too. The end roots of my blood are tied to the land and all the animals we tracked for families, some outsiders and ourselves. There is no place in Wallowa County we didn't go, no place we didn't understand and know like an Indian knows. Even the gulches and canyons, peaks and hidden gorges, we knew all of it; even the stuff shut from open view were seen by my brother and I, or Buck. It was all seen by us, that's for sure. My brother was a man's man, and Buck knew it. My brother was a decorated soldier, a Silver Star Medal, and the man was a ribbon winning bronco rider, a hell of a fiddle player, danced like a choir boy; was a true women's lover; a man's man. That's for sure.

I could feel hidden emotions popping up the middle of my body from the lower stomach past the heart to the lower throat, and my power drew the sadness within, my being actually connected with that power flowering within. I watched Buck as he glanced at an area right above my eyes, trying as he would to glimpse an area of solace, trying as he could to drag me from my deep grief, knowing full well that this task was impossible. Tell me again, Buck. Was J. Reed confessing to you directly, and what was it that drove a deacon like Reed to confess? Old J. Reed's a strange man Buck, a dignified and quiet man most of the time, yet one of the few of 'em that's got 'mud' and heart left in him. Reed was a man as I recollect not owned by anyone, a man free to his own heart not controlled by his affiliation with the New Church. Did he just walk into the jail house and confess what he knew straight out, no questions asked?"

"No, Billy. He called first, very politely, and asked to see me. In fact it was right after dinner last Monday night."

I know who killed him, Buck, I've followed the tracks, I know the footprints. Two died in the struggle. Did you know that, Buck?"

"Yes I did. Old Reed described the fight, said the group lost three of their own that night. Afterward, they all went somewhere to hide and bury them, somewhere near 'hidden like'. We'll find the bodies I assure you!"

I jeered at the sky turning red-rose purple behind Buck's head. The sky was all I could see. Maybe I could see a little of Frank's face there. Maybe I could see that, maybe!

"The story goes like this, Billy, and I want you to promise me directly, your word, that you won't go after Marten or any of 'em, you hear me?"

"Sure, Buck. I'll promise you that in white man's language, but not in Nez Perce, never in Nez Perce, Buck, never!"

Buck stood there and stared at me for several extremely silent seconds prior to speaking another word. "They came here, Billy, about twenty of 'em. They came in fact to get you late at night, in surprise like fashion, about two in the morning. I know you were in Spokane that night, or many more of 'em would have died. I know that full well, Billy."

"All right, Buck. You've made your diplomatic point. Now please continue with the damned murder story, the tale of Frank Onaben."

"When they surrounded the house with the lanterns and hoods, they called out to all in the house to come out, to come out unarmed and no one would be hurt."

"You say they had hoods on like some kind of racist Klan guys out to hang their 'red rigger' in good old 1930's style'?"

"Yes, they were spotted as hooded, and they were all trying to cover their identities. Reed was sure that Frankie knew each of 'em just by their voices and the shape and color of their shaded eyes."

"So, what happened, Buck? Tell me exactly what happened next, according to Reed?"

"There was approximately twenty men and they were quite tight around the house, but Reed did explain that at the northwest corner of the structure, to the side, there was an escape route. Next move, Frankie darts out between the men and he knocks one for a loop and smashes the other in the jaw with his rifle butt, killing him instantly."

"Who was the murder victim? Do you know who the man was, his name?

"As of this time, we have nothing. Not his name, nor his body, nor in fact, have we uncovered any physical evidence of any part of this confrontation. So continuing, Frank broke towards the granite and the bushes and as he jumped just clear of the crowd, at that point a shot rang out, and he was hit pretty bad in the center of the left calf muscle."

"He must have slowed down due to the intense bleeding. That right, Buck?"

Buck shifted his head in another direction looking up into the night sky taking a short breath before speaking again. He knew the words in his mouth prior to uttering 'em.

"The men pursued Frankie up some gully and down again. They went up there towards the north part of Paradise where it crosses Rye Ridge Road to Deer Creek."

"They bring out most of their dogs or horses, or did they just pursue him on foot all together?"

"No, in fact they knew they did have some dogs and old Hadley Williams was the handler; we know that much."

Hadley Williams used those bastard dogs 'a his on many a pursuit, never thought he'd bring them down on Frank. Never would think that, Buck, not in a thousands suns."

"Funny things happen to men when they're pushed by other men and sweetened to believe things which help motivate them to become both ugly and blind."

"White men have a dark history 'a those kind a things happening to 'em, but we can't let 'em off so easily, Buck. They hunted down my brother, my friend, like he was a wounded elk!"

"Now, Billy, I'm not here telling you this stuff so you can take particular and singular revenge out on these men. I'm telling you the truth as I've heard it and I want you to listen, you hear?"

Buck looked wide-eyed at me as he always did when he was making one of his major political points, but this time it was very hard for me to listen, very hard! I felt certain things inside me, which I hadn't felt since losing two friends in a booby-trapped foxhole just north of Da Nang, Vietnam. All of my internal guts burned, sizzled my every organ, starting at the spleen, ending up at the larynx.

Next, I really concentrated on Buck's green eyes, waiting for him to spew out the next few words. "All right, Billy, you ready for me to finish, or do you just want to sleep on what I've already said?"

"No, Buck, you continue, but I think I pretty much know the rest of the story, and I know where they eventually found him."

"You know that he fought them quite courageously through the back canyons and the deep gulches crisscrossing from ridge to ridge back- tracking all the way. Unfortunately, he moved too slowly and the faster group managed to surround him in a semi-open crater area. Your brother Frank slipped out again and headed towards old Paradise Cemetery, that old tiny plot of hallowed ground off North Rye Ridge Road. He took up a position with his seasoned army ensign carbine and a box of ancient shells and waited. First the dogs came at him. He killed three before the fourth got to his good arm."

"Did he get the fourth dog at that point or what?"

"Yes, he did. He did it with a large Indian fishing knife, but the dog apparently ripped into a good chunk of his left arm close to the shoulder blade. At that point, men began weaving between the old head stones and flashlights were seen pointing in every direction, just pointing everywhere."

"Did he kill any more of them? Did he shoot at the flashlights?"

"Again, let me emphasize one thing here. He was pretty well surrounded by the twenty men and he was crawling through the headstones. He did manage to shoot two men in the legs and stop their pursuit. He shot and killed two other men, the story goes, before the mass of cowards got to him. He was hit in the upper thigh and couldn't run anymore. It was a hell of a bloody mess up there according to Reed. Other than Frank, we found no other bodies, not even the dog's bodies were found. Best guess; they dragged them away and buried them."

You're planning a massive forensic search up there I hear. Did you find a lot of blood or evidence of a bloody fight?"

"Yes, they couldn't hide the blood. It was everywhere, even splattered on tree bark. No doubt there was a brutal fight before they put the fifty-some bullets in him."

"You're telling me they put over fifty rounds in my brother's body before he died?"

"Indeed. They put fifty-five bullets in his body, which one actually killed him, who knows, or one could say they shot him dead fifty-five times."

"They couldn't kill him quite enough so they had to puncture his body with fifty-five holes. When do you figure I can pick him up, Buck. I'd like to take him out there and bury him the old way."

"You can get him in a few days, after the forensic boys and coroner do their job. Then there's the coroner's report."

"No Buck. Do not do a full examine. No complete autopsy. Do only a cursory examination. You know full well what he died from. Tell 'em it's the damn Indian's religion or something. I don't want the body damaged beyond its current poor state; my brother's body cannot be spoiled any further. You hear me, Buck?"

We crossed eyes in deep peculiar silence before he spoke again, and this time Buck knew what I wanted. "All right. Let me make a call the morgue and I'll stop anything more they might have thought to do beyond your family request."

"You will repeat my request to them, won't you, Buck? I'm asking you to do this as an old friend, and now my friend is the law in Wallowa County."

"Now, Billy, I don't want you tracking anyone on your own. Please honor my request. I need you to help me finish this thing. 'Bout time for it all to end."

"Do exactly what I want, Buck, and after I bury my brother, I'll join you and your law, so we can finish this thing as you say. I do want to be part of the finish!"

"You will be part of it, my old friend, but you must listen to me prior to our last pursuit on this thing, all right?"

"Right. You have some of 'em in jail already don't you, Buck?"

"Yes, we have eight suspects in the county jail at the moment; eight men who were out there that night."

"Where's the rest? Do you know where the rest are? Do you have any idea where the rest are, Buck?"

"One man skipped the state and went to Seattle, and two others were spotted in Boise, Idaho. The rest are holed up in a massive log lodge just north of Robert's Butte up at Elk's Creek somewhere."

"You say they're holed up in a large log lodge up Elk Creek? Did I hear that right?"

"Yes, you heard me correctly. At this point there's no escape. Both the state and the county boys are there, and the feds have come in to help cut it off. At this point there's no route out."

"Heard that before, Buck. I've heard that many times before."

The sun was low that day as it doused the trees in shooting shadows. The wilderness was always Frank's. He was a man attuned to both current times and the past. My brother was a man, he was a man from the top of his head to his narrow feet, every horse he broke, every woman he tamed, in all ways, he was always a man. I put my brother up in the old Sioux way facing him into the setting sun, his face caught by the last streaking shadows before full night. I checked the support poles

215

and then doused the body in kerosene watching the oil soak into the bed of straw I built for him. I gave him to the Great Father, his spirit to soar with the many great spirits who've passed. I waited for sounds of the forest which he loved, the sounds of animals he wanted to be part of, animals he was part of and now forever. I thought of all the ancient beings, both two legged and four legged, that had passed before him, and tears flowed from my eyes. I thought of the devoured land that once was this place and would someday again become this place, and Frank would be there with them when it all came around. I backed off as the fire burned. It was an immense fire that consumed both my brother's body and the night itself. His essence was an imposing spirit, you see, and the dark sky knew it.

thirty-eight

Will A. Carson

"You know, I loved my brother, loved him more than just a brother. Miles was so much more than a brother; fact is he was the one who raised me. He did all he could his whole life to keep me straight. He kept me outta jail. I just don't believe Miles was killed the way they reported it. No sir, don't believe it, not for a horsehair of a minute. My brother knew all these backwoods' roads night and day. He traveled 'em; drove through 'em in all kinds of hard weather and everything in between. Old Pete Moss and my brother were the best eastern county sheriffs these parts will ever see, period. Thing about each of 'em was that they're men, nothing in between. Well, old Pete's still alive, no past tense there, but Miles should be remembered as a very strong man. That guy's the best lawman these damned mountains will ever know. For more than thirty years, Miles T. served the people of this county as well as possible; best he could! The man never swayed an inch and rarely said 'no'; and he always did as the judges said. Miles served the people unwaveringly. Yes, he gave himself fully to all the citizens of Wallowa County."

Will was being interviewed by Art Bell who was writing it all down in his notebook. "This personal interview, Will, is a kind of memorial thing; so don't be afraid to tell me how you feel. Feel free to tell me personal stories about you and your brother. The rest we have on record. I can pull out a vast number of personal stories. We got a crop of arrests on record that Miles T. was involved in during the last thirty years. Believe me, we got a lot of stuff," bragged Art Bell.

Will continued. "My brother knew Buckhorn Springs' viewpoint and he knew it well. We hunted up there many times, Elk in fact. Hunted up there many times right near Cherry Creek. At least fifty times, we camped up there. Miles understood that area too well, Art. So, unless he was stoned drunk, no quote here please, there is no way he could have driven off that two-thousand-foot granite cliff to those jutted up impaling rocks below. There's just no way! The body was real burnt up, in fact, 'cept for the teeth there wasn't a lot of other identification on him. Anyone find that two-caret sapphire and gold ring on him? That was quite a gem; wished my kid got it. The ring was never found, was it?

"No, and as a matter of fact, I know the ring you mean. I always admired it; but, I never did talk to Miles without looking at that magnificent ring."

"Right. So no matter how much you or Buck say or anybody else says, there is no way his ring could have been gone. There's also no way he could have driven off that ledge without help. I've requested a full autopsy report from Buck, a complete report on the corpse, no short cuts. I'll bet evidence or blood tests or DNA will show that old Miles was 'out' prior to his crashing death. I can assure you of that, Art."

"Will, they found two bottles of Red Label on the passenger side of Miles' truck. The truck was pretty blackened up and the coroner said the body had a great deal of alcohol in it, more than the normal amount. That's what he said."

"Art, as you know, my brother drank but he held his booze well. My brother could drink you and me under the table together and I'm at least twenty pounds bigger than he was. Scientifically, none of it makes sense.

"The coroner determined a three point five percent alcohol level on him prior to death. That's mighty drunk!"

"Coroner better find something else because that booze wasn't the cause of his death, not for one split second do I believe that. His friends, or friendly enemies, caused his death, pure and simple. There's no other way a man could get that close to Miles, believe me! If the coroner doesn't come up with more of an explanation, then Judge Buchanan wants Buck to bring a forensic specialist down from Portland to run my brother's body 'through it'.

"I've heard about the judge's order, Will, and I do know that they're flying Malcolm Cobb in from Portland tomorrow for the examination. Therefore, I guess you're going to get what you want."

"Good, and now you'll see that my brother's reputation will remain untarnished. He won't go down dirty and defamed like an old common drunk dying on the side of the road. Miles was a solid man, pure country lawman. He was the best man in this county and should never go down as a damned drunk!

"They did find your brother's law journal behind the seat along with his 44 Colt; yet all of it was burned up pretty bad. Maybe forensics can get something out of those pages."

"They've got their ways, Mr. newsman. They can find shit in nothing; now that's good forensics and I can assure you, Mr. Bell, they'll find solid evidence soon and some of it will get my brother cleared."

"Have you read the paper today or heard the local news?"

"No, if you haven't noticed, Mr. Bell, I'm grieving. I granted this interview only 'cause I'm waiting for my daughter, Tammy, to come along; her uncle's funeral is tomorrow."

"Yes, and I'm planning to be there with two of my assistants. We know there'll be many state and county dignitaries. By the way, just to let you know, we'll be there; and we'll be part of the event."

"I expect many people will come. We may just see the funeral of a lifetime. A great many people loved Miles T. Carson, and someone, Mr. Bell, will surely pay for his killing! I can assure you, sir, 'time'll come due'."

"Hope you're right, Will, if it proves to be a killing, then I hope you're right. This interview is over now. See you tomorrow at the funeral."

I nodded my head and watched the little man pack up his briefcase and sound gear. I knew the interview had exhausted me.

~~~

thirty-nine

Charles 'C' Marten

"Yes, I do remember that posse. A good many of the men were from the New Church same as me. I remember hunting that black man. I remember that chase pretty well. The game-hunt lasted a week, and the search was nothing like that 'running Negro,' nothing at all like him. That black man was a coy son-of-a-bitch trained in the military as a scout. He was tricky and he represented a real challenge, at least as a chase."

"Tell me a little more about it. Maybe we can draw some similarities. Maybe some people might just remember a little more. It makes a good story," encouraged Art M. Bell.

"It was my very first posse and my dad, J.C. Marten, who's dead now, used to talk about it all the time." I replied. "I remember very well, although I was young when we went on that hunt, very young."

"I've written several articles about that track over the years," said Art. "Is there anything in particular about it you'd like to share, something that might just add to the excitement?"

I remember my pause and how I took a couple of long moments to answer Bell. "Well, Art, at that time, my dad was also the president of the Umatilla State Bank. I had only been with the bank for about a year and a half when my dad got the call from Miles T. Carson to join in the damned chase. We closed the bank that day about two hours early. Dad didn't say much except, 'Close the bank now, get down to the house and put together some hunting gear and a couple of solid horses.' He was a man who rarely got fired up about anything, but that day, you could see it in his eyes. There was something special about the call from Miles T. Carson.

"Were you and your dad sworn in that day as deputies by Miles T. to track down that black man?" asked Art Bell.

"Dad and I were sworn in with the second group. Plus, old Jasso, dad's gelding, was acting strange and wouldn't load easy, so naturally, both dad and I were late to the party."

"You smile about that. It seems to me that you boys would have been the first to be sworn in, but you were part of the second group, is that right?" asked Bell.

"Yeah, old Jasso was acting strange and was refusing to load easy. We would still have been there first if it hadn't been for a stone in Jasso's hoof, which got stuck right next to the under-bone, and must have smarted against Jasso's flesh. Dad picked that rough stone out of Jasso's hoof and as soon as he did, that damned horse turned and kicked him right in the calf muscle. Nothing was broken, but dad had a lot of severe pain and it took about two hours for that swelling to go down. I asked dad if he still wanted to go, being that he was in all that pain. Do you know what he said? He said, 'No, it'll take a kick right in the balls from an old mule to keep this damned old son-of-a-bitch from running down this raping Negro we're chasing here.' Don't think I've ever seen J.C. Marten so damned angry as he was that day, and nothing short of death could have stopped that old man from attending that 'shoot'. Nothing."

"Why do you keep referring to the posse as a shoot? What exactly do you mean?" asked Art.

"Nothing really, Art, it was just an expression they used in those days; just a figure of speech like some of those missing words I used to use as an architect. You know dad used to say words changed their meaning just about the same speed as people's personalities."

"You sound like you were pretty fond of J.C.," Art said.

"Art, don't think I've ever been closer to another human except for Nathan Bork and the good Pastor Chrisp of the New Church."

"Can I quote you on that?" Bell asked.

"No, I don't want to be quoted on that. I got a sister who might not understand my exact meaning. Know what I mean, Art?"

"Sure, I think I know exactly what you mean. I'll kill that one. Let's try tying up the manhunt and get to our current search party."

"We got down to Union County at about 4:30 p.m. and it was bitter cold, just as the sun started passing shadows on the graying cloud cover nearby Umatilla National Forest mountain range. Some of that county down there was as rough as the Chesnimnus Creek area where we searched for the missing girl. We were in the fourth posse around Rock Creek Butte when we saw one of our men, Josh Adams. He took a 30-caliber bullet in the right thigh. Luckily it hit nothing critical. We knew that damned black man was one hell of a shot. You never should train black men to shoot 'cause there always comes a time those bastards'll change up and turn on you. Southerners were right about 'em you know. They had those black sons-of-bitches under their thumb, lock and key. That's the way they should all be treated."

"Your attitude couldn't exactly be considered modern on that subject," said Bell.

"Never said I was modern, but we're all solid Earth Christians with an eye on Jesus and the Lord Almighty. Get my point, Art?"

"Yes, I think I understand exactly where you're coming from here;" the conversation slowly digressed to last week's subject...the rigorous search for Kaelin.

forty

Buck Parrish
Battle of Robert's Butte

Nothing in my life, except for the firefights in Vietnam that I went through and was wounded, actually compared to the Battle of Robert's Butte. I recall driving back to Enterprise down Highway 3. Oh, it was about twenty miles from Robert's Butte to Enterprise, and that day it seemed to go on forever. Billy Onaben sat next to me dressed in his army green flack jacket and black-green camouflage pants. He stared out the window at the pitch-black forest and nothing passed by at the side of the road, nothing lit up except for an occasional birch reflecting the fog lights of the truck.

"Don't believe I'll ever track another man, Buck. My time for it ended at Robert's Butte. My brother, Frank's, death has been avenged. Yet, my friend, I feel 'blood falling on me' and the image of my fallen kinsman's body."

"I've been in battles, Billy, many brutal confrontations in the war, and never before have I experienced conflict with zealots primed and ready to die. The last time I saw anything like this was in Vietnam with a group of radical Montegard tribesmen who had been educated and reared by religion and tradition to die in and for battle. We, our government that is, took advantage of their backgrounds and used them for holy war, and gruesome attacks took place everyday using their fundamentalism as a wedge. What we heard about Charlie Marten's pep-rally at the New Wallowa Church of Christ must have been true. I've never seen twelve men so ready and willing to die as those around that lodge, not since Vietnam that is. Old Byron Frank was hit flat against his forehead by a thirty-ought-six round. The man looked like he'd been scalped by a lost tribe of Indians who butchered the job."

"They were ready for us, Buck, sons-of-a-bitches were well armed and they were plenty stored up for the fight. They were ready and had planned for the fight. I'm sure 'a that! Too many of 'em shooting at me from every direction, don't under-stand how I lived through it. Dr. Oliveson and Mr. Carter both had scopes, which must have been set improperly, or I wouldn't be talking to you now. Quite lucky I guess."

"If you're not with a weapon all the time, the weapon won't serve you well. My old 'Top' in the infantry would say that all the time."

"Maybe I was lucky to get a shot off at Oliveson just as he nicked me. That boy was directly involved in Kaelin's murder, you can bet on that. Losing him could never bother me."

"Billy, he was a lost man. That man was lost both in vision of himself and in his position and stance as an honorable church deacon. That bullet of yours in the neck was well placed. No way that son-of-a-bitch ever wanted to be taken alive, there's just no way!"

"That was a man who was scared to be taken alive. Death by police fire was the bravest way for the bastard to exit," said Billy.

I thought about it for a few seconds as I drove, so many men did choose to go that way. May have been a secret in their heads even to themselves, but I'd run across many who chose that death through the years. "Billy, you're probably right in what you're saying, but it cost us two good men to take that twelve out, and two fine men died in legal action just 'cause of Charles C. Marten and that mad and bloody church of his. There was two too many I'd say! We got too close to that place, Billy, 'cause it's evil. That place stirs darkness. We got to set upon destroying it like they'd condemn black-witch churches in the 1600s. What do you think Billy?"

"Don't really know what I think or feel now but I can easily say this, seems to me most of the perversity in that church is dead now; most of 'em are pretty dead."

"We never found Charles Marten picking through those mangled bodies did we? No one ever found the son-of-a-bitch's corpse. I got at least twenty men searching the bush for that bastard. You'd think we'd find him by now, Billy?"

"No I doubt that you'll ever find him there, Buck. Guys like him always avoid their deserved end."

"Got Nathan Bork in the gunfire. He died like a true believer. It took at least seven shots to kill him; sorry he was part

224

of it, lost a goodly number of neighbors and friends in that clash today, Billy."

"Bet you're pretty sorry it all came down to this, aren't you, Buck?"

"Yes, my friend. I never ever wanted it to come down this way. So many people dying, and for what?" asked Buck.

"Guess they died more or less for what they believed in like those thirty-nine Heaven's Gate whackies who died in California searching for some mythical comet. Remember in the news how those thirty-nine folks just committed some kind of mass suicide so they'd make it to the asteroid or meteor together? Buck, do you recall that? It was some five years back."

"Yes, I do remember that. But I could never believe for a moment that rock-solid citizens of our community would 'vote themselves out' just like that such as they did."

"Probably why old Miles T. Carson decided to end it like he did. That man was smart. He knew it was coming, I think, fact is, he knew it was coming, Buck!"

"After all, this is done I'll try to prove that Miles was neatly executed, as sure a death as any of the Robert's Butte twelve."

"It'll take a lot of work, Buck. Don't think you'll have the time or patience for it. Buck, don't you think it should all end here, my friend?"

"It won't end until I have Mr. Charles C. Marten in my grip. I recall grabbing the handle of my Colt 357 magnum, which had the same grip. I used to slap a hockey puck into the goal when I was about sixteen. Pushed those muscles tight then. Miles and I were very close for several years back in the early '80s. In fact both of us were divorced no more than a month apart and the two of us enjoyed some solid frolic time with a few of the local women."

"Is that when Miles got deep with Annabelle MacCrothers?"

"Yes. At the time, Annabelle was the sexiest horsewoman I'd ever seen. She was a young 'ball tweaker' for sure."

"She's still got one hell of a figure; not many men throw her out even in her fifties, I'd say."

"You're so right, Billy. Annabelle's still one fine-shaped woman with a quality heart to match. We've been good friends for a long time. She took the death of Miles kind of rough, don't think she ever really got over him, nor did he ever get over her, not really.

"Never slept with her, did ya, Buck?"

"No, Billy never did. Can't say I didn't have the urge many a time but it seemed better for me to stay away from that, and I don't actually know why."

"Maybe it was because of Miles. Maybe it was out of your respect for him?"

"Maybe, Billy. I don't really know. All I do know is as I've said before; she took Miles' death awfully hard. No one's seen her in town since he died."

I watched Billy turn to put his face in the truck window staring again at the passing trees brought bare in the headlights quickly jutting through them. "Yes, Billy, Annabelle MacCrothers is as charming a woman as a man could visit. She was smart, sexy, and one hell of a drinker and a dancer; now there was a fine dancer! I filled my mind at that point with the warmth of the friendship that Annabelle and I had shared for all those years. I glimpsed back to times she and Miles and I 'grouped up,' at times, Willa Shannon would come along; those, my friend, were some great times. Miles got as high on pure bourbon as any man I'd known; fact was one night he finally broke down and described a spiritual sex dance between him and Annabelle. They did the dance up somewhere near Mt. Howard. Now, maybe it's a coincidence, but Annabelle built her place up there; maybe it had something to do with that night with Miles. At least that's what Miles believed. Annabelle to this day is always a straight shooter about loving and she cared quite deeply 'bout Miles, did for years. They even talked about marriage at one time. Think they lived together for a couple of years; didn't ever work out as a marriage. However, neither of 'em suited the package.

In my head, I was rolling around the idea of going to see Annabelle up near Mt. Howard. I surely planned it many a time for the future but I never got there. Much as I wanted to, I never did get there, just got too damned busy. "Billy, do you think about Frankie much? Bet you do, aye?"

"Not supposed to, Buck, but I do all the time. For an Indian like me, nothing closer than your womb brother or sister. That's just part of our way. Frank was a pure man. That man was a fine *'spirit-life'*…loved horses and even loved people. He was an exceptional human being."

"That's about as good as one can expect to hear about a man in this life, Billy. If people say that about me when I pass, that's about the finest memorial a man could have. Those words themselves are a memorial!"

I could see tears form in the shadows of Billy's eyes, never saw a tear near Billy before. This one was about his brother.

"My brother will always be in my heart, Buck. He will remain a deep muscled part of my spirit-being. He guards me. My brother shall always be partnered in my life."

"Do you believe that, Billy? Do you really believe that; what you're saying?"

"Yes, Buck, I do. No way in the world would I have lived through the battle of Robert's Butte unless he was at my side. I will not die until I'm old, Buck. When one's brother dies, the other lives for a long time."

I smiled at Billy, lost in his words; I guess I couldn't say much at that point. There was something in my throat regarding Miles and Nathan Bork, two friends dead. Now there were just useless memories of good men devoured by worms. "Did you ever flash on Nathan Bork? Do you picture anything about him at all, Billy?"

"I recollect something about him, Buck. Fact is, I spent a good deal of time helping him out at county jail some years back. Nathan was one hell of a lawman then, Buck. Being a warden's a real tough job, that's for sure."

"That job is beyond tough, Billy. A job like that gets the core of a man, starts to crawl inside a man like one of those

African brain worms that crawls through your ears and drives you insane. Life in those jails, fact is, life in any tightly closed place with people that hate you and the place being 'tight' with those kind of people every single day, drives itself into your body like those brain worms. After a while, even a good lawman such as Nathan Bork, even a good lawman cracks and warps. I thought about all those years I've known Nathan, all those years and all those times spent together, and today most of the men I grew up with are dead! What in the living hell was this all about, Billy? Every day of my life I'll ask myself this question, my friend. What was this bloody evil thing all about? Was it about Kaelin, Billy? Or was it about something more?"

"We lost too many, my brother. We lost Frank and Nathan Bork, Miles T. Carson, and Byron Frank, why did they all die Buck? All in the last couple of months."

"Somehow all of it came to a head. For all of us in the community, it came to a sudden head. Everything we knew or everything we thought we knew disappeared in a gut-soaked bloody mess, all in the last sixty days. Governor McCullum never should have sent in those two National Guard gun-ships. Bad medicine for everyone involved I'd say. I knew Tom McCullum in Vietnam. He was a captain and anytime he thought a situation was critical, he'd call in those gun ships. Tom's the kind of man knows nothing different today than he did in the war; so he's always calling in the gun ships; always! To those kinds of men, the battles there to be won at any price by whatever means necessary. There's not much honor in anything anymore, Billy; not much honor left in this world."

"The six men who were left to fight in the last assault tried to fight those choppers head on, but there was too much fire power coming too fast. Watched it tear the whole damned lodge to shreds, a 50-caliber's a gruesome weapon against flesh, Buck; terrifying!"

"It was a down right abortion, Billy, and we both know it. It was the newest slaughter of Christians, annihilation by law, period. A lot a people die 'by law' these days, Billy. What's the term 'execution by police'? Something in that, Billy, especially here, right here and now!"

I watched Billy staring out the window at the streets in downtown Enterprise. It looked as though the whole damned town was sleeping while the law was out there disposing of its primary citizens. There were citizens of distinction not just rabble entering in and out of town. They weren't just tourists seeking a piece of 'country life'.

"The men chose to stand their ground, Buck. They took their positions and held it and paid the price for it."

"They truly believed, and so they positioned themselves for a better world to come. The choice was just as much put into their heads as no choice was."

"Whatever drove them there put the law in a special circumstance of its own."

"Our 'stand', Billy, was purely an arbitrary one, and the whole damned mess at Robert's Butte just got out of control. It was totally out of hand and it erupted. That's what it did like some enormous volcano."

"Maybe, and quite possibly, it went exactly the way those twelve deacons scripted it to go."

"Maybe it went precisely the way those church elders wanted it to go; no evidence cleanly evaporated, end of entire story!"

Dropping Billy off at his truck in town, I watched him tote his weapons. They looked to me as if they were three of four times heavier than they actually were. He was an exhausted man lifting his guns to the rack behind the seat of the truck cab. I kept my lights on Billy so he could see what he was doing. My mind was stuck in those beams hazed across his body in the cold darkness of the early morning hours. Enterprise had always been a cold dark place in those early dew hours. It had been that way for the last thirty-five years of my life; I could say that and be sure I wasn't lying to any part of myself. It took me quite a while to come out of that staring, sure seemed to be deeply stuck in my own head.

The events of that day at Robert's Butte shook me deep to the core. Nothing I'd known then and in the many weeks before, nothing in my law-enforcement years had ever occurred like Robert's Butte, nor had anything ever been so powerful as this odd series of bloody events. It seemed like a tale of far-out fiction that no one could have directly been involved in, and yet dark blood stains of neighbors and friends were on my hands.

I sat there and watched Billy drive north up towards Paradise, just sat there in my truck watching and staring out at the clear brisk sky. For at least two more hours, I stayed there waiting in the cold. I was somewhat lost until I got a chill and headed home.

forty-one

Sister Mary Espanola
Article in the *Daily Enterprise*
December 14, 1999

The recent human slaughter at Robert's Butte should be an outrage to all within our community! Twelve men and three police officers were killed because our beloved Governor Tommy McCullum ordered in Marine Corps-style helicopter gunships to settle matters. Today, little is left of the old lodge at Robert's Butte. Most of the evidence of the destruction, if there was any left at all, was within the walls of the nonexistent compound which was further blasted into nothingness by a raging hell fire, which took place when the battles ceased. No apparent hard evidence exists now of the possible murders of three of our local teenage daughters. Additionally, Kaelin Jones, who disappeared two years ago and was never found; may just be another 'kill' subject. The slaughter at Robert's Butte may resemble some kind of master plan. Most, if not all, of the possible witnesses and culprits in the teen disappearances were themselves killed at Robert's Butte Lodge last week. Even my old friend Sheriff Miles T. Carson was brutally killed in a terrible rural county auto crash in early December 1999.

All the good citizens of this fine county must be personally outraged both by the needless deaths and the unthinking slaughter of our citizens, and the loss of any credible evidence to investigate the mess. So far, it's been proved conclusively that our young teenage girls have been viciously exploited for sex and other unspeakable uses right here in our own county! Other girls like Kaelin Jones have been missing for two or more years and most likely appear dead with their bodies scattered to the four winds by animals running around in our forests. Who is responsible for these catastrophes? Is it not prudent for our authorities to bring forward their evidence and answer many of the questions about the disappearances of these teens and the cults that destroyed them? Many churchmen lose their way as has happened in all churches since the beginning of the first millennium and before. Good churchmen and women who have twisted into 'cult pariah' whose sole goal is 'gratification' on the body of the innocent, these must be brought to trial and exposed.

Today, the truest leader of the New Wallowa Church of Christ, Senior Deacon Charles C. Marten, has vanished along with two-point-five million dollars, which somehow he managed to steal and 'suitcase' for his trip to unknown places. Some of this has to surprise and shock some of you. But please take the time to read it unless you're opposed to a nun writing it.

Mr. Charles C. Marten was one of our leading citizens and a pillar of committee authority in his own church. Mr. Marten was considered a man of sound values and business reputation. Fact is that many of the readers of this article are personally familiar with him. Mr. Marten was considered an outstanding Wallowa citizen.

It has been reported by good solid authority that Mr. Marten was the leader of the twelve deacons who fell at Robert's Butte. FBI agents, Jeb Hirsh and Shawna Thore, have uncovered further evidence that Mr. Marten ran two sub-cults at the New Wallowa Church of Christ. He both managed the sex rights of young runaways and was intimately involved in the 'lost girl' car facility operated by his same church. It has been additionally discovered that Mr. Marten was deeply involved in a sacrifice killer group that all of the killed twelve deacons of the church were also intimately embroiled in. Also, it seems that Robert's Butte may have saved the state and the county untold monies in trial and jail costs.

What, dear citizens, has happened to our magnificent way of life? It was once a way of life purer than the one we're currently living in this Wallowa County.

When I joined the Catholic church as a wayward young woman, I went into it to devote my life to Wallowa and the loving care of young girls. I did everything possible to shelter my girls from the horrors, the wrath which has risen concretizing my worst nightmares. The blatant escapades by good people at the New Wallowa Church, run by at least two notorious sub-cults with Mr. Marten as leader, has poisoned any possible cover the world should share with its young.

Where were the rest of the citizens of Wallowa? Why was it that not one of us reported anything to the authorities?

Were those authorities too corrupt in people's minds and hearts to do anything about any of it anyway? There are too many questions in our community without answers and certainly there are elements in the community who'd rather sweep all of it under the old proverbial table. These questions and the deaths of three girls with the disappearance of a fourth, these questions deserve further hard investigation and all of us must support these probes. It is our duty as humans, as citizens of this community to seek hard and long and to uncover all the truths about these recent horrific events. We must get ourselves fully behind Sheriff Parrish and his deputies in the continued uncovering of the details which lead to the butchery at Robert's Butte and the ruthless murders of at least three of our young women.

We must be relentless in our search for the truth. Naked truth itself must be put on trial by the Hon. Judge H.A. Buchanan and all the law in the county that he commands. I demand this search as a citizen of Wallowa County and as a human being who cares. Many of us care about young women and have compassion, not some twisted and contorted exploiting passions! It is almost impossible to imagine your young ones taken and fed to wild jungle beasts in the name of the holy one.

Let the obligation be Judge Buchanan's and the state's to uncover the real truth and expose that to our citizens so that nothing like this can ever happen again! Let our truths resemble the South African Truth Commission headed by Archbishop Desmond Tu Tu. Let it be a trial to unearth the vestiges of veracity with no further indictments, just exposure of truth.

In summing up, we must give the law its time to reach conclusions on all the items I've mentioned, especially the uncovered truth. We must allow the law its space to close in on Charles C. Marten and his companion, Stella Frank, who both seem to have neatly vanished with the two-point-five-million dollars that Marten embezzled from the Bank of Wallowa. (Mrs. Frank was the sometimes wife of Deputy Barney Frank, killed at Robert's Butte.)

I have worked and grown up in this county for most of my life, and a scar on this place is an imprint on all of us. This deep mark will affect us every day we live here and it will be difficult to forget. So then, we must find a way to mend many of the wrongs, some of the grief caused by past and present groups and institutions within our beloved county. This, dear brothers and sisters of Wallowa, is the only way to heal those sharp mental wounds freshly inflicted on our collective citizen psyche.

With Admiration for the good citizens of Wallowa County,
Sister Mary C. Espanola;
Inmaha Runaway Center For Wayward Girls.

forty-two

<u>Diary of Jillian Doud</u>
December 25, 1999

Christmas day was a time for prayer and joyful meditation to some, but for me there was still great pain regarding the indescribable deaths of three young girls. After the siege at Robert's Butte and the deaths of most of the remaining cult deacons or 'The Demons of Death', my heart goes out to all of the young girls these men killed. Here, I can describe without remorse and recount what has happened to my community during the last two years. For me, at this point in my time, it seems that life itself has been turned topsy-turvy, right-side up; every which way except the way I thought was right. More than that, it seems there are few out there who listen, and even fewer who much care. Some care if it meets some personal or financial criteria for them. In this community, in less than two years, there have been twenty-five people killed brutally and some were even grotesquely killed.

The leader of this murdering spree is Mr. Charles C. Marten, and he has completely vanished with the deputy's wife along with over two million dollars of stolen money. Charles C. Marten has many friends I'm told, and he has many cult brothers and sisters in several of the surrounding counties who'd help him get out of the country if they could. Imagine normal people smuggling a mass sex killer out of the countries from Umatilla to Union, to Grant and finally, to Harney County?

From the channeling mouth of Millie Roberts has come the tale of his note-worthy escape along with Stella Frank. From what I've been told, the two of them sit on some wonderful remote island off the coast of Indonesia eating, drinking, fornicating, and devouring 'blood money' stolen from the state bank.

Believe it or not, Millie Roberts has seen this. She passed this information through the voices of Kaelin Jones and Tilly Wallis. They've seen Marten and Stella Frank, and they know what island they're on, exactly, yet to no avail because no one will listen, period. Oh yes, I'll listen and Annabelle MacCruthers will listen; yet we are not heard and we are viewed far less seriously than any other citizen by the rest of our normal community. Is a community ever really normal after something like this happens to it, ever?

The fact is we do what we know, and what we believe. We, at least do exactly what is truth for us. Amos T. Blackburn and Dr. Oliveson killed Kaelin and Tilly. Still, all or most of the evidence was corrupted by insiders and those that wanted to point that evidence in another direction. According to the black message coming through Millie, Ms. Tilly was raped, beaten, sodomized, and slowly and brutally killed. Kaelin had no better fate except they finally strangled her after beating, sodomizing, and raping her, not a pleasant way for a young girl to leave this world. In addition to all of the above, Kaelin was stabbed forty-one times, Millie claims. Anyway, it was Amos Blackburn who was the twisted horrific young-woman serial killer. For years, his friends and supporters hid his true identity from the community. According to new evidence, the FBI will expose seven other girls who have been savaged unmercifully by Blackburn. It's a good thing that Sheriff Buck Parrish rightfully killed the man. Good that his nightmarish ways were finally put to an everlasting end, for the sake of our county.

The final FBI investigation will substantiate everything channeled through Millie's mouth. Shawna Thore and Jeb Hirsch have assured Mr. Parrish of that truth. According to Millie, conclusive forensic evidence will show the complete and verified pattern of these heinous crimes. The National Security Agency will work with INTERPOL to discover the exact where 'bouts of Charles C. Marten and Stella Frank. Marten was conclusively found to be involved in the cover-up death of Kaelin Jones as well as two other girls. As it turns out, Kaelin was segmented in a special sanctuary prayer room in the New Wallowa Church of Christ.

"She was literally butchered in a quiet sacred room in one of the retreat marriage-saving 'come together' cabins above and behind one of the main church buildings," Millie said.

In the name of Jesus, so many inhumanities have been committed, and yet so gloriously loving and peaceful was our Lord. In spirit, Kaelin and Tilly came to the three of us many times to relay their stories, to decry their loss, to communicate

Steve Dreben

our loss. Finally, my words that are written here are being systematically exposed as 'truth' in the disappearances of these two girls and the seven or eight others…a definite count we may never know. All of these young ones have been savagely obliterated from this earth by Blackburn and his pack of craven cult monsters.

Marten and Stella Frank will be found. All of the rest of the original cult members are dead. Any other deacons or church members associated with these killings who might be hiding within the deacon groups will be discovered. Local citizens will eventually burn the New Wallowa Church of Christ; all the unholy buildings will be leveled. A county park will replace the church grounds and buildings. Nothing will remain of this 'false body' but the trees and the grass landscape. A plaque will be put up on the site and it will say: "Humble County Park; A Peaceful Place."

Another large memorial will be placed in the north corner of the park and it will read thus; according to Millie Roberts: "THESE GROUNDS ARE DEDICATED TO THE MEMORY OF OUR LOST AND STRUCK DOWN YOUNG WOMEN: KAELIN JONES AND TILLY WALLIS."

The memorial plaque will read in small letters as follows:

These grounds are additionally dedicated to the eight other fallen young women and the thousands of others lost to vicious unsolved crimes. It is further honored by thousands of other world victims who pay the price for the twisted deeds of the few who commit such heinous deeds. SO WALK THESE GROUNDS and feel for the souls of those that were innocent and are now gone. Remember to listen to those who call out truth and know it when it is spoken. It might make a difference!"

These combined memories of all the killings in the communities and the shootings and deaths have scarred my soul. My good heart still bleeds for the innocents who have been taken from us. It is my wish that all those who committed these piteous crimes be castigated and sanctioned for their deeds, now and forever. This is my wish as a sister of LOVE'S eternal spirit!

Jillian Douds

forty-three

Arthur F. Bell

As an experienced newsman, I had to think of a way to bring some closure to both the town and the county after the death of so many of our rooted endemic citizens. I've written for newspapers and news-organizations for thirty-seven years; nothing like this situation had ever happened in this county or in any other that I know of, at least not during all of my experiences. Twenty-five people had died violently and literally. The county was littered with corpses. The county mind was consumed with a never-ending cache of dead, and the bodies were a constant reminder of the carnage, which had taken place during the last three months in Wallowa.

Articles have appeared in newspapers and on the Internet across the country, and probably even across the world, reacting to the deaths in Wallowa County Oregon. Some of this related in an archaic way to the stories coming out of the Old West. It was as if we were caught up in some time warp or another 'dime novel'. Most of our semi-intelligent citizens had either written some commentary in the local press or had been interviewed by national magazines or national news organizations. Yet nothing seemed to have touched home. After reading some of the local personal reports and articles by people like Sister Mary Espanola, I decided to extend my Radio One News Show to an hour format. I even got sponsorship to support me. Additionally, I decided to publicize the show for two weeks before starting and then the plan was to invite selected guests to debate the murder of Kaelin right there live on my new show.

The disappearance of so many other children both locally and nationally was not just a parochial problem; it was a national one, maybe even one of an international concern. I did significant research every night before ever attempting to air the show 'live' and it was very important that I did air it live. In the publicity, I included an enhanced written statement on the show's participants but my commentary and editing never cut important and true information nor guests' quotes and self-content.

239

Sister Mary Espanola was the first guest. Sheriff Buck Parrish was the second, Judge Buchanan the third, Jeb Hirsch of the FBI fourth, and Teddy Cochran a rancher/builder and our state representative currently running for congress was the fifth guest. I called the show 'A Sense of Justice' because that is exactly what the community needed, to get an impression for healing. It was all set up as a type of 'healing need' thing, which was creeping through our very air currents everywhere I traveled within our small valley towns. It all reminded me of Bishop Tu Tu's African Truth Commission, the Commission on Truth and Reconciliation, a kind of purging of truth for all the dead- the dead of course who couldn't come back, yet there must be somewhere some sense of truth/justice or something out there worth coming to grips with. There had to be something! Let me play the tape of the show unedited, there is no doubt it had an effect, it thoroughly cauterized the wounds I suspect. So let's start the audiotape of the show, which again, I called 'A Sense of Justice'.

After introducing everyone to my guests, we'll start the tape with Sheriff Buck Parrish.

"What is there about the case of Kaelin Jones and Tilly Wallis which forced you to pursue the culprits so feverishly?"

Sheriff Parrish: "Well, Art, let's focus the discussion on the real reason for us being here. What went wrong in Wallowa County and what happened to Charles C. Marten, Mrs. Stella Frank, and the two-and-a-half-million dollars they stole form the community."

Jeb Hirsch: "A community must be able, no matter how small it is, it must be able to control its own activities and trusted provincial personnel."

Sister Mary Espanola: "A civic group which refuses to see darkness when that type of horror is confronting them is one that will pay a price for its laxness. Wallowa has paid a dear price, my friends! Seven precious young women have been brutally assaulted and murdered and no one caught the 'bubble of that evil' breaking in time."

Teddy Cochran: "A small community like ours must trust the hard-working people working within it to do the right thing in times of stress. That's a civil community's responsibility and it's also an individual personal concern."

Judge Buchanan: "Sure it is, Teddy. However, the community itself must open its eyes sometimes. As you know, I lost a son in this mess as many of us have. The law itself cannot stop these types of 'moral intrusions' run amuck. The law alone can't halt it without proper citizen support."

Jeb Hirsch: "Your position is well taken, Judge. We did have a solid enough law group in this county who by every shred of evidence was uncorrupted."

Sister Mary Espanola: "That's not actually the point here. The point is that several murders and/or disappearances went on for years before anyone noticed or cared to notice, because the girls involved in all this stuff were tainted as 'poor runaways.' When prostitutes are killed on the streets in many of our big city streets in such ghastly ways, how often do the authorities catch the killers?"

Sheriff Parrish: "You have a good point, Sister. There is the perception here of moral evil, which the society has embedded in itself regarding certain classes of victims."

A.F. Bell: "So is what we are saying here in order to clarify, certain victims are not worth as much in society's mind as in others?"

Sheriff Parrish: "That's correct. And any solid law officer will tell you that in private, certain victims take precedence over others. Whores are generally near the bottom, if they're even there at all. It's sort of a massive sense of profiling the genetic victim."

Sister Mary Espanola: "Question. Where then do these girls fit in? Or, are they automatically somewhere near the bottom?"

Jeb Hirsch: "For the FBI, children are never near the bottom. Even our computers stack them at the top, but we do have a massive number of missing children nationwide. It's almost epidemic!"

Sister Mary Espanola: "So according to the FBI and Mr. Hirsch here, the numbers control the levels of involvement, not the nature of the killings nor the tactile evidence presented."

Jeb Hirsch: "Seems like the Sister is trying to put words into my mouth. So let me clearly repeat what I said earlier. The FBI nationwide has a massive number of these types of cases. Some of them are real; but many of the children reported missing are really missing. It's difficult to use finite resources on loose evidence and in many cases, just hearsay."

Judge Buchanan: "By the time all this stuff gets to court, it had better be supported by good documentation even when a child is killed. Yes, even then, without strong evidence, we must tough it out. There's too many cases, too little time."

Teddy Cochran: "The state has fine laws on the books and we have powerful police reinforcement of those laws, yet it remains very true that without substantial documentation or effective evidence pursuance of certain cases, it becomes impossible."

A.F. Bell: "Let's get back to the murders of Kaelin and Tilly by local citizens performing those killings from within a 'morally higher' group."

Judge Buchanan: "After an analysis, a brief analysis of the cases by my staff and interns, it's hard to imagine that any citizen or pre-legal inquiry could have been duly accomplished in these murder cases. There was in fact never enough legal indication to begin an investigation into the civil or church authorities connected with the two cases. We only had the scanted rumblings of psychic searchers and those who record, assist, and confront them."

Sister Mary Espanola: "Your statement, Judge, seems slightly unfair. Along with the psychic evidence, there was additional hard legal data produced which was sidestepped, lost, or immorally misplaced by certain county personnel in the legal system. Remember, we have two specific dead legal personnel involved here. We have Deputy Byron Frank and civilian Deputy Amos T. Blackburn."

Jeb Hirsch: "It is true that the FBI did an analysis of hard bone evidence not originally viewed as animal. These bone fragments were analyzed several times. The analysis was done only after they were formally received and that was one and one-half years after the murders of Kaelin Jones and Tilly Wallis. The other so-called evidence Sister Mary talks about was never received for forensic analysis, nor was it received by Sheriff Parrish until eighteen months after the original non-human bone material was handed in to the authorities. Hard evidence must be received!"

A.F. Bell: "Was there any proper documentation of the original finger-bone evidence handed in by two of our citizens who uncovered it as part of what you call their psychic search?"

Sheriff Parrish: "Deputy Frank obtained this bone evidence. The actual nature of this evidence was never determined, but this evidence was lost or misplaced two days after it was formally received by the department."

Teddy Cochran: "Sheriff, did this not seem somewhat unusual to you? That in this case, didn't it seem strange for some good solid evidence to disappear? After all, it was the first evidence lost from the police lock-down vault."

Sheriff Parrish: "First of all, it's not totally bizarre that a piece of evidence is misplaced or for it to disappear. Every police department in the country can statistically sight similar things that have happened in their lock-down evidence facilities."

Sister Mary Espanola: "Buck, the misplaced evidence gathered and delivered by the psychic group, as you call them, misses the point. At every level in this legend-like investigation with its search and chase elements included, and all the confrontation with evidence reality. The fact is that the entire struggle seems terribly garbled. In this matter, even the truth seems to have been exaggerated because of the circumstances in the extended cases. Either law enforcement was eventually proved to be corrupted, or more importantly, citizens refused to believe the complicity levels of good Christian people attending and belonging to a solid church organization."

Jeb Hirsch: "I've worked for and with the FBI and its labs for twenty years. During that time, we've run into several kindred cases, ones similar to the one Sister Mary describes here. But let me say this, never in my years have I confronted all of the conditions that lead to vast corruption of the legal system as in this case. We have citizen and church compliance and outright public blindness on apparent major legal system cracks, which have happened here in Wallowa County. The evidence was here in our own mitts; with in fact more than normal documentation as post-examination of that evidence has shown, and yet there was a breakdown."

A.F. Bell: "If it was all here or somewhat here at times, why didn't anyone admit that it was here? Why didn't they do anything tangible to expose its existence?"

Sheriff Parrish: "Here's where we get into belief; no one wanted to see it. No one would believe the evidence if they saw it and there were those who refused to accept the base reality of obvious evidence. It's part of the group seeing, or in this particular case, not seeing the flying saucer nor the planet Uranus flying overhead just above the earth. It's just hanging there so one refuses to believe truth. The point is the same, it's there like ink on your fingers from a leaky pen but citizens turn away from the reality of acceptance."

A.F. Bell: "I like that theory, Sheriff Parrish. A group hypnosis, inner rejection except for belief as to what is acceptable to the mind as belief."

Sister Mary Espanola: "It's not true that deep blind belief like this accords lies and unseeing in itself."

Judge Buchanan: "As a nun in the Catholic church, you may be one of the least likely of persons to disuse the concept of 'belief as blindness.' Your church itself has been teaching absolute dimness to idols since the first coming of Jesus Christ, two thousand years ago."

Sister Mary Espanola: "That statement may be somewhat true but our church also teaches faith with understanding, not total attachment to symbol, especially within my order of Jesuits. We are perhaps the most liberated group in the church when it comes to blind faith or concealed belief."

A.F. Bell: "A point well taken, Sister Mary, but let's get back to the discussion at hand rather than fight the impossible fight of religious faith and belief within an institutional structure. Sheriff Parrish do you have a comment regarding the details of the murders, the cover-up and the escape of Charles Marten with two-point-five-million dollars of our citizens' hard earned funds?"

Sheriff Parrish: "I can only speak as to what I've heard and read as recorded evidence regarding the murder and cover-up, and of course, Mr. Marten. Actually, Interpol still searches for Marten and his companion, and in fact, Mr. Hirsch can give you a lot more on that sacred subject than I."

Sister Mary Espanola: "Is it true that an out-band or an in-band of deacons at the New Church of Christ Wallowa was responsible for child rape, child molestation, sexual depravity and child disappearance, not to mention forcing young women into sexual bondage and pornographic favors?"

Sheriff Parrish: "Yes. A group of deacons, evidently led by Umatilla Bank President, Charles C. Marten, were proven responsible for all the illegal and reprehensible acts you've accurately outlined."

Judge Buchanan: "After several months of shifting through piles of evidence, both forensic and non-forensic, several solid conclusions were reached regarding the New Church of Christ Wallowa. The deacons at the church were undeniably involved with most of it. Much is still unknown about the case. Also much still remains unproven. It seems that for many years, inside paranoia and group paranoiac activities took place. This surface band of deacons and a deeper band of deacons had subverted hones spirit and quest within the legitimate Christian walls of the New Church. Studying the mounds of documents regarding the church, one does begin to reach the conclusion of mass denial, both specific and group, and within a group. A kind of justified abstaining, a look-the-other-way philosophy congealed in the hearts and minds of the people attending the church. There of course was another base contradiction within a major church subgroup, and then of course there was community dismissal taking place on the outside and within the town itself. So, we at the time had many counter-leaning forces playing with the community, all during the same time period. People had known something before and after the disappearances, and there was personal knowledge from within the deacon groups. Yet knowledge itself was avoided and denied and put somewhere else as if whole new worlds were built up for the self-benefit of the groups fomenting both their own and their group disavowals and mass abridgement of any acceptable reality. Remember, over twenty-five people from our little county have been killed in one way or another, including my son, Pastor Filbert T. Buchanan, who was obviously involved in one of the deacon groups. How did this kind of abnegation happen? Who caused it? What caused it, and how did this cancerous growth evolve in our sacred community? Who knows? Still, it can be determined to have come about due to a number of possible factors and yet no secular or Christian explanation can be uprooted. Can you understand it? Really, Sheriff Parrish? Or has it been as much of a mystery to you as it has to me?"

Buck Parrish: "Understand it? Actually today is the third anniversary of this dark cloud that somehow moved into the bowels of our little community. A flirtatious and loathsome nefarious force gripping some of the best of our people driving them into illegal and corrupted actions somehow moved into our community's innards. As consolidated and scientifically accurate evidence continues to mount regarding the murder of Kaelin Jones and others, the documentation uncovered is hard for the average human being to grasp. People whom we all grew up with seemed to have coiled up and started to rot from inside and outside their cores. Human acts only read about in fiction and displayed in our fantasy-lased news media took place right here in Wallowa County. Abominable acts were committed and then denied as the judge has just stated and yet these heinous acts have been proved irrevocable beyond all refutation. Sister Mary, Judge Buchanan, and so many others have discussed the subject at great lengths. Yet none of our so-called rational people have the answers as to 'why'? Why did it happen here? How did it happen here and more than all of that, in what ways could it have been stopped or defused? In all, twenty-seven lives have been lost. Most of these departed were our beloved citizens. How could it all have been averted?"

A.F. Bell: "Seems it's too late to do anything to avoid the past, but a community healing must begin to take place regardless. That is what must happen here. We have a wounded community that must do what it can, as was done in South Africa in 1999, to heal itself, period. What do you think about my statement, Mr. Cochran?"

Teddy Cochran: "Art, and to all the folks here and in the listening audience, my offices are completely open for any help we can give in this matter. Come to my office and talk to me. Talk to my people if you like and air your grievances. We are there for you! I myself, I'm here for our community to move forward toward renewal and restoration. I'd like to see us move toward rehabilitation and melioration. Come to our offices, your offices for a place to be heard in complete privacy and comfort; come!"

Sister Mary Espanola: "Convalesce is needed just as if we've all received a major operation. The community needs added rejuvenation time to recover. I offer this to all with a total wholeness and sectarian acceptance as personally required by each visitor. I do remember the South African Committee for Truth and Reconciliation. Maybe that is exactly what we, of Wallowa, need and I offer it openly, or then again, I offer something close to it, quite publicly."

Teddy Cochran: "The community has choices here and in the future, other possible decisions may arise which offer some help. Remember, regarding everything we are, we must exist as a law-abiding and religious community of concrete human beings and citizens of this honorable state. We shall, all of us, recover from this horrific tragedy. More than that, we will move on; we have to move on as none of us have another choice. So, if you need a strong shoulder to cry on or to just have around, come down to my office, or to Sister Mary's chambers at the Runaway Center in Inmaha"

A.F. Bell: "Yes, indeed, and next week, this station, KPFJ, will be open at this same time for an open show on any subject related to the murder of Kaelin and the aftermath. So now, I want to thank my guests and the Wallowa Enterprise Gazette for sponsoring "Open Talk" with Art F. Bell. Goodnight and thanks for joining us!"

THE END